⟨⟩ ⟨⟩

"Take me to bed...." Orielle began again. "and take what you *really* want from me."

"I can't," Alex said softly, lowering both her voice and her eyes.

"But you can...."

Alex realized her hands were shaking. She hid them behind her back and leaned against the wall, staring up at the ceiling and away from Orielle. "Really, I can't."

"Tell me you do not want to, or that you will not let yourself...but don't tell me you *can't*."

"No..." Alex said. "Honestly, I can't because..." she paused, daring to meet Orielle's eyes again. "Because I don't know what I'd do if I ever...ever fell in love with you."

Orielle stroked Alex's face, affectionately searching her sable eyes and seeming to understand the mixture of fear and desire tearing Alex from within. "You already love me, Alex...you loved me long before you ever met me."

"Orielle, I..."

"Alex," she whispered, taking Alex's hand and pressing it to her breast. "Come inside my heart tonight...and in it you will find your own again."

⟨⟩ ⟨⟩

NightShade

Karen Williams

RISING
TIDE
PRESS

HUNTINGTON, NEW YORK

Rising Tide Press
5 Kivy Street
Huntington Station, NY 11746
(516) 427-1289

Printed in the United States on acid-free paper.

Publisher's note:
All characters, places and situations in this book are fictitious and any
resemblance to persons (living or dead) is purely coincidental.

Publisher's Acknowledgments:
The publisher is grateful for all the support and expertise offered by the
members of its editorial board: Bobbi Bauer, Adriane Balaban, Beth
Heyn, Hat Edwards, Pat G, Marianne Miller and Marian Satriani.
Special thanks to Edna G. for believing in us, and to the feminist and
gay bookstores for being there.

First printing February, 1996
10 9 8 7 6 5 4 3 2 1

Edited by Alice Frier and Lee Boojamra
Book cover art: Peggy Mocine
Photo credit: Gloria J Marino
Williams, Karen 1959-
        Nightshade/Karen Williams
                p.cm
ISBN 1883061-08-3
Library of Congress Catalog Card Number 95-68823

Acknowledgments

To the following people I express thanks:

My publishers, Lee Boojamra, and editor, Alice Frier, for their support, expertise, and for giving me creative freedom, when they should have been giving me hell....

Gloria Marino, for her feedback, technical assistance and undying support.

Lady Lucina of the Blue Crystal Star, for teaching me about candles, oils, potions and spells, and for inviting me to a solstice ceremony—even if I did chicken out the first time!

Dr. Koshi, physicist, for putting so much *energy* into discussing the *matter,* as it were.

Annette Adler, for the soul talks; Donna Ramirez for the spirit walks—we've traveled many places in that little room.

Kim Hamilton in the UK, for editing my British English, chasing after opium lords and showing me how to properly brew a *real* pot of tea.

Edmond Witkowski, historian and antiquarian, for enchanting me with stories about 19th Century America; and Ron Grassullo, urban cowboy, for dance lessons.

And all the women at Pure Silk Productions. Special thanks to Laurie the songstress, Coleen Cantrell, and to Nancy B.—New York's hottest D.J.—who so willingly discussed and demonstrated her sound equipment...then helped break into my car at 4: 00 a.m.

DEDICATION

To Gloria, and the memory of our pal, Allen, who left us
quite suddenly to fly with the angels.

And to my father, who is relieved to know that *someone*
finally discovered the Fountain of Youth.

❦ 1 ❦
Case of the Stolen Poppies

Alex Spherris had run out of milk—a minor inconvenience you might say, but for her it was a horrible discovery. There were, after all, certain things in life a woman could rightly excuse herself for running out of—time, luck, patience, lovers. But when the milk ran out? Who could you blame but yourself?

With an aggravated huff she tucked her T-shirt back into her khaki shorts, stepped into the Timberland boots she'd just kicked off, then marched to the wood-framed screen door and surveyed the ominous sky. A thunderstorm watch issued earlier that afternoon had since been upgraded to a warning, and judging from the looks of things, Alex estimated it to become an immediate threat right about now. It wasn't yet five o'clock, but over the low lying hills an unnatural line of darkness was building, expanding along the horizon and coiling as it did, like a black viper set to strike and spray its venom on the town of Halfmoon.

Alex studied the swirling nimbus clouds, doubtful she'd have time to drive four miles into town and back before the downpour came. Better to get the milk from Raspberries, she decided; the cafe was only half the distance, and Ana Mae never ran out of anything.

It wasn't that Alex minded getting caught in the rain—no upstanding naturalist would—as long as it was a warm, daytime rain. But nighttime storms in the country were a different story altogether. Even in summer they were nasty, apt to chill you to the bone, and any woman with a bit of sense knew that nights like this were best spent indoors—dining, slow dancing, romancing. Of course, if your romantic prospects happened to be as poor as the weather, a good book, cozy chair and gourmet brew would always do. That and a small fire, perhaps, to take the nip off the mountain air.

Alex had all those things tonight—the book, the fire and the brew, that is—but she couldn't well enjoy any of it without milk for her coffee. Basic comforts were at stake here, the lack of which, she theorized, would inevitably reduce even the finest of women to explosive outbursts—like the swift and sudden kick she gave the screen door. Alex stepped down onto the green-painted planks, letting the wood-framed door snap shut behind her, then shuffled over in untied boots to a bushel basket at the edge of the porch. It was stocked, as usual, with overripe fruit—fare for the resident opossum who'd claimed squatter's rights to the otherwise vacant barn. The marsupial probably wouldn't be out for dinner tonight, though. Animals were smart that way. Whether it was the drop in barometric pressure or the smell of sulphur and ozone in the air, animals could sense a storm a day before it struck. And unlike humans who like to complicate life by desiring milk in their pecan coffee, animals were never caught gallivanting around in a thunderstorm.

Alex bent and plucked an apricot from the basket anyway, impatiently tossing it up and down in her hand a few times before drawing back her arm on impulse and pitching it at the shed. But the apricot collided with a maple tree instead, the yellow fruit splattering against the trunk and the pit ricocheting off the bark and plopping somewhere in the middle of her poppy field.

Atop tall flimsy stems the orange poppy flowers seemed to vie for attention, each bobbing and bowing and curtsying in the breeze, their black centers staring at her like unblinking eyes, beguiling in their lack of emotion. Against the storm-darkened sky, their papery petals were brilliantly phosphorescent, so big and crimson-colored that they seemed to jump out from the landscape.

Alex stood there, her black curls tousled by the wind, and frowned at the flowers. There weren't nearly as many as there should have been.

Last night a good third of her poppies had been stolen—just as they had last year and the year before that one. The thought of it made her ears get hot. Abruptly she turned away, squatting on the porch to tie her boot laces, then flung open the screen door and grabbed an orange slicker from its hook. The same slicker, in fact, that made Alex *look* just like a poppy—at least that's what Mrs. Southworth, the Realtor, had said the day Alex first came to see this house.

It had been drizzling that late spring day, and when Alex arrived, getting out of the car and pulling up the orange hood so that it hung loosely around her thick black curls, the stout, bulgy-eyed Realtor—who, rumor had it, moonlighted as a psychic when she wasn't selling houses—could hardly speak.

"Alex? Alex Spherris? My!" she began in a high-pitched twitter that gave her voice an operatic sort of sound. "Do forgive me," she apologized, sliding stubby fingers inside her trench coat to nervously fiddle with the neck of her pink, pearl-buttoned cardigan, "but...but...oh, *goodness!*" she exclaimed. "You look just *like* them!"

Mrs. Southworth's cheeks grew flushed and blotchy, and with a dramatic sweep of the hand she gestured toward the blooming poppies, her eyeballs jiggling as though about ready to burst with psychic energy. She stared deeply into Alex's dark eyes, the corners of her mouth beginning to quiver and turn way up in a spooky sort of smile. Alex regarded the Realtor hesitantly, then gave an awkward nod of greeting, unsure as to whether Mrs. Southworth might be experiencing a premonition or a hot flash.

"I do believe *fate* is at work," the Realtor announced. "Why...why, it's as if these poppies have been waiting for you—

growing for you." Her eyes narrowed with the conviction of a preacher. "You *belong* here, Ms. Spherris."

Mrs. Southworth told Alex that her physical resemblance to the poppies was a good omen; that Alex's dark eyes were as intoxicating as the opium-filled poppy heads, and that their mysterious allure was bound to seduce any young gentleman in the town of Halfmoon. Of course, it was the ladies Alex hoped to seduce, but she thanked Mrs. Southworth just the same, and in the end bought the house—but not because of Mrs. Southworth's nonsense about good omens. Alex didn't believe in good omens; only bad ones. So naturally, the annual disappearance of her poppies had become cause for concern over the years.

This year, however, Alex had decided to bring the culprit to justice—to change the course of fate—and only yesterday, as the poppies came into bloom, had gone so far as to rig the entire field. Armed with a pail, some transparent fishing line and a ladder, Alex set out to build a trap. Around the whole field she inconspicuously staked the fishing line, then to the end of it tied a tin pail. Finally, she climbed a ladder to the roof and hid the pail behind the chimney.

The intruder, Alex calculated, would trip on the invisible line and send the tin pail clanging to the ground, at which point Alex, awakened by the commotion, would jump out of bed and catch the poppy-picking phantom smack in the act of thievery. It was foolproof. A fine plan, really. But it failed.

Just this morning, Alex awoke to find the poppies gone and the fishing line cleverly clipped. Pruning shears, no doubt—the same shears probably used to snip and steal her poppies. The sight of the decapitated stems, the thought of having been outsmarted—outright robbed—made her ears even hotter. And she might have stood there fuming for hours if not for the cold wind blowing against her feverish lobes and reminding her of the impending storm.

Alex stomped down the porch steps, marched straight out to the field and picked one of the remaining poppies. She had a right to pick her own poppies, didn't she? And with black curls blowing wildly now like tassels in the wind, she headed for the white Subaru.

The light was fading fast, and in a matter of minutes the sky had deepened to a dark and eerie green, turbulent clouds churning overhead like whitecaps on a raging sea. Alex zippered her orange slicker, pausing as she opened the car door to look up at the nautical sky. She felt as though she were staring *up* at an ocean.

Here and there in the wavelike clouds, shadowed shapes resembled dorsal fins of storm-drawn sharks, fanning tails of sky-bound whales. It was as if something otherworldly were coming this way, turning the whole world upside down; as if the universe itself had decided to alter its laws—change the game plan, so to speak—and had set about redesigning the cosmos, all on a most unlikely whim.

❖ 2 ❖

As the Crone Flies

The weather-beaten shutters blew open with a bang, and a cool wind, smelling strangely of the river, wafted through the cottage window. It gusted toward a potbelly stove over which the old woman hunched, first freeing wisps of white hair from her ponytail, then whirling down to set the tips of her wings to flapping and fluttering along the edge of her house dress.

From a cast iron kettle steam lazily swirled, and against its heat Batilda squinted, her black eyes shifting suspiciously from the window to the cluttered table and back again. She'd be damned if she'd let some ghostly wind blow her hard day's work to bits. Snorting her annoyance, she let go her wooden soup spoon and, with a quick wipe of her hands on a berry-stained apron, made a shuffled dash to close the shutters. She might even have reached them in time, too, if not for a slipper getting caught up on the droopy tip of a membranous wing.

"*Bah!*" Batilda hissed, "Cursed wings, wretched things!" She stopped short and shoved a hand into her sleeveless dress, tugging on and yanking up the bones of her avian appendage the way another woman might have pulled up a fallen bra strap, then switched hands to reach in and grapple with the other one.

The featherless things had been bothering her all evening. Forecasting the weather was all they were good for these days.

Why, even years ago they'd been nothing but trouble; way too long and flimsy to get her rotund body high enough off the ground. To *think* how many times she'd nearly killed herself getting tangled in the tension wires. And now? Now they'd completely lost what little muscle tone they'd ever had—hung as low as her breasts, in fact—and as if that weren't enough, they were getting as stiff and crooked and knobby looking as her fingers; plagued by rheumatism and arthritis and—what else? Age spots, probably, if she cared to inspect them closely enough. Truth to tell, aging was a nasty business.

"*Bah!*" she scowled again, as another gust swept through, this time making a beeline for the kitchen table.

The table's planked surface took up the better part of the kitchen—probably weighed more than the cottage itself—and in the center burned a railroad lantern, its light casting a glow on a black cat perched fast asleep in the rafters. The feline's ears flickered, whiskers twitched, as if it were currently involved in a thoroughly disturbing dream. And its pendulous tail swished back and forth, batting a bunch of cord-tied poppies dangling from a beam, and all but hypnotizing a Scottish terrier sitting on a chair at the table.

Heaped upon the table itself were all sorts of oddities: at one end, a mound of hastily opened Priority Mail envelopes, at the other, a bottle of Advil, a scattering of scribbled notes, and a bowl of plucked poppy heads. There was a thesaurus there, too, along with a leather-bound cookbook and any number of mortars filled with roots and herbs and unspeakable things now finely ground to powder. And somewhere in the middle of the hodgepodge rested a box of Mumble Munchies. *Pets Love 'em*, the label read. And beside it, a bag of Fritos and two bowls of stew, one of which was being eaten by the terrier.

Silhouetted in the lantern light, Boogawoog sat with her back to the stone wall while she ate, her eyes upturned to the swinging poppies and the cat's pendulum-like tail. From under coarse bangs jutting out from her brow, the dog's eyes began blinking. Soon her chewing slowed, and just when it seemed her snout might fall into her stew, the wind whacked the shutters again and snapped the dog to with a start.

Batilda cursed. Boogawoog growled. Poppy petals set sail around the room. And in the rafters, the cat sprang to its feet, hissing and spitting and arching its back. Through yellow eyes it surveyed the room, worried, perhaps, that its dream-antagonist had somehow crossed realms.

"Cursed wind! Dang!" Batilda grumbled. "Dang, dang, dang!" And with wings finally tucked into place, she resumed her shuffled dash for the shutters. She lunged this time, thrusting her plump torso out the window, and with outstretched arms struggled to grab hold of the shutters. But before she could, another gust of wind swept in.

The bottle of Advil was the first to topple over, and as it rolled rattling to the floor, bits of herbs and powders blew up from mortars, notes whirled about like paper airplanes, and in the flickering lantern light, pages of the cookbook began flipping wildly, as though the ghostly fingers of an uninvited guest were frantically seeking to steal some alchemical recipe.

The box of Mumble Munchies was the next to go, and as it tumbled over, Boogawoog shifted her weight from paw to paw. The whites of the dog's eyes flashed expectantly, almost criminally, as she stealthily gripped the cardboard flap with her front teeth, and with quick little jerking motions of her head edged the box forward until it, too, plunked to the floor. Then Boogawoog was off the stool, using her oversized nose to nudge and steer the box clear under the table and out of sight.

"We got a squall kicking up, girls," Batilda called to the animals. But just as she grabbed the shutter knobs and began drawing them in, the wind let go as fast as it had taken hold, suddenly changing course to skate figure eights around the budding trees. Batilda paused to catch her breath, blowing a strand of hair from her face and craning her neck as she did to spy a faint half-moon rising in the afternoon sky.

A *half*-moon in the *town* of Halfmoon—her favorite monthly coincidence. The sight of it caused a crooked grin to spread across her face. And this month she had good cause to grin. It was June, the month of the solstice, of the strawberry moon. But this solstice would bring a full moon—and not just any moon...this was the year of the devil's moon.

For years she and Dr. Birdwhistle had plotted and planned, tracking the celestial calendars and finally succeeding in their acquisition of the bell in time for the planetary arrangement. And now, after all these years, their time was close at hand—which meant time was running out. There were still things to be done; laudanum to be made, tinctures to be prepared, and Benjamin Birdwhistle—that crackpot of a wizard—was still putzing around Manhattan, fiddling with his sound machine and having his Mercedes tuned-up for his trip to Halfmoon. And to top it all off, this God-awful headache was doing nothing to alleviate her writer's block.

Did *anyone*, Batilda wondered, ever think of crones suffering from writer's block? Probably not. It was always the pampered novelists, the temperamental poets, the high-strung playwrights who received all the sympathy for creative blocks. Oh, sure, there was something to be said for a poignant play, a pretty poem...but let any of them try writing an incantation—an incantation that *worked!* A spell that could raise a skeleton and have it tap dance atop a piano. Now *there* was a literary genius! Just once, just once before she died, she'd like to see a crone honored, awarded—*acknowledged*, for heaven's sake—for a spell well-written.

"Soon, my beloved Lilah," she snickered to the moon, whispering her promise to the woman she once hated to love and now loved to hate. "Soon, my belladonna...when the moon hides in the earth's shadow, I will stop your heart with a poison arrow." It enraged her to think of the precious years she'd lost, the lifetime she'd wasted, of the many lives she'd taken...and of how, without hesitation, she'd have given her own life all in the name of— what? Love? "*Bahh...!*" she snarled, transforming her pain into anger, and through clenched teeth, hissed the words to her newest recipe.

Moonseed, Jimsonweed, color me a solstice spell
Opium, laudanum, give Morpheus a dream to sell

Nightshade, forestmaid, sing your song for Orielle
Pound your heart where evil dwells
and free our healer from the bell.

"And while you're at it," Batilda sneered, "let my belladonna rot in hell! "

Batilda's lungs swelled with air, her chest puffing with
pride, and with her plump torso still suspended out the window,
she broke into the uncontrollable cackle of a madwoman; a woman
made mad by love. Indeed, she looked mad, with eyes as black as
the sky, white hairs poking out every which way, and cackle after
cackle echoing on the wind.

And then, before her eyes, the half-moon disappeared,
its faint outline instantly obliterated by a darkness overtaking the
afternoon sky. Suddenly the sky was so black that even the silhouetted treetops could not be seen against it, and then, as if responding to her laughter, the tempest wind whipped back around
and rushed at the cottage again. It howled as it raced along the
ground, stirring up smells of moist toadstools and flowering foxglove, and then the most sickeningly sweet smell of all...Lilah's
favorite flower.

With a sudden dread, Batilda craned her neck again, this
time peering down to see lily of the valley blooming along the
stone foundation. Pearly white strings of the tiny bell-shaped flowers glistened in what little lantern light emanated from the cottage. As if the seductive sweetness alone were enough to poison
her, Batilda's chest suddenly deflated. Her shoulders slumped, her
face sank, and her jowls hung loosely under the weight of her
own despair.

Funny thing, the olfactory sense—stronger even than the
sight of an old photograph, or the reading of an expired love letter, wasn't it? One minute you'd be going about your business,
and the next minute the smell of a distant memory, the perfume
of a past lover, would pass you in the breeze and—*wham!*—hit
you in the nose like a rubber mallet. And for a moment you

wouldn't be where you were at all, but catapulted back in time to passions foul and best forgotten.

That's how it was with lily of the valley. It never failed. Every year when the earth thawed and the sun grew near, there they'd come like clockwork to haunt her, breaking through the rocky earth and poking out their pale heads like ghouls rising from a winter grave.

For a heart-wrenching moment Batilda stared at the blooming strands, oblivious to the screaming wind, and paying no mind to the bubbling brew in her kettle, nor even to the crunching of Mumble Munchies being gobbled beneath the kitchen table.

One whiff of the white bell-shaped flowers, and it seemed like only yesterday she was young again, wrapped naked with Lilah in those lily-scented sheets that always laced the early morning air with such romantic sweetness. Just the thought of it—the very thought of it—made her want to run outside and squash the flowers—stomp the pistils right out of them.

"Why, Lilah...?" Batilda whispered, heaving a sigh of regret. "Why did it ever have to come to this? You fool...you wicked, *wicked*..."

"WI-WI-WI-*WICKED-FOOL!*" came a gravelly shout from under the kitchen table.

Batilda spun around, forced from her trance, her glazed eyes zooming in on Boogawoog and the spilled box of Mumble Munchies. "Booga—? Oh *dammit*, Boogawoog!" She turned back to latch the shutters, then turned around again, waggling a reprimanding finger in the dog's face.

"What'd I tell you? I said *no* Mumble Munchies tonight. *No* talky treats. I've got recipes to write, potions to brew, things to do. I don't have *time* to listen to a dog mumblin' and mopin' around here all night!"

Being caught in the act, or perhaps the fact of eating too fast, brought on an instant case of the hiccups. The whites of Boogawoog's eyes resembled half-moons themselves, as she sat peering up at Batilda with her head lowered in shame. Each jolting hiccup made her bangs bob and her body heave.

"Ah...*shoot*, Boogawoog," Batilda muttered, her reprimands becoming halfhearted as she waddled across the room. She fumbled through her apron pocket for a wooden match, struck it on the fieldstone, reached up to light a candle in a sconce, and in the added light, went about tidying the mess, using the edge of her gnarled hand to sweep bits of herbs back into their respective mortars. And when she'd created some semblance of order, she lifted the burning taper from its sconce and shuffled over to the gas-fueled refrigerator and stared at the bottled contents. Gold water or Blackened Voodoo lager from her favorite New Orleans brewery. It was a toss up. But with Boogawoog mumbling and hiccuping and carrying on, it was nearly impossible to decide.

"BALL...TOY...BOOGAWOOG's BALL. CAT...CAT... BOOGAWOOG'S CAT. BED...STICK...BOOGAWOOG'S—"

"Will you please *shut up!*" she yelled, the vibration of her shout sending hot wax dripping down the candle and over her fingers, and splattering to the floor.

Boogawoog stared sheepishly, her bottom teeth exposed, her mandible moving soundlessly up and down like the mouth of a puppet. But as soon as Batilda turned away, the dog went off again, vocalizing variations on her own name—*affectionate* variations Batilda used when she was in a *good* mood and didn't have wicked Lilah on her mind. "BOOGIE...? MAMA LOVES BOOGIE? BOOGA-WOOGA-WOOGIE? BOOGIE *LOVE* MOMMA."

"Mama loves you, too, Boogie. Now just *put a lid on it*— I can't hear my damn self *think!*"

Boogawoog flattened her ears and moped away, grunting self-reprimands all the way into the next room. "BOOGIE BAD GIRL, BAD BOOGIE, BOOGIE BAD..."

"Oh, stop now and come back in here," Batilda coaxed, her tone softening with guilt. "Don't go off pouting now. Mama didn't mean it. Want some more stew? Huh? How 'bout a bone? A pig's ear?"

Boogawoog stopped short in the door way and turned, her tail wagging softly. "PIGGY?"

"Is that what you want?" Batilda asked, her gravelly voice breaking into baby talk. "A piggy-wiggy for my boogie-woogie?" Batilda cooed.

Boogawoog held no grudge. She accepted the peace offering and pranced to a braided rug by the hearth, the hurtful exchange already erased from memory.

Batilda watched the terrier settle down and smiled regretfully. She hated to yell at Boogawoog. If there was anyone in the *world* she hated to yell at it was Boogawoog. She couldn't help it, though; every time she got carried away with thoughts of Lilah she got like that—snappin' and lashin' out, and ready to chop the head off anyone who looked at her the wrong way.

On impulse, she went back and slammed the refrigerator door, deciding to forget the whole matter of a drink, but just as she did, the muffled rings of her cordless phone sounded and sent her into another frenzied shuffle to locate the damned thing. At least when a respectable cord was attached to a phone you didn't have to spend half your time remembering where you'd last put it. "WHAT!" she finally shouted into the receiver after the fourth ring, cradling the receiver and fiddling with her wings again.

"Batilda...?" a gentleman inquired, his British accent offering a sharp contrast to her gruffness. "Is it you?"

"No Birdwhistle—you *idiot*—this *isn't* me," she snarled. "You're talking to a harpy. You know, one of those big ol' nasty birds with a hag's face? I ate Batilda for dinner and was just sitting here flossing my teeth when the phone rang. What can I do for you?"

There was a sigh of resignation on the other end. "My *dear* woman...must you *constantly* antagonize me so?"

"Must you ask such *stupid* questions? What do you want?"

Benjamin cleared his throat nervously. "Well, as planned, I expected to arrive tomorrow, but..." He stopped and cleared his throat a second time.

"Go on, Birdwhistle—speak up and spit it out. I've got a squall kickin' up and static on the line."

"Well...as I was about to say...my equipment seems oddly to have disappeared."

"Disappeared? *Disappeared*? Just *say it*, Benjamin—they ransacked your apartment. You got yourself followed by those damned imps and they ransacked your apartment, didn't they?"

"I'm afraid so."

"And they got your sound machine."

"Afraid so...."

"*Afraid so—afraid so*," she mimicked, gritting her teeth and swatting the stray hairs from her face, just wishing she could reach into the phone and ring the old buzzard's scrawny neck. *Count to ten*, she told herself, *hold the anger in and count to ten*. That's what a witch-doctor friend in Louisiana had advised her to do—a tactic to temper her temper, as it were. But she'd never mastered the trick, never been able to hold her tongue much past the count of three. By the count of four she felt her brain catching fire, by five her ears were smokin', and by the count of six it felt as though her whole head would explode.

"You're a sorry excuse for a wizard. You know that, Benjamin? A damned, stinkin' sorry excuse!"

"Dear lady, do compose yourself...please!"

"Don't *lady me*, Birdwhistle. I'm no *lady*—never was, never will be. And *don't* tell me what to do," she scoffed, her gnarled hands shaking with adrenaline-powered rage.

"I do have my notes on disk at the bank. That is why I am calling," he said, pausing a moment. "I'm afraid our safety deposit box might be the only safe place for the bell...until the solstice, of course." He hesitated. "I was hoping to convince you to travel here by train."

"I've got work to do. My packages only arrived today. And what about the *animals*? No way, Birdwhistle! I'm *not* coming to Manhattan," she yelled. "I can't take the *heat* and I *can't stand* the crowds. Besides, your cat misses you. She hasn't eaten since you left her here."

"No!" he cried. "My Sheeky hasn't eaten?"

"Nope," she lied, "your Sheeky hasn't eaten. Last time she came down from the rafters I mistook her for a skinny squirrel.

So get your butt up here, Benjamin. And make it snappy—before you ruin *everything* we've worked for!"

Batilda clicked off the phone and sat it on the base on the floor. Then she hurried over to collect her iron kettle, cursing Benjamin all the way, as she plopped the pot on the stone hearth then stopped to rub her lower back. Her hands were shaking, her heart pounding, a deep ache growing in her bones. Maybe it was the dampness settling in, or maybe fear creeping in. Whatever, she wasn't feeling herself—of course, she hadn't *felt* herself in a hundred years, but that was beside the point.

Still rubbing her hip, she looked around at the rafters, the door, the shutters. It was the wind, she finally decided, the sound of the wind she didn't like. Even the cat and dog seemed to vaguely sense some sort of portent. From the rafters, Sheeky gave a low and steady cat-growl, her tail batting so hard that there were no more petals on the dangling poppies. And Boogawoog, lying on her belly with hind legs outstretched, suddenly dropped the pig's ear between her paws and sniffed the air. Batilda stood silently, listening to the wind, to the logs burning on the hearth, and to the low warning sounding from Boogawoog's chest.

Something was coming. Something evil was riding in on this wind.

✎ 3 ✎

Raspberries Cafe

Ana Mae was sitting at the bar, sipping a cup of cappuccino as she counted the money in the register, when a cool breeze blew through the cafe door. She leaned sideways and peeked through the archway to see the ruffled Cape Cod curtains on the windows puffing out, the corners of raspberry-patterned table-cloths billowing up. Then both the curtains and cloths settled, and the door clicked softly closed.

"Hello?" she called, her voice hinting of a Southern drawl. She supposed it might be the same odd traveller who, only minutes ago, had come in asking for directions. Sunny days brought out such ordinary people; but leave it to a storm to blow in the strangest lot of characters.

"Who is it?" she called again, and when no answer came, took off her eyeglasses, set her cup on the bar and quietly slid off the stool.

"Is someone there?" Ana Mae questioned, pausing in the archway to scan the room. She took another step, and then another, and as she passed through the archway, something feathery, like fingers, lightly brushed the back of her long, frizzy blonde hair. "Oh!" Ana Mae shouted, nearly jumping out of her skin as she spun *smack* into a rubber-coated body.

"It's only the wind..." Alex whispered.

For a startled second Ana Mae's hazel eyes showed no recognition of the shadowed figure, but then they filled with anger. With open palms she pounded Alex's chest and growled through clenched teeth. "Son of a bitch! Don't *do* that to me—you always *do* that to me," she scolded, her Southern accent more pronounced with emotion now. "I hate when you scare me—I hate it, *hate* it! One day you're going to scare the wrong person—someone who's gonna shoot first and ask questions later."

Sporting her orange slicker and a mischievous grin, Alex stood holding the poppy by its stem. "I didn't *mean* to scare you," she lied, extending the floppy flower. "I only came to bring you this...and borrow some milk if I may...Ana Mae. May I, Ana Mae I?"

"Stop *toying* with me, Alex." For good measure she gave Alex's shoulder another swat before reluctantly accepting the proffered poppy. "Thanks," she said. "One day, when you've finally succeeded in scaring me to death, I hope you'll think to bring some of those poppies to my grave."

"Would I ever show up anywhere empty-handed?"

Ana Mae ignored the question. Instead she said, "I got your message this morning. Your tin-pail-trap didn't work, huh?" She stared into Alex's eyes; eyes which, aside from their perpetual gleam of mischief and mystery, were as black and velvety as her beautifully arched eyebrows. Ana Mae made a face. "Serves you right," she said. "You want coffee or something?"

"I have a pot waiting at home."

Ana Mae glanced toward the windows. The wind had stopped, but the afternoon sky was black as night. Not a single thing moved outside. Even the pink and white flowers in her window box were still as a picture. "You better hurry then. It's gonna hit any minute...and they're saying it's gonna be a bad one. Is milk all you need?"

Alex winked at her. "I wouldn't mind a little sugar."

Ana Mae rolled her eyes as she sidestepped Alex and made her way back to the bar room. Alex trotted behind, grinning as she eyed Ana Mae's denim shirt and the tight blue jeans that always accentuated her full figure. It was Ana Mae's usual attire, and Alex always teased her about looking like an inmate in her blue denim clothes.

"I love it when you wear your prison suit."

"Yeah, yeah," Ana Mae humored her.

"How about coming home with me to do some *time?*"

"Oh? You're sentencing me? But my wife's upstairs. What will you tell her?"

"I don't know..." Alex gave a playful shrug and hopped up on a bar stool. "Just tell Laurie I've given you work release. I'm your *work*, and you're my *release.*"

"Uh-huh...sure, Alex." Ana Mae regarded her sarcastically, then ducked behind the bar and disappeared into the kitchen. She turned on a radio just loud enough to hear a weather update while filling a bottle of milk.

Alex's propositions were in jest, Ana Mae knew, and it was easy enough to shrug them off. But it hadn't always been so easy. Before Laurie had come into her life, it had taken every ounce of discipline to deny herself Alex. But she had, and in retrospect was glad for it. Because even back then, Ana Mae knew that sleeping with Alex would mean losing her, and in the long run she knew Alex was worth more as a friend and business partner than as a memory of a miscalculated love affair. And so for eight years now—since she was thirty-two and Alex was twenty-two—they had remained close friends, although sometimes she wondered if she was any closer to Alex than the day they met.

At a financial low point during those years, before Half-moon had caught on as a popular resort for women, Alex had come of age to access her trust fund. She had insisted on helping the cafe and becoming a silent partner. And silent partnerships were what Alex was best at. They suited her well, just as they did in her private relationships. Of course, *relationship* was hardly a suitable term for Alex's liaisons with women—liaisons, in fact, were exactly what they were. All they'd ever be.

Suddenly a white flash of pulsating lightning lit the kitchen, followed by the low booming of distant thunder. Ana Mae grabbed a milk bottle, sealed it, and hurriedly sponged it off.

"And so what makes you even think," she finally retorted, looking out at Alex before reaching for a can of sugar, "that I might still have a soft spot for you?"

Alex drummed her fingers, frowning hard at the poppy lying on the bar. But then she looked up and smirked. "A *soft* spot? Geez, Ana Mae, is that all you've got left for me? I was hoping you still had a *hard* spot—"

"Alex Spherris, you're disgusting!"

Alex shook her head melodramatically. "I don't know, Ana Mae. You used to call me witty and charming—now your hard spot's gone soft and you think I'm disgusting. I guess I really *have* lost my touch with you."

Maybe with Ana Mae she'd lost her touch, but certainly not with the women who came to vacation in Halfmoon. Alex, most would agree, was witty as a weasel, charming as a snake. What they didn't know is that Alex was, quite truthfully, full of cow dung. For Ana Mae, listening to Alex's lines was like listening to an overtold joke—one you've heard so many times that it just doesn't get you laughing anymore.

As they continued their banter, Alex briefly thought about the predictable pattern her life had fallen into lately. During winters she lived quietly—writing, illustrating, playing her violin—but when summer arrived she came out of hibernation to play at the cafe. Most evenings she'd dine at her *reserved* corner table, and after she finished would go behind the bar, make a blender full of raspberry margaritas, then climb on a stool with violin in hand and serenade the house of prospective suitors. Usually by ten o'clock Ana Mae would walk by, drop a cowboy hat on Alex's head, and on cue, Alex's classical violin would turn into a fiddle. She'd have the whole crowd two-stepping clear past midnight on Raspberry's sawdust-covered dance floor.

Without fail, a handful of single women would glance shyly at Alex, each dancing and giggling and whispering to their coupled friends until, eventually, each in her own turn would work up the nerve to mosey over and compliment Alex on her fiddle-playing. Trying to predict which woman would strike Alex's fancy had become somewhat of a game for Ana Mae. The trouble, though, was that Alex really didn't have a type. Tall, short, light, dark, thin, full-bodied—it didn't much matter—as long as the woman had, as Alex always said, that *certain something*. And if she had it? Well then, Alex would order raspberry margaritas on the house. And when that happened, Ana Mae knew it was a matter of time before the fiddler fiddled her way into someone's pants.

Of course, when interested women learned that Alex was a trained forester and local writer of tracking and field guides, they'd suddenly feign a love of nature, hinting at their interest in a private *tour* of the native flora and fauna.

You couldn't find a better guide than at-your-service Alex. Over rolling hills of wildflowers, she'd lead you on a breathtaking tour of natural springs and caves and waterfalls, and eventually back to her cozy fox den for dinner and a pre-copulatory glass of wine.

Alex was a lot of fun, no doubt, but beyond good sex and a good time, she didn't have much to offer. And Ana Mae always dreaded the part that followed Alex's rendezvous. Inevitably, some woman would come around the cafe—her original smile having dissipated—to inquire about Alex's whereabouts and to ask if she might leave a message with Ana Mae in hopes of contacting Alex before leaving Halfmoon.

Ana Mae politely accepted all messages, although some-times she was tempted to tell the woman not to take it too per-sonally—to tell them that Alex wasn't as insensitive and uncaring as she seemed. On the contrary, Ana Mae suspected that Alex's emotions ran very deep; so deep, in fact, that Alex could barely *feel* them. And that, in a nutshell, *was* the truth. Alex had buried half her heart when she buried her parents at the age of five, then buried a good portion of the remaining half when her first lover died at nineteen.

Ana Mae could have tried explaining this to all or any of the women with whom Alex slept and then avoided, but for some reason she never bothered. Perhaps because, instinctively, Ana Mae knew that no respectable woman would care much for listening with a sympathetic ear to the reasons why she'd been, quite literally, screwed and scorned.

Alex was standing by the window when Ana Mae came back out. Tree branches scratched the roof and shingles, the first drops of heavy rain hitting the glass panes, and when lightning struck Ana Mae could see her flowers now blowing wildly in their boxes. Approaching Alex from behind, Ana Mae propped her chin on her partner's shoulder and held out the two filled jars in front of her. "You better get a move on it."

Alex took the jars in both hands, acknowledging the milk in one, then holding up the other to inspect its white contents.

"What's this?"

"Sugar."

"I don't need sugar."

Ana Mae raised her brow, on the verge of being fed up again. "You *said* you wanted sugar."

"It's not the kind of sugar I had in mind," she said, "but thanks anyway."

Ana Mae grabbed the jar from Alex. "You put me to all that trouble?" She pursed her lips, thinking to swat Alex again, but instead just shook her head and put down the jar. "Get—" she pointed, gripping Alex's waist from behind and steering her through the archway and toward the door. "Go on now—get out of here!"

Alex pulled up her orange hood and put her hand on the doorknob, then turned back to kiss Ana Mae on the cheek. "Thanks for the milk...I'll be back for the sugar."

"Whatever, Alex. Now go. And be careful," she warned, shooing Alex out and quickly shutting the door on a spray of windblown rain. She watched from the window until Alex was safely in her Subaru, then turned off the flood lights and bolted the door against the fury of the night ahead.

❧ 4 ☙
Hit-and-Run

Rain drummed down on the metal roof of the Subaru wagon. It fell in such torrents that in the short time it took Alex to run the length of the walkway and sprint across the rubble parking lot, the cuffs of her shorts and socks had gotten soaked. She started the engine and bent down, feeling the hair on her arms stand on end beneath her slicker sleeves as she rubbed the goose bumps rising on her bare, wet legs.

The air was heavy with the smell of clay and river weeds, and in no time at all, the dampness emanating from her own body began fogging the windows. Alex blindly patted for a rag beneath the seat. She ran it back and forth across the windshield a few times before flipping on the wipers and backing out to edge her way onto the stormy road.

Sheets of wind-driven rain swept across the windshield, making it nearly impossible to see, and for the better part of the trip Alex inched her way forward, driving the way she always accused senior citizens of driving—accelerating and braking, accelerating and braking, as though the whole concept of motion was a confusing matter to the aging mind, and their failing senses could no longer be trusted to tell them whether they were going too fast, too slow, or whether, in fact, they should still be driving at all.

Alex leaned into the steering wheel, struggling to make out the road through rippling waves of rain. The wipers were doing little, and although the fog lamps helped somewhat, the headlights themselves only accentuated the raindrops, turning them into a mass of lighted dots and dashes that made Alex feel as though she were a figurine trapped inside a snow globe.

Everything beyond the curtain of rain was black, not a single light shone on the winding road, and soon Alex found herself relying on the lightning; waiting for a bolt to strike and illuminate the yellow road line that guided her around the dangerous bends. The thought of pulling over and waiting out the storm occurred to her, but there was no telling when it would let up; she might very well sit there all night. Besides, she had little more than a mile to go. A fire in the hearth was only a matchlight away, and a pot of pecan coffee was waiting for that fresh milk.

Strong winds shook the car, causing it to waiver from side to side, and once more the windows fogged. Keeping a white-knuckled grip on the wheel, Alex pushed on, cautiously rounding a bend before again retrieving the rag beneath her seat. But as soon as she straightened out and wiped the window, the smudged glare of oncoming lights appeared. At first, the car looked to be on the wrong side of the road, then, an instant later, it appeared to swing back to its own side.

The shimmering lights grew brighter, Alex's visibility improving as the distance between the two cars closed. The next moment, though, the car seemed to be coming straight at her, then swerved back again, trying, perhaps, to come out of a skid. The turnoff for Alex's house was half a mile now, at most, and she thought to accelerate and chance passing the car just to get out of its way. But instead, she slowed to a near stop and moved to the shoulder for fear of colliding head on.

As a warning, Alex turned on her flashers and honked the horn, preparing to steer clear of the car. But then, out of nowhere, a third object appeared, darting recklessly about the road and blotting out the headlights of the approaching vehicle as it moved back and forth in front of the car.

Alex watched as a jagged flash of lightning lit the road, outlining for an instant a large black figure—an animal, maybe— bouncing up on the hood of the oncoming car. The vehicle screeched and skidded wildly now, the object apparently obliterating the driver's view of the road as he tried to come to a stop. The car swerved, swinging from one side of the roadway to the other, and nearly sideswiping Alex before finally skidding to a stop only inches from her car. And as it did, the storm-distorted figure on the other hood was thrown toward Alex's car.

The thing tumbled toward her headlights and windshield so fast that all Alex glimpsed was a wide-eyed face and a mass of white hair, a pair of arms held stiffly out in front of her, as though intending to break her fall. Lightning struck, thunder boomed, and then came the sickening thud of flesh hitting metal.

Alex gasped and shut her eyes, and when she opened them an old woman's face was pressed up against her windshield, those wide eyes still open with shock—either still seeing, or so newly dead that they hadn't yet lost their expression. They stared fixedly at Alex as if to say, *I can't believe this just happened to me.*

Alex yelled and shouted, although she didn't know at whom she was yelling. Generic shouts of urgency, they were. And the shouts continued as she turned off the engine and jumped out, expecting the other driver to do the same. But as she ran around to the victim, the other car—a white car, she could see now—suddenly accelerated, its tires spinning uselessly on the slick road. The back end slid out, almost hitting Alex, tires throwing up muddy sprays on to her legs and slicker.

Alex leaped out of its way, then lunged back at the side of the white car, pounding a fist on the trunk in a feeble attempt to stop it. But there seemed to be some sort of ruckus going on inside the vehicle; people arguing, shadowed figures moving, someone accidentally switching on the dome light in the process. And as Alex struggled to make out a plate number, a bunch of dimly lit faces popped up in the rear window—a row of children turning around and springing to their knees to have a look. Ugly children—the whole lot of them. So ugly that she could only stare in disbelief as the car's tires finally gripped the road and the car sped away. And as it did, Alex could have sworn the children were laughing at her. In the red glow of the brake lights and zigzags of lightning, their maniacal grins flashed like neon signs. A second later, the car and the faces were gone, the horrid image swallowed by the darkness.

How utterly atrocious, Alex thought. A hit-and-run had taken place, a crime committed—an old woman *killed*—and the driver's children were in a silly uproar as if they'd all just come from the circus.

Using a forearm to shield her eyes against the pelting rain, Alex rushed back around to the front of her car and began tugging on the woman's sleeves when, above the pounding noise of the thunder and rain, she heard a groan. *Alive...she was still alive.*

Alex tugged harder, attempting to turn the body over, then stopped. "Hang on," she shouted in as calm a voice as she could manage. "It's all right, it's going to be all right—just hang on, okay?"

Slipping and nearly falling, Alex rushed to the back of her station wagon, hauled out a camping blanket, then ran back around to spread it on the ground. Get the woman out of the rain and into the wagon is what she wanted to do, but there was the possibility of adding to her injuries—maybe even killing her for sure.

Carefully, she placed her hands on the woman's heavy body, flinching when she felt the bony protrusions on her back— broken ribs, Alex was sure. She did her best to gently slide the old woman from the car, bracing herself and easing her down onto the blanket. Then Alex tore off her orange slicker and covered the victim to shield her from the beating rain.

"Boog...Boogie...?" the woman whispered. Then, "The bell..." she mumbled.

"Shhh...help is coming, okay? I'm going to get you help. I'll be *right* back. I'll be back as fast as I can," Alex assured her, looking around and wondering exactly *where* it was she planned to go and how fast she'd get there. The house was not too far up the road—a few hundred feet at most—but she couldn't chance leaving the woman at the roadside to get hit by yet another car. Better to run the distance on foot, she thought, thinking the flashers and the car itself would safeguard the woman's injured body. But before Alex could get to her feet, gnarled fingers crawled out like a tarantula from beneath the slicker and fastened a grip on Alex's wrist. "The bell," she gurgled.

"Easy," Alex said nervously, certain all this talk about boogies and bells was a sign of head trauma. "Just try to lie still while I get some help."

The old lady's grip only tightened. "The bell..." she instructed, her voice barely audible. "In my pocket...."

"Your pocket?"

"Take it...take the bell."

Still kneeling, her shorts and T-shirt drenched, her knees burning from scraping the asphalt, Alex lifted the slicker, patting the pockets of the woman's black trench coat until she felt the round, metal object. "In here?"

"Take it."

Nervously, Alex reached in, pulling out what appeared in the headlights to be a small brass bell, the clapper secured to the inside wall by a piece of sloppily cut duct tape.

"Ring," the woman wheezed, her breathing weak and labored. "Ring and she will come...."

"Easy now, don't try to talk," Alex soothed her, convinced that the old woman—and she was old, wasn't she? Certainly too old to take the beating she'd just taken—might be slipping into some sort of shock-induced delirium. But then she appeared to lose consciousness altogether.

Alex wriggled her wrist from the old woman's grasp and bolted down the road with the bell, shoving it in the pocket of her shorts as she ran.

Thunder crashed and shook the ground. Her boots kicked up floodwater from the river bank as she staggered through the storm, squinting her eyes against the rain that poured off her dangling curls. Midway down the road, though, she heard the motor of another car, quickly followed by the slamming of doors and what sounded like argumentative shouts muffled by the storm.

Alex stopped short and turned back toward the commotion, but in the blinding headlights couldn't see a thing. In a breathless panic, she glanced in the direction of her house, then at her car, and bolted back toward it, thinking it wise to instruct the passerby to stay with the body while she ran to call for an ambulance. But in the seconds it took to run halfway back to the car, another series of shouts rang out, doors slammed again, and the car—the same white car, Alex would have sworn—made a wild U-turn, sideswiping the guard rail as it screeched off, its red tail lights glowing like the eyes of a demon until it disappeared into a curtain of darkness again.

Breathing hard, and thinking what an amazing night this was turning out to be, Alex finally reached her car. Beneath the headlights of the station wagon Alex saw the open blanket...but both the old woman and her orange slicker were gone.

⊰ 5 ⊱
Ring My Bell

The polished bell shone like gold in the firelight, but Alex stared past it, losing her thoughts in the flames instead. Rain still fell steadily, but the wind was dying and the ticking of a clock on the split-log wall muted the rumble of fading thunder.

Alex sat in the Windsor rocker, tugging at the collar of her terry cloth robe and pulling it tighter around her otherwise bare chest. She was still cold. A hot shower, robe, and sweat pants had initially done the trick, but now it felt like her whole body was vibrating from the inside. No matter how much wood she threw into the fire, the room just wasn't getting any warmer, but there was nothing else with which to associate the shivers, other than the fact of her bare feet and wet curls. Certainly, she wasn't one of those hysterical types who stood strong in the face of danger only to feel dizzy and weak-kneed *after* the fact. Not Alex.

She raised a cup to her lips, barely able to hold it still, and wondered if she shouldn't be sipping something stronger than pecan coffee. She'd be surprised, in fact, if the night's tragic detour—all for the sake of milk—wouldn't serve as some sort of aversion therapy in teaching her to take her coffee black.

The drumming rain on the roof began to sound like a dirge, and visions of the gray-haired woman's face floated in her mind's eye like the flickering afterimage of a camera flash. Almost equally disturbing was what Alex could have sworn had been the oddest, almost imperceptible glint of recognition in the dying woman's eyes. But Alex was sure she'd never seen her before. She'd probably never see her again; God knew there were a thousand places for a murderer to dump a body along these desolate highways.

The scene of the accident kept playing itself over and over in Alex's head—the thud, the body, the gnarled fingers and powerful grip. Every once in a while, though, images of those hideous children popped teasingly into her head until, finally, they, too, were replaced by more morbid flashbacks of another car crash long ago.

Alex stared into the fire, struggling to ward off memories of the way her father's bloody head had looked suspended in the windshield, and of how pretty her mother had looked—so pretty, in fact, that she hadn't really looked dead at all. Only five-year-old Alex—spared by some miracle—had survived the crash, along with Fink, a pet white rat who fancied Sunday drives and, save for a bloody nose, had been left unscathed, too.

Alex never saw her parents after that—never saw the men who came to cut her father's body from the car, nor the white van which came to give her parents a postmortem ride to the morgue. An ambulance had arrived before the cleanup, whisking little Alex away and taking her to a big, noisy place—a hospital, she was told—where lots of strange people rushed in to treat her for shock. But now she couldn't even remember having been in shock; what she did remember was waving and smiling to her dead family from the ambulance window. *See you later Mommy, see you later Daddy*, was what she keep calling out, as though expecting that some wizardly doctor, some magical person would come right along and simply *fix* her mother and father; patch them up and make them alive again. Alex took a gulp of her pecan coffee, spilling a few drops as she set it back down, then tightly pinched the bridge of her nose and tried to laugh at that stupid child she once had been. How *silly* it seemed, in retrospect, that a child should not understand the permanence of death.

After that fateful day, Alex and her Rat Fink had no one
to take them for Sunday drives. No one to do much of anything
with anymore. And it wasn't long before the same cruel God who
took away her parents got it in his mean old head to come down
and snatch Fink from her, too.

"Stop," Alex scolded herself. "Just stop it...*stop!*" She
pressed her hands to her temples and squeezed away the haunting
images, focusing on her breathing and trying to match it with the
clock's rhythmic ticking. That was how she'd taught herself to
stop hyperventilating as a child. But now *this* had to go and happen. A car accident, no less. And *she*, of all people, had to be the
one to witness it. Alex hated when things like this happened; hated
when something happened to make those old feelings come back
and undermine the ways she had learned to cope with her tragedy.

Alex looked away from the fire, her long black eyelashes
damp with tears trained never to spill from her eyes. And just as
it seemed they would, she jumped up, scoffing at herself, as she
threw another log on the hearth.

Put your head before your heart, she would have told anyone, because at least the head had eyes and ears and rested on a
relatively logical foundation. But the heart? What was it, anyway,
but a senseless little blob, mindless and spineless and condemned
to *feeling* its way through life's philosophical muck? And if you
made a habit of following it, why, it would lead you into a whole
lot of metaphysical dilemmas from which it wasn't bright enough
to find its way out. The *head* was the way to go.

Alex paced the hunter green carpet a couple of times, then
poured a shot of Grand Marnier before returning to her rocking
chair.

Sheriff Silber had taken a report over the phone, promising to put out an APB, even call the local hospitals in case an
unidentified woman, dead or alive, showed up in any of the county
hospitals. But without a body or a license plate, and without Alex

having actually *witnessed* someone making off with a body, there
was not much anyone could do but wait. Breaking into an agitated rock, Alex rocked in her chair
as though she were in a swing at a playground. But just before she
bowled herself over, the log on the hearth caught fire and sent a
violent spray of frenzied flames reflecting off the polished surface
of the brass bell on the coffee table. Abruptly, she stopped herself
and focused her eyes—her thoughts—on the shining bell. Its black,
wrought iron handle stood silhouetted against the yellow fire. Alex
studied it, thumbing her chin. So feminine it was; maybe a dinner bell, a servants' bell, belonging, somewhere in time, to a
maiden or a wealthy mistress. Alex lifted herself, leaning forward
to carefully grasp the bell by its stem, then sat back down and
dangled the bell in front of her face for close inspection. The
handle's art-nouveau design was exquisite, a vine-like pattern
artfully woven into a leafy, heart-shaped tip.

Alex ran a still-trembling fingertip over its cool and shining surface, traced a slow finger along the circular line of its flared
and golden mouth. Then she turned it over, peering into the bar-
rel. She was puzzled by the frayed duct tape sloppily securing the
clapper, and wondered at the bell's possible significance. What
value could it possibly possess to send an old woman out in the
middle of a storm? Maybe it was a collector's piece, an antique of
some value; possibly a family heirloom that the old woman, upon
her demise, would have wanted Alex to deliver to a relative—a
grandchild, say. But *deliver* is not what the woman had said, was
it? *Ring,* she had said. *Ring and she will come....*

Alex didn't like the bell, didn't like the idea of a dead
person's belongings in her home. And it occurred to her that she
didn't have to assume responsibility for it. She could open the
door and toss it outside if she wanted—pitch it like an apricot
and let it sink unseen into the muddy poppy field. Maybe next
year the poppy-picking thief would steal it and rid her of it.

But the bell, she reminded herself, was her only tangible
link to the old woman, the only physical proof that what happened tonight had, in fact, really happened. Maybe that's why she

hadn't mentioned it to Sheriff Silber. Without the bell, there would be nothing to help her distinguish between reality and what was fast beginning to feel like a dream.

Part of Alex wanted to phone Ana Mae, get her opinion on this awful matter. But Ana Mae wouldn't believe any of it; she'd accuse Alex of being up to her usual pranks—of trying to spook her. *Get a life,* is what she'd tell Alex, and then she'd probably hang up. And really, that's what Alex would want her to do, because it would be embarrassing—shaming, quite truthfully, to let Ana Mae see her in this present weakened and indecisive state— even if it was only over the telephone.

Alex set the bell in the palm of her open hand, as though estimating its weight, and watched it sparkle in the firelight before turning it upside down and curiously peeking in. With a thumb pressed against the clapper, she gently peeled off the frayed duct tape, stuck it to the oak arm of her rocker, then grasped the black heart-shaped handle again and rang.

The tiny clapper swung back and forth, striking the brass sound bow and sending forth a series of chime-like tings which resounded throughout the sparsely furnished room. Then Alex stopped ringing and listened. There was a strangeness about the resonation. Rather than diminishing in intensity, the reverberations grew stronger, their frequency quickening to a higher pitch that sounded like a computer starting up.

With each second that passed, the echoes continued to increase, climbing to an inaudible pitch that would have set a dog to howling. Then it transcended sound, and suddenly there was nothing—no ringing at all—only a sharp clinking sound, like two crystal glasses meeting in a toast.

"What the...?" Alex leaned forward and set the bell on the table, looking in open-mouthed amazement at the crack in her liqueur glass. Then, with the caution of someone walking around an explosive, Alex gripped the arms of the Windsor rocker, eased herself up and slowly stepped back, gazing incredulously at both the bell and the oozing Grand Marnier.

But as she stood wondering at the phenomenon, her thoughts now absorbed entirely by the bell, something blew by; something light and breezy and draft-like. The skin on her neck prickled where its warmth touched her. And unless it was merely an auditory illusion, Alex heard the faintest tinkling noise, as though the sound waves were, by some force of nature, making a U-turn and coming back at her—traversing the room in a quad-raphonic manner so that she couldn't tell from where the sound was coming.

Apprehension rose in Alex, that deep-down gut-feeling that tells you to *run like hell!* There was an energy about the room, an unmistakable presence softly blowing in past the flames. Alex sensed she wasn't alone anymore. She glanced behind her, quickly noting her spatial relationship to the front door—the nearest exit, should she need it momentarily—then turned back to see the oddest mist forming in front of her hearth. Like a mirage it was, creating for Alex the optical effect of heat rising off a summer road. But then it thickened, glittering and fizzing with specks of pastel colors and distorting the hearth behind it. And for a mo-ment, it seemed Alex's whole living room was a big flute being filled with champagne. She watched, paralyzed by a mixture of fear and fascination as the sparkling effervescence worked itself into an image, colors arranging and grouping themselves like some celestial paint-by-numbers, until, finally, the colors began taking on a human shape—the shape of a woman, if she wasn't mistaken.

Alex's lips were pursed so tightly, her nostrils flaring and her breathing so forceful, that she sounded like a cornered bull. But she wasn't about to lose control—she'd fight herself on this one—because if she lost control now, she'd do nothing more than call attention to herself. *Nonchalance*, Alex told herself, was the key to survival tonight. There was no point in alarming the appa-rition, prompting it to chase her.

Ever so slowly, Alex began stepping back, a ready hand positioned behind her to clutch and turn the doorknob the minute she felt it touch her palm. No sooner had she taken three steps, though, than the shape changed again, the lower half radiating white, the top a mass of red, gold and brown pigments, all losing their translucence and solidifying into what looked to be a flowing mane of auburn hair. Alex stepped backwards steadily, finally jolting and startling herself when she bumped into the door. She gasped slightly, forced a polite and trembling smile as the shape took on the form of a hologram. It stood with its back toward her, undulating and wavering like an image mirrored in water. And although the figure was fast becoming three-dimensional, the flames flickering in the hearth still shone through it.

No sense in waiting for the hologram, or ghost—or whatever the hell it was—to turn around, Alex thought. Who's to say the face would be as pretty as its hair? What if it was rotten, decomposed, half eaten away; a hollow-eyed skull set to angrily clack its teeth when it caught Alex staring?

Alex quietly turned the knob, opened the door, then bolted, slamming it shut behind her and breaking into a frantic search for some makeshift form of defense.

"Out," she hollered, her bare feet slapping the rain-dampened planks as she ran the length of the porch in search of a suitable weapon. "Get out of my house!"

<&> 6 <&>

Damsel in Distress

Behind the porch swing Alex spotted a broom leaning up against the log wall. She gripped it like a tribal spear and
tiptoed back, creeping past the door and over to the window, un-
aware that in the midst of the commotion, the sash of her robe
had come undone.

Barefoot and now bare-chested, she crouched like a warrior, fully prepared to impale the hologram if necessary.

"Hey!" she shouted, popping up at the window and rapping on the glass with the broomstick. "Hey...*you!*" But the figure
wasn't a hologram anymore. It—*she*—was substantial, as real as
any other woman, her physical weight made evident by the fact
of her bare feet sinking into the pile of the green carpet. She was
facing Alex now, wispy bangs ablaze with color from the firelight,
her rosy skin and high cheekbones highlighted by the fire. But
Alex could not see the woman's eyes. They were cast down, her
head hung slightly forward, as though she were reaching to pick a
wildflower in the ethereal meadow from which she'd just been
plucked and transported.

Alex peered in, her breath fogging the window, her black
curls and the tip of her nose pressed against the glass. "Hey..."

Alex tried again, but the exclamation had drained from her voice. She gave the fogged glass a wipe with her forearm.

The woman noticed the movement and looked up in the direction of the window. Her eyes were so light—blue or maybe gray—that they shone like sequins in the firelight, disarming Alex with their strange and impersonal compassion. And when they finally met Alex's, Alex felt her muscles go soft. She lowered her broomstick, holding it like a staff, her earlier fear now replaced by unspeakable awe. "Who are you...?" Alex asked, intending to yell, but managing only a whisper.

But the woman seemed not to know where she was, let alone *who* she was. A crinkle of confusion appeared between her eyes, and she began pivoting; first circling clockwise, then in a counter fashion, then back to face Alex. She looked all about, her starry eyes roaming the entire room, and when she regarded Alex again, her focal point changed. She stared now, quite indifferently, at something below Alex's eye level.

Alex squinted questioningly, looking down to follow the woman's line of vision, and when her chin hit her chest she saw it was her own breasts that held the woman's attention.

"Christ...!" Alex yelled, dropping the broom and groping wildly for the ends of her sash. The sudden embarrassment drove her back into her previously frenzied state. "Out!" she ordered, and picked up the broom. "Get *out* of my *house*!"

The woman's look of confusion only intensified. She slowly shook her head, her lips parting as if to say something.

"Speak up," Alex demanded, unable to make out a word of it through the closed window. Huffing, she held on to her broom and with a free hand pushed up the window a bit. "Did you say something?" she shouted in.

"What is it you would have me do?" the woman asked weakly, pausing between words.

"Just go—get out."

At first her expression was blank, as though she had no idea how to go about initiating such a task. She glanced at the door, then slowly down at her own feet and took one unsteady step.

"No, not that one! Behind you...the door *behind* you," Alex instructed, thinking to get the woman out the back while she slipped back in the front and locked both doors. There was no sense in a confrontation; no sense having the woman join her on the porch. "Turn around." She used her broomstick as a pointer, directing the woman to the back door at the near end of the kitchen.

But the woman paid no mind to Alex's demands. She seemed intent on exiting via the front door—even lifted an arm and pointed to it. "Out this door...?" she asked.

And before Alex could think to solve their communication difficulties—before she could even utter another word—the woman took two more unsteady steps, spun halfway around, then collapsed on the carpet.

"Hello?" Alex shouted. "Hello...?" And when no response came, Alex's eyes widened with panic. "Shit," she shouted, looking wildly around, then peered up at the porch roof, addressing some higher power. "Why can't you *ever* leave me alone?"

Alex didn't bother to wait for an answer. She knew better than to expect one. Holding the broom in both hands, she rushed to the door, turned the knob, then booted it open with a foot. Crouching once more, she cautiously crept inside to approach and circle the woman like a jackal moving around a carcass.

Alex edged the broomstick forward and gave the woman a poke, ready to drop the broom and run, should the stick pass right through her. She'd had just about all she could take tonight: a hit-and-run, a dead body...and now a swooning ghost in her living room. But the broomstick met with resistance against a solid body.

Drag the intruder outside is what Alex had a mind to do—drag her out, shut the door, forget that *any* of this ever happened. Maybe by morning she'd disappear, or at least wander into someone else's house. And suddenly it struck Alex that perhaps the woman had done just that—*wandered* in—and hadn't materialized from thin air at all. Maybe the whole damned thing had been staged; the trick of an illusionist masterminded by any of a dozen women out to get even with her—maybe even Ana Mae.

Alex gave the woman a second and a third poke, glancing suspiciously at the bell and wondering if ringing it again might reverse the process, send the woman back. But in the end she didn't for fear of conjuring up yet another uninvited guest. Who could say if the second one would be as nice and pretty as the first? With her luck she'd get the clacking skeleton.

The woman stirred just then, a soft whimper issuing from her mouth as she blinked open her eyes. They were gray—Alex could see that now—and they twinkled like crystals through shags of chestnut bangs. She stared up at Alex and breathed softly, deeply. "You...?"

Alex's brow shot up in surprise. "Me...?"

"Your name...."

"Who—me? Mine?" Alex stammered. "Alex," she said.

"Mmm...Alex...." The woman smiled a weak but tranquil smile, her rosy lips moving ever so slowly to form her words. Then, "Alex..." she murmured again. "I am bound?"

"I don't know *where* you were bound," Alex blurted, "but you ended up here!"

"Here...?"

"In my house."

"Your *house*...?"

"Halfmoon."

"On the moon...?"

"No, the *town*. In New York," she added. "North America...on the east coast. Earth, to be exact."

The woman lay on her back, a thousand questions dancing in her firelit eyes. She seemed drugged, Alex thought, intoxicated. And it was rubbing off; there was something strangely intoxicating about the way she said Alex's name; the way she gazed so peacefully into Alex's eyes. All dressed in white, she looked like a wounded angel lying there on the carpet.

"Sleep, Alex...."

"What, you want to sleep? Here? You can't sleep *here*."

"Take me...please...."

"Oh geez. Please, no, I—I can't—" Alex got up and wiped the perspiration from her forehead. What was she to do? Refusing to cooperate might only worsen the apparition's present condition, maybe even cause her to die. Alex couldn't stand to witness yet another death tonight. There was, after all, only so much a woman could handle in one day. She looked around the room in a quiet panic, wondering where a suitable napping place might be. Perhaps that's all she would require—a nap. Then hopefully she'd awake, feeling strong and refreshed, and simply fly away.

The sofa was a possibility, but having her in the living room would limit Alex's access to the kitchen, the phone, the front door, should she herself decide to suddenly take flight. Better to tuck her away in the bedroom, Alex thought. But when she looked back down, the woman's eyes were closed again.

"Oh no—you're not going to die, lady, are you? Please don't die on me—not here." Alex knelt on one knee, making to touch her, but not sure how to go about it. "Lady...?"

"Orielle..." she whispered groggily, her heavy-lidded eyes opening halfway.

"What do you mean?" Alex asked, her tone almost frantic.

"My name."

"Your name? Your name is Orielle?"

"Mmm....take me, Alex," she pleaded. And then her eyes closed again.

Cringing, Alex gently took her arm and hand, helping her into a sitting position. So far, she felt ordinary enough; tangible, at least, and not unnaturally cold as Alex had feared she'd be. Yet there was a weightlessness, a buoyancy about her, too, which made Alex feel as though she were dragging someone through water. And when she looked up at Alex with those sleepy gray eyes, Alex felt a little on the light side herself.

"Alex..." Orielle repeated for no apparent reason.

"It's all right...I'm right here," Alex managed in a hoarse voice, then helped Orielle to stand and secured an arm around her waist.

"Lead me, Alex. I cannot..."

"Okay, okay...the bed is just down the hallway here. Can you make it down the hallway?" She was more worried than frightened now. In truth, there was actually nothing frightening about Orielle—save for the unlikely means of her arrival.

Halfway down the hall she began almost to feel the woman's weight bearing down upon her shoulder. It was as if with each step Orielle was getting a slight bit heavier. Alex strengthened her grip around Orielle's waist—held tightly to the arm slung over her shoulder—and when she had reached the bedroom door, leaned against the frame and freed one arm to grope for the light switch.

As Alex helped her uninvited guest into bed, she was still furious with the *forces*. And what bothered her most was the idea of being, once again, a randomly selected target tonight. A woman's life was supposed to be a willful one, wasn't it? A pick-and-choose-and-mix-and-match affair. She hated it when someone else—*something* else—came along and did the picking for her. It took the predictability, the nicety out of life.

"Are you thirsty?" Alex asked once she had drawn the covers up over Orielle's waist. She'd remind herself to strip the bed tomorrow.

"Thirsty..." she said with a sigh, "...but I cannot hold it."

Oh, great, Alex thought. Here she'd saved her, accommodated her needs, and in a show of gratitude the spirit woman—or whatever she was—would go and wet her bed. But she left a glass of water on the nightstand anyway, just in case it might speed up the woman's recovery.

Alex was beginning to seriously wonder if the night's events didn't signify something too grand for her comprehension. And when it was over and done with, she decided she'd need to give serious attention to this matter of external forces. Perhaps if she just learned to give in and go with the flow the *powers* would lose interest in harassing her. Take the opossum in the barn; now *there* was a fine example. When powers beyond his control threatened to strike, he simply submitted, happy to stay cozily curled in the barn. He didn't insist on defying the elements for the sake of indulging himself in pecan coffee—nor *milk* for the pecan coffee. And he was clearly a better animal for it.

Alex wondered if maybe she wouldn't do well to take a lesson from the opossum. Maybe in the morning she'd pay the marsupial a visit; sit in the barn and treat herself to a heart-to-heart monologue with the pouched Zen master. It might help shed some light on the subject of eluding the powers that be. And it would certainly beat hanging around, waiting for Orielle to disappear.

⋘ 7 ⋙
The Healer

Alex awoke slumped on the couch in her jeans, her legs planted wide apart and her hands tucked warmly in the pockets of her blue terry robe. She couldn't have said for sure whether she'd slept or merely spent the night in a state of suspended consciousness.

Last thing she remembered was listening to the drizzling rain, warding off sleep and dumbly watching the embers burn out. Now geese honked overhead and the sun fought its way through the louver shutters. It was a fruitless fight, though; the living room faced north, with no eastern windows, and the log walls were simply too dark to be lightened up by much of anything. It suddenly struck Alex that the entire room was a rather gloomy sight by day. Only at night did the hurricane lamps and a firelit hearth bring out the room's more cheerful points. But then Alex wondered if her dreary perception of things had to do less with the lack of sun and more with the night's tribulations.

Horrid thoughts of the dead old woman made Alex's stomach flip-flop. And a glance at the bell instantly set her heart to racing. She forced a quick look down the hallway to her right, wanting yet not wanting to know if Orielle was still there. Alex wanted to pray the woman would be gone, but prayer, she knew, wasn't a viable option for the poor in faith. She could always wish, though, couldn't she? And wish she did. With all her might. She wished that Orielle had simply evaporated during the night—that she'd saddled up some waves and ridden them away as fast as she rode in. And if her wish came true, she decided she'd be more than happy to chalk up the whole incident to posttraumatic stress—a reactive psychosis induced by witnessing the old woman's violent death last night. Then she'd shower, dress, bury the bell and gladly get on with her day.

Alex listened intently. The house was dreadfully quiet now, the floorboards creaking as she stood up and slowly crept across the room. The hallway was dark, and the bedroom door would have been lost in its shadows if not for hazy sunshine seeping out along its four sides, outlining it like an aura. As Alex approached the bedroom door it seemed like a proverbial light at the end of some metaphysical tunnel. And behind it, of course, was the very real matter of the metaphysical guest in her bed.

❨ ❨ ❨

Sunlight fell in lines across Orielle's sleeping face. She stirred beneath the rays which played warmly on her closed lids, turning the darkness of her dreams into a visual field of radiating red. And somewhere in that field of shut-eyed color, she recalled the dark and handsome face of the woman who had led her to this bed. Alex....

Orielle ran her legs dreamily over the cotton sheets, so refreshingly cool and soft against her skin, and breathed in a familiar, Sambuca-like sweetness in the morning air. And from somewhere, not far off, came the low humming of honeybees.

Orielle's gray eyes sparkled like faceted crystals, her silky russet hair spilling over the pillow as she rolled her head from side to side and settled her eyes on a garden window. It had been left open just a crack—enough for the sounds and smells of early summer to find their way into the room. Like tears from a rainbow, sunlit raindrops clung to the glass. Just beyond them, grape-like vines of wisteria cascaded past the window like a violet waterfall. And all about the purple, pea-shaped flowers honey-bees drunkenly droned, stopping here and there to sit and drink from floral chalices. The humming was like a Gregorian chant to Orielle, a hymn to her ears...the sweet wisteria a balm to her weary mind.

She closed her eyes and lay still, succumbing to these earthly seductions, while wondering where she was. The air seemed light, and she felt her body at a higher altitude. But there was another kind of lightness about this space. Her spirit was still bound, she knew, yet freedom seemed to fill this room, and Lilah's presence no longer bore heavily upon her. But just how the black-eyed woman had come to take possession of her she did not know. Perhaps she was an *adept*, a descendent of the Magi—one of a new generation sent to keep an old promise. A member of the Guild had subverted Lilah, Orielle speculated, stolen the bell, and entrusted it to Alex for safekeeping until...until *what*, she did not know.

A clock on the oak nightstand read 6:22 a.m. But the time was not enough. Orielle needed to know the month, the day—she needed Alex. But just as she thought to reach and throw back the covers, a floorboard squeaked in the hallway.

Orielle stopped and waited with an expectant smile as the doorknob slowly turned. Knuckles of a hand on the knob appeared first, then the edge of a second hand pressed flat against the door, as though the person entering were attempting to sneak in on her. Bit by bit the door opened, just enough for a cluster of black curly hair to fill the open space. Then the curls were fol-lowed by the emergence of a nose and one dark and suspicious eye. But the instant the eye met hers, a single eyebrow jutted up in surprise, and the door quickly closed again.

Orielle crinkled her brow, perplexed by Alex's sudden re-treat. There was not a sound in the hallway now; not a floorboard creaking, nor even the sound of footsteps descending. Orielle knew Alex was still there; she could feel her presence, almost hear her breathing on the other side of the door.

"Alex?"

There was no answer, only a series of creaks, as though the person behind the door had just shifted her body weight. "Is it you, Alex?" She waited another moment. "Alex...?"

"Yes...?" Alex's voice was low and hollow-sounding in the hallway.

"You may open the door."

There was a long pause, and then, "No...it's okay."

"Please *do* come in," Orielle offered.

There was another pause, longer this time.

"Alex...?

Slowly, then, the knob turned again, the door opening only halfway, and there in the doorway Alex stood stiff and motionless, her countenance rather zombie-like.

"Good morning...." Orielle pleasantly greeted.

Alex began fidgeting, putting clenched hands in her pockets so that her fists bulged beneath the fabric of her blue plaid robe.

"G'morning...." she flatly responded, her lips barely moving.

The blue of the robe complemented the mass of dark curls that hung down on her forehead, just far enough to touch the peaks of her arched eyebrows. But beyond the colors Alex wore, Orielle could not read her aura. The mixture of emotions swirling inside Alex's heart was too erratic to decipher in the bedroom's bright sunlight, and Orielle's powers were far from restored. She needed her own energy, she needed to eat soon, to bask in the sun. But for the moment, she was content to delight in seeing this new and handsome face. Her senses were clear now, her vision sharper than it had been last night. She thoughtfully gazed at Alex's full chin and slightly squared jaw—the jaw of a stubborn and independent woman, Orielle surmised, worthy of being her protector. But the eyes appeared soft from where she lay, a black, velvet-lined abyss that seemed to unknowingly call Orielle into them as though some part of Alex were in need of healing.

"Are you not well?" Orielle asked softly.

"I'm fine...." Alex said, regarding her strangely.

Orielle patted the bed. "Won't you sit, then?" she asked.

"No...."

Orielle tilted her head in puzzlement over Alex's oddness. She seemed determined not to budge from the doorway. "At least come in...?"

Alex looked at Orielle as though she were speaking another language. Finally, she took a few hesitant steps toward the foot of the bed, coming at Orielle mechanically, clenched fists opening and closing inside her pockets like the kneading paws of a cat.

Orielle smiled softly again, bemused by Alex's apparent shyness. "You are of the blood?"

"Huh...?"

"The blood," Orielle repeated. "A Crafter. You *are* with the Guild, no?"

"The *Guild*? I don't know what you mean—I don't know what you're talking about," Alex stammered. I don't belong to any *guild*!"

The smile disappeared from Orielle's face, replaced by a look of confusion. She studied Alex silently, careful when she spoke again. "Then who...who *are* you?"

"Nobody," Alex protested, as though held at gunpoint. "I'm nobody—honest."

"Then how is it you have come to own me?"

"*Own* you?" Alex's eyes bulged. "But I don't—I swear. There was a car accident last night—a woman was hit. She made me take you—take the bell, I mean."

Orielle threw back the sheet and swung her legs over the edge of the bed, only vaguely aware of Alex's eyes wondrously roaming the length of her bare legs. She stood, absently pulled down the white gown that had worked its way up around her waist during sleep, then walked to the window.

"Where are we, Alex?"

"Halfmoon," Alex answered abruptly, "I told you last night."

"It is in the north?" she asked, surveying the misty crowns of mountains against a pastel sky.

"Northeast."

"Near the Fountain ..." Orielle murmured.

"What?"

But Orielle did not answer. "What is the month?" she asked instead.

"June."

"And the solstice...has it come?"

Alex took a moment to process the question. "Summer, you mean? No, not until the twenty-first."

"And when would that be?"

Alex's fingers moved in her pockets, as though she was using them to help her to count. "Less than a week."

Orielle whirled around as though in slow motion. "This woman you speak of...who is she?"

"I don't *know*. I told you, I don't know anything."

"Take me to her, Alex."

"But I...I *can't*," Alex pleaded. "She's *dead*!"

The peace drained from Orielle's mind, the threat of Lilah weighing down upon her. "What did you do to the bell?"

Alex's eyes grew wide with worry, and she felt about ready to snap under the pressure. "There was tape on the clapper, and I...I peeled it off and rang it. She *told* me to ring it, she—"

"But now," Orielle interrupted. "Where is it now?"

Alex gestured toward the living room. "In the living room—I left it on the coffee table. You can have it."

Orielle's eyes narrowed calculatingly. "You saw me come through the bell...."

"Yes..." Alex said, both her voice and her eyes dropping. "I watched you...."

Orielle nodded solemnly. "I am enchanted, Alex...my spirit is bound by the magical properties of that bell...by the power of my mistress."

Alex's eyes grew wide and seemed even more blank now. And when she tried to swallow, her tongue did little more than cluck against the roof of her mouth. "But she gave the bell to *me*, so I'll give it to you, okay? Just take it, and take yourself back, too—I don't want the damned thing. Honest!"

"It's not that simple, Alex. The woman you saw last night could not possibly have been my mistress. She was someone else... although I do not know who. I suspect the accident you witnessed was not an accident at all, but that the woman struck by the car was an unknown guardian—someone who managed to steal the bell in hopes of freeing me. I can only believe she was being chased."

Orielle looked about the room, her thoughts racing, then zeroed in on Alex once more. "What are you, Alex?"

Alex's volume built defensively again. "Nothing—I told you, I'm nothing, I just—"

"No, no...your work, Alex, your talents," Orielle whispered, trying to calm Alex. "What is it that you do?"

Alex stared at her. Simple questions seemed to be causing her such strain. "I...I'm a forest ranger, but I...I mostly publish guides now. *Look*," Alex blurted, "I'm sorry I rang your bell, okay? Really, I am, but—"

"Guides?" Orielle asked, her gray eyes lighting with hope as they searched Alex's face.

"Field and tracking guides...trail maps..."

A smile broke on her face. "A pathfinder..." she mused. "Huh?"

"A pathfinder...you make *paths*." A certain sense of comfort returned to her again. "Take me, Alex. Find me a way to her."

"But I can't! A car took the body away. How can I track a *car*? I don't know where—"

Alex stopped abruptly and Orielle waited, holding Alex's gaze until a look of silent confirmation appeared in those dark and beautiful eyes.

"You mean...where she was coming *from*...?" Alex asked.

Orielle nodded encouragingly. "I need you, Alex, to find the path from where she came."

Alex gave a nervous shrug. "The ground would have been soft enough to hold prints. But the rain was heavy...any tracks might have deteriorated by now." Alex looked up with a promising intelligence Orielle had not seen before.

"But we will try...and you will be my pathfinder...?"

Alex, willingly or not, gave in. It didn't seem she had a choice. "All right," she finally said.

Orielle heaved a sigh of relief and smiled warmly upon her pathfinder. "Good," she said. "We will breakfast now?"

"Breakfast...?" Alex asked, that comforting air of intelligence fading to a look of dumbfounded wonder once again. "You eat food?"

"My body has stabilized. I must eat now, and replenish my energy."

Alex only stared at her.

"Shall I prepare something for us?" Orielle offered.

"No! No," Alex said, taking one hand out of her pocket to gesture toward the hallway with a thumb. "I'll a...I'll fix something."

"No meat, please. Bread and fruit will be fine."

"Bread and fruit?" Alex nodded. "Bread and fruit," she mumbled, then turned in a disoriented fashion to leave the room.

Orielle watched her pathfinder's every movement with pleasure. She had confidence in Alex—she couldn't afford not to. Alex was her guardian now; the keeper of the bell. And if she succeeded in making a path, it might well serve as her path to freedom. It was not by accident that she—that the bell—was here so close to the solstice. Someone's plans—plans unknown to Orielle—had failed, but destiny now acted in her favor; it had led Alex to her...and now Alex would lead *her*.

⊰⊱ 8 ⊰⊱

Pathfinder

Fruit, jam and hot buns were spread out on the blue-checkered tablecloth, and from the kitchen window came the lament of a mourning dove. Alex was glad for the bird's incessant cooing, for it filled the awkward silence and gave her time to think of something appropriate to say. Elbows propped on the table, Alex held her mug in two hands, and over the rim studied her improbable houseguest. She had already watched Orielle eat three cinnamon buns and the better part of a mango, and now stared wondrously as Orielle—like a dislocated princess from a fairy tale—went about making an erotic art of berry-eating.

Beneath the table Alex's knee bounced up and down, but above the table she feigned indifference, pretending not to be distracted by the sensual appeal of Orielle's table etiquette. Discard both the sensual *and* the supernatural circumstances of this unlikely happening is what she'd need to do; opt for a pragmatic approach to coping with the ethereal problem at hand.

Did it really matter *where* Orielle had come from? Whether she was prisoner in a jail cell or an enchanted bell wasn't the point, Alex convinced herself. The point was getting the woman where she needed to go. And the faster Alex got her there, the sooner she'd be rid of her.

Maintaining a logical framework was the key to her emotional survival; she'd simply pretend Orielle was like any other innocent captive in need of speedy relocation. And while she was at it, Alex decided, she'd do well to speedily relocate her own eyes. They were fixed, at the moment, on Orielle's white silk dress. It was shear, nearly see-through in the morning light, and revealed beneath it were shadowed nipples as taut and rosy as the strawberry Orielle now lifted to her fruit-moistened lips.

Alex set her coffee mug down and drummed the table with her fingers, and Orielle, in response, stopped in mid-bite and held the half-eaten strawberry away from her lips. "Is something wrong, Alex?"

"No...nothing's wrong, it's just that...that..." Alex paused, struggling to keep her eyes off Orielle's aesthetic aspects, "you'll need to put something on before we go."

"Something on...?"

"*Clothes,*" Alex self-consciously clarified. "You'll get scratched up in the brambles in that thing. Besides," she said, releasing an index finger from the handle of her mug and with it making little circles to indirectly gesture at Orielle's chest. "Your dress is sort of, well...*you know*," she finished, awkwardly flailing her finger one last time.

"No, Alex, I don't believe I do."

"See-through," Alex grumbled, trying her best to appear aloof. "Your dress is see-through. You can't go out walking around like that...."

Orielle looked down at her chest, then back at Alex. "Oh," was all she said.

Alex puffed her cheeks as she exhaled and gave the table top another drumming. She hoped Orielle had no recollection of last night's accidental baring of her own breasts. "So...I'll, uh...I'll find you something to wear," Alex offered, then compulsively eyed Orielle's breasts again before looking down and taking inventory of a crossed leg and bare foot jutting out from beneath the blue-checkered tablecloth. "You'll need shoes, too," Alex added.

Sunglasses wouldn't have been a bad idea either. Orielle's crystal-gray orbs were getting to her more and more by the minute; the color of a storm they were—the *calm* before a storm—so beguiling in their quiet turbulence, and so settling as to be *unsettling*. That impersonal compassion still shone in them, too, only now it was losing its universal appeal and taking on a more personal focus which made Alex feel terribly transparent; as transparent as Orielle's silk dress.

"Something troubles you, Alex. Are you not well?"

"Who, me?" Alex facetiously pointed to herself and forced a chuckle. "No. No, I'm not well, now that you mention it—I haven't *been* well since last night."

Above gray eyes, Orielle's brow furrowed in an expression of worry, a note of genuine concern rising in her voice. "What ails you?"

"You want to know? You *really* want to know? I'll tell you," Alex said, her own voice growing higher until it nearly cracked. She stared incredulously for a moment, amazed at how commonplace their sitting here seemed to Orielle. "Last night I went out for milk. You understand? *Milk!* I was minding my own business, just wanting to get milk and get home before the storm broke. But what happens instead?" Alex paused, trying to keep her words even. "Instead, I witness a hit-and-run, an old woman hands me a bell, dies in my arms, then her body mysteriously *disappears* and *you* appear. That's what ails me, okay? I mean, no offense, Oreo—"

"Orielle."

"Orielle.... But, look at me. Look at *us*!" Alex forced another laugh of mocking disbelief. "I'm in my kitchen eating strawberries with an apparition!"

Almost imperceptibly, Orielle winced at the insult, then lowered her head subserviently. "What is it you mean to say?"

"That I'm still counting on you to be an illusion, a figment of my imagination—or how about a prank? A hoax? I'd even settle for a—" Alex cut herself short and, leaning in, narrowed her black eyes in clever suspicion. "Do you know Ana Mae Wingo? Did *she* put you up to this?"

"No...."

"You swear?"

Orielle looked truly insulted by the accusation, and for the first time Alex detected a note of huffiness in her voice. "I know no such person, Alex. I am *not* a prank, nor a *hoax*—nor an *apparition*. You saw me come, did you not? You witnessed my arrival?" She lowered her head submissively, her cinnamon hair falling forward, then peered intensely up at Alex with truth-seeking eyes. "How is it, Alex, that a pathfinder should have such little trust in her senses?"

Alex rubbed her face, scratched the back of her neck. "Then...then how'd you get in there?"

"Where?"

"The *bell*. Where did you come from—where do you go?"

"It all depends," Orielle answered calmly. "Should you ring while we are apart, I will come to where you are...but if you ring when I am here...you will send me back."

"But where? Back *where?* Where's *there?*"

Orielle shrugged. "I am not certain, Alex. Wherever sounds go, I suppose."

"What do you mean, you *suppose?* You don't *know?* You don't *know* where you go?"

"Time stops there...I am not fully conscious, nor able to expend the psychic energy necessary for thought."

Groaning, Alex rubbed her face again and shook her head wearily. When she spoke again her voice deepened to a whisper. "What are you...?" she asked. But as soon as the words left her mouth, she regretted having asked the question. She wasn't sure she wanted to know.

Casually, Orielle took another berry from the bowl, slowly chewed and swallowed, then gathered the napkin from her lap and daintily patted her berry-stained lips. "A sylph."

"A *sylph*," Alex repeated, mockingly nodding in consideration of the idea. "I see." But then she suddenly broke under the pressure of it all. "And just *what the hell* is a *sylph?*" she demanded.

Orielle calmly reached across the table and plucked another berry from the bowl. "A fairy," she said, then put the whole berry in her mouth.

"A fairy?"

"Mm-hm."

"A fairy. You're telling me you're a *fairy.*"

"Yes, Alex," she said when she had finally swallowed.

Alex tried to raise her brow matter-of-factly—as casually as she would have in response to someone offering up their occupation during the course of conversation. But her one foot was tapping the floor, the other knee jiggling and bouncing so violently that it prompted Orielle to lean down and have a look beneath the tablecloth to see what all the commotion was about.

"My mother was one, but I was sired by a human father...and humans, even *half-humans,* cannot survive in the fairy realm for any length of time. I lived with my father, in this world...until my capture."

Abruptly Alex stood, pushed the kitchen chair back, then tightened her blue robe and began to pace. She was too agitated to sit. She needed to walk soon—get out, move around, breathe some fresh air—get fairies off her mind and her mind off the fairy's breasts.

Orielle didn't say a word. She sat there, hands folded demurely in her lap, and with those omniscient gray eyes followed Alex's movement along the length of the kitchen.

"Listen...I'm sorry, okay?" Alex blurted, sorry for insulting the fairy, and angry at herself for even *feeling* sorry. "But I—I can't handle this. I'm not experienced with mysticism or spiritualism or any of that New Age stuff—I don't even have a religion!"

Orielle regarded her appreciatively. "You need only believe your eyes."

"My eyes. Right," Alex sighed, "my eyes...." Facing the window and the kitchen sink, she turned on the faucet and leaned on the counter for physical, maybe even moral, support—God knew she could have used a little of each. Then suddenly, she splashed her face with cold water and raked back her black curls with a wet hand. "I don't see *how* I can help you."

"You underestimate yourself, Alex. I was quite weak last night, not yet molecularly stable." Orielle paused, smiling empathically. "You could have done as you wished with me...turned me away, cast me into the storm...rung me back into the bell."

"Oh, great, *now* you tell me."

Orielle's face softened even more, her crystal-gray eyes surveying Alex with a kindness approaching that of adoration. "But you didn't, Alex. You gave me your bed, instead...a place to rest, to sleep, to eat. And now...? You offer to clothe me...to find a path for me."

Alex doubted she could walk a straight line right now, let alone find a path. Her emotions were confused, her earlobes awfully hot, and the dove's monotonous repetitions were beginning to grate on her nerves. From a cabinet above the sink she retrieved a glass and an aspirin bottle, washed down two pills, then impulsively opened the screen and tossed the remaining water at the bird. The cooing stopped.

"Like I said," Alex began, wiping her mouth and turning back to Orielle, "I'll try to help you find something—but then I'm out of this."

"As you like, Alex," she said, acutely aware and respectful of her hostess's apprehension.

"Okay," Alex agreed. "But if we uncover anything—*anything at all*—I'll call the State police in to help you—"

"No! No police, Alex." Orielle's words seemed more a command than a plea. "I'm afraid this matter is outside their jurisdiction. They are no match for her."

"*Her*...? Your lover...?"

Orielle appeared a bit confused. "She is not my lover. Why do you honor her with such a title?"

Embarrassed, Alex shrugged. "I don't know...you called her your mistress in the bedroom."

"*Mistress*...yes, the one who has power over me. She is *not* my lover."

Alex didn't know what to say next. Orielle seemed to sense her discomfort and tried to explain. "Lilah did have a lover...she keeps many lovers," she said. "There were two at the time—a man and a woman—who aided in my capture."

Orielle stared dreamily at the kitchen window, partially closing her eyes as though in reminiscence. "One of them...the man...was a brilliant young physicist out of Oxford. It was he who crafted the bell you possess. And the woman," Orielle went on, "was an equally gifted apothecary—a chemist who might have gone on to make great contributions to the healing arts, had she not turned her talents to the infernal science."

"Infernal?"

"Death by poison.... She was one of the most notorious assassins of her time. A formidable adversary of anyone interfering with her lover's pursuits."

Temporarily distracted from her anxiety, Alex stretched her arms along the sink, waiting for Orielle to continue.

"Benjamin and Batilda weren't inherently bad people," Orielle explained. "They were simply in love...but their loyalty and devotion to the wrong woman caused their downfall. Each one, you see, would have done anything to win Lilah's love—to be the sole object of her affection. And Lilah likely intended it that way. She pitted them against one another, so that each, in attempting to win her heart, would work harder at their respective crafts. In doing so, they unknowingly gave Lilah her true desire. What they failed to realize, however, or realized too late, was that it was immortality, not love, which Ms. Ponce de Leon so desperately sought...."

At the mention of the name de Leon, Alex regarded Orielle questioningly. "De Leon..." she murmured, the name triggering memories of the Spanish explorer from high school text books.

"Yes...why? Do you know of Juan?"

"Well, sure...everyone's *heard* of him. He founded Florida while searching for the Fountain of Youth." Alex stuck her hands into the pockets of her terry robe. "What does he have to do with this?"

"Lilah is a descendent."

"Wow..." was all Alex could think to say.

"A paternal descendent," Orielle qualified. "As for Lilah's mother, no one is certain of her origins. It is said she was born of devils."

Alex felt a tightening in her throat at the mention of devils. She didn't like devils—didn't want to talk about them, didn't want to think about them. When it came right down to it, Alex decided she'd much prefer to continue her dealings with fairies.

"You see, Alex, the Fountain of Youth was a family legend. The Ponce de Leon archives contained many writings about the Fountain. Juan, however, was the first to draw up maps and set sail in search of the immortal waters. But, as you mentioned, he founded Florida instead. In 1429 he was attacked by Indians and died from a fatal arrow wound...and, needless to say, never *did* discover the Fountain."

"Well, of course he didn't—it's not *real*. It's just a story, just a *legend*, as you say....isn't it?" Alex said, hoping for some sort of confirmation.

"What I said," Orielle began, holding Alex's gaze with her soft gray eyes, as though carefully monitoring her hostess's reactions, "is that *Juan* never found it. Lilah did. Four centuries later. And it's not in Florida, Alex. The Fountain is here...in New York."

Alex opened her mouth, but all that came out was a sound amounting to no more than a snort. "That's...that's impossible!"

"As impossible as I am?"

Alex couldn't very well argue Orielle's point. She didn't even have a point of her own to argue, did she?

"I can't tell you of its exact location, Alex, but of its proximity I feel certain. There is no other reason why I—why the bell—would be brought here so near the solstice."

Alex walked across the planked kitchen floor, then crossed it again. "It can't be," she insisted. "Trust me on this one, okay? I've gotten wet in every body of water in this region— every creek, spring, pond, bog and river and, well..." she held her arms out, "*I'm* not getting any younger."

"It's not the water itself that possesses rejuvenating properties, but the energies generated by it when the nymphs gather to dance on that water."

Alex fell silent, her lips stupidly twisted, a lost look in her eyes.

"Sound waves heal, Alex—any physician will tell you this—and it is the foundation of fairy magic, the source of our healing powers. Every solstice the nymphs join together in celebration. Their dance is called a *fairy ring*." Orielle smiled and, to Alex's surprise, it somehow soothed her.

"It is the most beautiful sight a mortal could ever behold," Orielle said. "But the ring is very dangerous. No human has ever survived a dance in one, for the ring moves so swiftly that it attains the speed of light. And once the ring is formed it cannot be broken until the dance is done. If you, a human, tried to join in the dance...you would be danced to death."

Being danced to death was the least of Alex's concerns; she wasn't up for dancing and didn't plan to be any time soon—not at home, not at Raspberries, certainly not in a fairy ring. "And exactly where do you come in?"

"To the ring?"

"To the picture! To this whole...*hoopla!*"

Orielle seemed cautious when she spoke again, as though increasingly attuned to the tenuous position in which she had put her hostess. "I possess the healing powers of my mother, Alex. Lilah knew of my birth. She knew I was born of a fairy and that, as such, I possessed the powers and the secret knowledge of fairy magic. And since I also was of human blood, she knew she could capture and coerce me under the right conditions—induce me to reveal the knowledge which would become the blueprint for Benjamin's work in quantum physics. And with that knowledge Benjamin was able to devise a way to make objects move at the speed of light. And then he crafted the bell."

Alex returned to her chair, buried her face in her hands and peeked at Orielle through the spaces between her fingers. Then she groaned. "And so...what?...she continues to keep you in that bell because you're just beautiful to look at?"

"Why, thank you, Alex...."

Alex rolled her eyes. "It was just a question, not a compliment."

"I am her physician, Alex. As I said, fairies heal with sound waves emitted from their bodies. And when they join together during specific planetary arrangements, their healing properties are magnified. The collective energies emitted are then strong enough to drastically slow the aging process."

"Planetary arrangements...?"

"The moon must hide in the earth's shadow."

"An eclipse," Alex clarified.

Orielle nodded. "Of June's full moon."

"June's moon...."

"Yes...an eclipse of that moon is known as the devil's moon...and it must land on the night of the summer solstice."

Alex glanced at the Farmer's Almanac on her telephone stand. She could have turned in her chair and consulted the wall calendar, too, but she didn't need to verify what Orielle was saying. There had been talk all week of a lunar eclipse, and with the moon already half full, she knew the calendar would probably confirm what she didn't want to know right now.

"Lilah's lovers," Alex said, releasing a troubled sigh, "you said they realized their mistake...?"

"Yes...."

"So why can't they undo what they did?"

"They wanted to. By the time they realized their error it was too late. The power was Lilah's and they could do nothing to repossess it."

"But things are different now, right? Why don't you contact them? Use my phone!" Alex encouraged. "Do you have an address? We'll call information—get their numbers, track them down. I'll even drive you somewhere, get you on a plane or train or limo—"

"I'm afraid neither one is alive, Alex."

"You don't know that—they can't *both* be dead! One of them has to be—"

"No."

"Well why not? What makes you think they'd both be dead?"

"Alex..." Orielle interrupted, regarding her solemnly. She attempted a reassuring smile, but it was a thin and hopeless one at best. "All I have told you happened a very long time ago—almost one hundred years. Benjamin and Batilda were already in their late twenties at the time."

"But you said you *knew* them—you said you—" Alex stopped herself short and swallowed, a wave of nausea undulating in the pit of her stomach as she mentally calculated. "But that would make...that would make you..."

"Only thirty." And this time Orielle's smile *was* reassuring. "There is no time beyond the bell, and where there is no time there is no physical aging process. Only when I am called upon to serve Lilah in this realm do I age. She summons me usually no more than one day a week."

"So maybe it was Lilah who was killed last night...."

"No," Orielle said, without the slightest bit of doubt in her voice. "Lilah is still alive."

"But the woman was very old. She had dark eyes, wrinkles, long white hair and..."

"Lilah has no wrinkles. Her hair is black, worn back in a French braid to reveal the prominent widow's peak which is the mark of her mother's family, and her eyes are very light—as cold and blue as a winter sky. You would be struck by her beauty."

"And she just stays that way?"

"For one hundred years...but over the past few years she has begun to show signs of aging. You see, on that first night, when Lilah came to bathe in the residual energies of the fairy waters, she knew the powers were not enough to keep her young forever...she knew that within a hundred-year period she would need to bathe again. That is why Benjamin, combining the ways of fairy magic with his own theories on quantum physics, devised a way to bind me to the bell...so that I, forced to serve and heal Lilah, would care for her physical needs as the end of the century approached. I can only do so much, however. And I certainly cannot give her immortality...only another bath in the midst of a fairy ring can do that."

Alex felt herself begin to sweat. "Well, we are expecting an eclipse...and as for a full moon?" Alex said, daring to get up and stagger over to the wall by the phone. "It looks like you'll have your moon." A strange numbness slowly replaced her jitters as she tapped the square on the calendar. Her hand dropped to her side then, and she turned, waiting for Orielle to respond—to offer some sort of reassurance or, better yet, to slap her knee, burst out laughing, and tell Alex the joke was on her—compliments of Ana Mae Wingo.

But Orielle didn't. She only stared off into space, Alex's own worry mirrored in her stormy-gray eyes.

❀ 9 ❀
Here a Nymph, There a Nymph

By late morning Alex and Orielle were on the road, padding their way around puddles and hummocks of violets and buttercups that blossomed everywhere. They had only travelled a few hundred yards, yet getting Orielle even this far had proved an accomplishment. From the moment they had stepped off the porch, every little thing had captivated her: the wisteria and white lilac trees, the blue sky and swarming honeybees, even a white butterfly that chanced to flutter by. It was as if the insect had curled an antenna like a summoning finger, causing Orielle to about-face and follow dreamily after it.

"No!" Alex yelled, dashing ahead to cut Orielle off at the poppy field. "Not *that* way—*this* way!" she reprimanded, insisting that Orielle cooperate and follow her lead. Now, at least, they were on their way, although to *what*, Alex had no idea.

In the far distance a hawk glided in circles around the sun. Warming rays burned through the fog, turning it into a golden mist that made mountain peaks look like the floating parapets of some heavenly fortress. Across the road the sun shone on the water, too, but their side of the road was shaded by poplars and alder trees that grew on an incline and retained the night's cool dampness. Alex was aware of crows cawing somewhere in the woods, of cardinals singing above the rushing river, and then the faint rumble of an eighteen-wheeler, which quickly erased the morning's mystical mood.

On reflex, and without looking back, she held out an arm, signaling for Orielle to stay close. As she did so, Orielle said something, but the rumbling tractor trailer made it impossible for Alex to understand exactly what it was she was saying.

"*What?*" Alex hollered back.

"Cross." Orielle shouted again.

With growing impatience, Alex abruptly stopped and turned, her face softening involuntarily the moment her eyes settled upon Orielle. Standing there in Alex's clothes, Orielle seemed so ordinary—as natural as a dozen other women who had unexpectedly spent the night and borrowed clothes. Although Orielle wore Alex's clothes well, the olive L.L.Bean shorts were a size too big—fashionably so—and the sleeves of her yellow sweat shirt were long enough that they hung down to her palms. She clutched them as she shrugged sheepishly in acknowledgment of the deafening noise.

Alex waited as the truck-made wind blew her own black curls and then the fairy's russet locks. "What is it?" she demanded when the truck had passed and only the birds were heard again.

"Can we cross?" she repeated, looking toward the other side.

"What for?"

"The river," Orielle said, stretching out her arms in anticipation.

"What about it?"

"I hear it moving...and the sun shines there."

"So?" What did rivers have to do with anything? This was hardly a time for scenic detours, Alex thought. Orielle was supposed to be in crisis, wasn't she? Had she forgotten that?

"I need them, Alex...I need their energies. They will strengthen me."

Alex studied Orielle, still puzzling over how wonderfully ordinary she looked. Why couldn't it have been some hairy monster she'd summoned from the bell—some repulsive creature she might have guiltlessly beaten to death in self-defense? Why did

Orielle have to be so pleasant, so agreeable? Why did she have to be so damned beautiful?

Motioning with an exaggerated sweep of her hand, Alex rolled her eyes and gave a conceding sigh. "After you," she said.

Orielle's lips parted in a smile. Not the thin or sad sort of smile she'd shown earlier, but a genuine pleasure-smile. Without further regard for Alex, she crossed the storm-littered road, side-stepping the guard rail and turning back to extend a hand to her pathfinder.

But Alex shrank from the fairy's proffered hand. She didn't mean to; she'd touched Orielle last night, after all. But last night had been another story. Last night she hadn't had time to *think* about what she was doing. And that was the odd thing about thoughts; if you spent too much time thinking about them, you'd think yourself right out of them.

Lowering her eyes in unspoken respect, Orielle casually withdrew her hand and quickly dismissed the incident. "Thank you, Alex, it's beautiful here...." she whispered, gazing dreamily at the water below them.

Alex didn't say anything. She quietly swung one and then the other leg over the rail and came up behind Orielle.

Sunbeams glistened on the wet backs of river rocks, the rocks themselves arranged in such a way that it seemed the blue dragonflies were striking up a game of hopscotch. And in between the rocks the river mirrored the women's images, Orielle's watery, undulating reflection reminding Alex of her arrival last night.

A fairy...an honest to goodness, palpable fairy. Why was it so hard to believe? Alex wondered. Respectable people believed in angels, didn't they—invisible spirits flying about, meddling in our daily lives? So what was the big deal about fairies?

Alex stared at the back of Orielle's head. Her long, wavy hair was the color of cinnamon in the sun, its highlights an intermingling of reds, golds and chestnuts. And standing this close to it, Alex could smell the windblown fragrance of wild honeysuckle in it. She closed her eyes for a moment, thinking that if Orielle were not Orielle, but an ordinary woman—a woman she'd met at Raspberries, say—she'd have leaned forward and buried her nose in that floral-scented hair. But she resisted.

Alex walked on, leaving Orielle to her meditations. She shuffled pensively through the ankle-high violets and buttercups, the tips of her hiking boots stirring up iridescent dragonflies here and there. Like miniature helicopters, they rose up in front of Alex's feet, propelling themselves forward and out to hover over the river. They were young, recently out of the nymph stage, but pondering dragonflies and nymphs only reminded her of the two-legged nymph following behind.

Alex turned back, glimpsing Orielle's sideways figure, then turned forward again, her thoughts caught between the fairy behind her and the mystery of a murder ahead.

☾ ☾ ☾

Tracking was like walking through a storybook, each print a page on which was told the adventures of a living thing. Sometimes in spring, just after dawn, Alex would throw on a jacket and come to the river with a thermos of coffee. And there she'd sit, timing how long it took for the elements to change or obliterate the prints. It's how she'd learned to guess the age, the freshness of a print, to put the story in its proper time frame. But last night's story already had a time frame. It had an ending, too. All she needed to do now was figure out a plot and tell the tale backwards. Until she reached the beginning.

Alex stepped over the guard rail and crossed the road again, surveying the lush, shaded growth and an enormous willow leaning out from the poplars. The sun hit its straggly branches in such a way that they seemed bleached-white, like the lightning-lit hair of the old woman. And somewhere in the middle of the tree, where a face would be, Alex imagined a pair of dark, omniscient eyes.

Alex nudged the debris with her foot, kicking around the twigs and buds drying on the sun-warmed asphalt.

"Come on," she coaxed, waiting for Orielle to finish her meditations—or whatever it was she was doing—and catch up.

"Coming, Alex," she peeped from a distance, but even without the rumbling noise of an engine her soft voice was almost lost in the breeze.

Have faith, Spherris, Alex thought to herself. *You're gonna wake up from this nightmare real soon...and in the morning you'll be lying to Ana Mae, teasing her and telling her about the erotic bell and the hot little fairy you seduced in your dreams.*

She watched as Orielle moved toward her, strolling along the bank and finally crossing the road to catch up with her. Orielle walked quietly, her gait so smooth that it seemed she'd just sprouted from the river and not from Alex's living room carpet.

"Are you energized?" Alex asked with a hint of sarcasm.

"Oh, yes, Alex...I am whole now."

"Glad to hear it," Alex mumbled, wondering how it was that Orielle kept feeling stronger and stronger and wholer and wholer, while all she could do was fight to keep from falling apart.

❧ 10 ❧
Dung-ho!

Grabbing a handful of willow branches, Alex pulled herself up the eroding incline. Mud-washed shale and clay soil made the five-foot climb a slippery one, and when Alex reached the top she turned, mindful of her manners, and extended a hand to Orielle. It was the least she could do to reciprocate, to make up for having recoiled and insulted Orielle earlier.

But this time it was the fairy who recoiled from Alex's touch. "I can do it myself."

"Touché," Alex said, and for the first time found herself smiling. Something about the fairy's sarcasm eased Alex—it made Orielle seem more human.

Alex pursed her lips and stared down, watching Orielle's calf muscles work as she, too, grabbed hold of the willows and climbed to Alex's level.

"Not bad," Alex commented, her smile turning to a smirk. "I'm impressed."

Orielle brushed her cinnamon bangs to the side, leaving a smudge of mud on her forehead. "You forget the forest is my natural home, Alex. My mother bore me in a forest."

"And you lived in a polka-dotted mushroom, next door to a couple of hobbits, right?"

Alex waited for her to retaliate. But Orielle didn't. Her gray eyes twinkled serenely. "It is good to see you smile, Alex...even if it is at my expense. If it helps relieve your nervousness, then I gladly give myself to that need."

"I don't *need* anything—from you or anyone else." Alex frowned. "I was just kidding," she said defensively. "And if you're so much *at home* in the woods, why am *I* leading? Why don't you find your own path?"

"Because it is not my own path, but another's which I seek. You are the tracker...."

"Then stop talking and let me track."

"You underestimate me, Alex...."

"Whoa! Wait a second," Alex said, holding up her hands. "After seeing you come out of thin air, how could I possibly underestimate you? I'll probably never underestimate anything in this world ever again."

"Then it is a good thing that I came...already you have learned something."

Alex looked up, opening her mouth to speak, but then forgot what it was she was about to say.

The road was below them now, hidden by the rain-washed slope and stand of trees. And in the woods ahead the poplars grew sparse, patches of Indian pipes and green ferns covering the open ground between them.

It felt warm and humid suddenly, and Alex stopped to roll up her sleeves while she took a look about. *Logic*, she thought. She needed to find the logic of these woods. There was no point in focusing on details—not after so hard a rain. It was the overall pattern she sought.

Not until you learned to see the pattern—understood that pattern—could you see disturbances in that pattern; only when you saw the logic could you see breaks in the logic. Like the patch of flattened vegetation up past a scattering of birch trees. "This way," Alex said, skirting the papery white trunks and making her way to a trail of trampled ferns. And when she reached it she got down on one knee and touched the vegetation.

The path was heavily traveled. Seasons of ferns mashed and worn thin extended beyond Alex's line of vision.

"Animals?" Orielle asked.

"A deer run...but it might tell us something."

Alex stood up and rested her hands on her hips. True, the run was a disturbance—a communal trail by which animals came down to drink from the river at night—but it was natural, logical—an intrinsic part of the pattern, as it were.

Signs of panic is what Alex looked to find; that one, *illogical* break in the pattern. Panic cared not for logic, only self-preservation. It never looked for the most sensible route, never looked to negotiate obstacles—it trampled anything in its way. Alex had seen it hundreds of times—the aimless tracks of disoriented campers, circles of the lost hiker at nightfall, the frenzied run of prey from predators...the hunted old woman running with her bell...if, in fact, she had passed this way.

And isn't that what had happened? Hadn't the woman appeared out of nowhere, aimlessly darting from the woods and around the road to elude her predator? So why wasn't there any sign of panic: a tear in the thickets, a crushed fern, a flower hanging from a broken stem? How could an old, lost woman come tumbling through these woods without making a mess of things?

"There's nothing out of place," Alex mumbled, more to herself than to Orielle. Still squatting, she rested an arm across her knee and looked up in the direction of the path.

"What do you see, Alex?"

"Nothing...but let's hope nothing is something."

"Perhaps the woman did not travel this way...?"

"Oh, she was here—I saw her run out from the woods with my own eyes."

"Then, as you said, Alex, the storm has washed her trail away."

"She didn't make a trail."

"How can you be certain?"

"Because she used this run." Alex got to her feet and brushed off a knee. "She knew where she was going...I'd bank on it."

❰ ❰ ❰

The trail ran straight up over ferns, around chamise and nettles and mountain laurel, then led them through a dense patch of blackberries.

"Watch the brambles," Alex warned, as they passed in single file through the berry bushes. Orielle stepped so softly behind her that every now and then Alex turned to make sure she was still following. She wondered suddenly what her odds were of ditching a fairy in the woods—of taking off and hiding behind a tree, say, then sneaking home alone. With her recent luck, though, the fairy would probably beat her back, and be waiting on the porch swing.

And if she did manage to lose Orielle, and the fairy *couldn't* find her way back—then what? Alex was invested now; she'd opened the book on this mystery, agreed to help Orielle *read* its woodland clues. If Alex left her stranded now, she'd only end up going back for her out of guilt.

A plant which had grown to a few feet caught Alex's attention, and she glanced back at Orielle mischievously out of the corner of her eye. "Maybe you should reach down and pick one of those," she said.

Orielle looked down, slightly confused, then at Alex.

"A wand," Alex said, pointing at the fuzzy end of a tall shoot that grew up from shiny spatula-shaped leaves. "We call them fairy wands. Every fairy should carry one."

"I don't need a wand, Alex, and neither do you...so long as you have a fairy."

Alex shook her head in defeat. "Got me again...." she mumbled, then walked on, giving attention once more to where the run was leading.

Soon, the land leveled off, and for a space of a good thirty yards, not one tree grew. Under the full sun, Alex glanced up at the blue sky, the breeze moving softly across her face, gray-green spears of sedge moving with it and tickling her calves.

To each side, the stretch of open land continued beyond her line of vision. Alex guessed it might have been a road back a hundred years or so ago. But now the ground cover grew thick, and here and there were colorful splashes of hops and wild strawberries, blue-beaded lilies and bittersweet.

"Foxglove..." Orielle whispered.

Alex regarded her suspiciously. "So?"

"It is the sign of a witch."

"No it isn't!" Alex said. "Don't start spooking me with any witch stories, because I'll turn right around and go home, I swear. This whole thing is getting creepy enough as it is...."

Orielle didn't pay any mind to Alex's threat; she had that confused look again—a look which seemed to suggest that Orielle was engaged in private and exceedingly complex thought processes. "Foxglove..." she murmured a second time. "Do you know what drug is derived from it?"

Alex glanced down at the oval-shaped leaves. The pink spotted buds hadn't opened yet. "Digitalis," she said.

"*Very* good, Alex...now I am the one impressed," she said. And then she smiled, but her eyes remained focused elsewhere as she recited from memory, "'...the rapid pulse it can abate, the hectic flush can moderate....'"

Alex raised a brow. "What *are* you *talking* about?"

"It's a poem by the physician who discovered its medicinal qualities. He used it to cure dropsy. But long before that the witches used it to—"

"Will you *please* stop talking about witches?"

"Then choose a path."

"What?"

"Choose a path for us, Alex."

"Why not just take the yellow brick road?" Alex scoffed, as she studied the layout of the copse ahead, and the path to either side of her.

Orielle was oblivious to the remark. She slid her hands in the pockets of her shorts, looking like a model for an Eddie Bauer catalog—then closed her eyes and lifted her face to the sun. "Mmm...I smell herbs," she said.

Alex smelled them, too. A sage-like fragrance was in the summer air. She wandered in slow circles, taking inventory of the ground cover. It looked as if someone had come out here, tossed a bagful of seeds, then left nature to mind the garden.

But just then the soft breeze shifted, and a horrible odor began permeating the air. Orielle's monk-like calm vanished. Her brow beetled and her nose crinkled. She raised each foot, inspecting the soles of her shoes, then waited for Alex to do the same.

"Well, it's not *me*," Orielle said. Alex felt put on the spot. But she finally gave in, lifting a foot behind her and peered over her shoulder. "Shit...!" Alex scowled to herself, then looked at Orielle and inanely walked back to the sedge, balancing on her heels.

"Fox?" Orielle asked.

Alex grimaced as she scraped her hiking shoe in the grass. "No."

"Coyote?"

"No...they eat a lot of berries sometimes—the dung usually has seeds. I think it's..." Alex hesitated and retraced her steps and stooping to examine them. "It's a dog's," she said.

"Whose?"

"How am I supposed to know? State land is on the other side of the river—this is private land. I don't know who owns every piece of property." She looked at Orielle. "Let's go."

"Which way...left or right?" Orielle asked.

"Neither," Alex said. "There's too much ground cover. Let's check the copse first—if there aren't any signs or prints in the soil we'll come back and take the path."

The humidity rose in the shaded grove of trees, and here and there in the humus a haunting array of mushrooms sprouted, some more colorful than the wildflowers. There were inky caps and toadstools, chanterelles and red russulas—the mushroom in which Alex had fancied the fairy might live. And there, in the damp humus, Alex found her dog tracks; fresh, perfectly formed prints moving like a wavy ribbon amidst the mushrooms. "A dog, for sure," Alex confirmed.

The tracks led them almost all the way through the copse before trickling off into a thick carpet of lichen and moss. But by then Alex didn't need the prints anymore; fifty feet or so beyond the edge of the copse was a wall of fieldstone.

Alex pointed, tilting her head from side to side to better glimpse the structure. "Look, Orielle, that's probably the house the dog came from."

☾ ☾ ☾

The land inclined again, and they worked their way up to what Alex guessed to be the north side of an old cottage. There was an abandoned look about it, and Alex imagined that had it been made of wood instead of stone, it would have collapsed by now. On each side of a single window, barn-wood shutters hung crookedly on rusty hinges, and the mortar between each block of stone was filled with moss. Even the roof was covered with green and yellow mosses, the low-hanging tree boughs giving it a thatched appearance.

"It looks as though no one lives here," Orielle whispered.

"Someone's been here," Alex said. "And not just a dog," she added, pointing to all the signs of activity around them.

There were deep marks, staggered ridges in the ground— as if someone in a hurry had crab-walked toward the copse, using the sides of their shoes to edge their way down and keep from slipping. Alex stood on her toes and gripped the splintered windowsill, straining her eyes to peek inside. But sun filtered in from the opposite side of the cottage, turning the whole room into a cloud of dusty haze. Alex let go of the sill and stepped back on her heels. "Let's go around to the door."

Without a word Orielle did as she was told, and Alex wondered if something was the matter with her. She seemed too acquiescent, too quiet; come to think of it, she hadn't said much since the foxglove incident.

In the front there were more of the pink-spotted flowers. The trees ended, the sun streamed down, and all along the stone foundation lily of the valley and an assortment of other flowers bloomed wildly. It looked as though once upon a time it might have been a well-groomed garden, but now everything grew rampant, covering the better part of the broken stone walkway.

There was another window here—larger than the one in back—the shutters apparently latched from the inside, and Alex suddenly realized the sun spilling in from the back of the house was coming not from this window, but from the front door. It was planked and dome-shaped...and ajar.

Alex came up to it cautiously and knocked. "Hello," she said. "Anyone here?"

"M-M-MAMA...?"

Alex's eyes widened and she glanced at Orielle. The voice was deep and coarse, like that of an old man—a man too old to be calling for his mama.

"I'll go in," Orielle offered. She seemed nervous, suddenly shifty-eyed, as though she already knew what Alex had yet to figure out.

"No," Alex insisted, holding out an arm to shield Orielle. "You stay here."

Alex knocked again, then gave the door a soft push so that it creaked open another few inches. "Sir...?" she called, squinting but still unable to see well. The visibility was just as poor from this side, sun and shadows making for nothing more than a fuzzy blur.

She pushed the door all the way back, stooping a bit to clear the low doorway. "Sir?" she tried again, this time in a more demanding voice. Then slowly she walked to the middle, startling herself when the tip of her shoe clipped a bottle and sent it rolling across the room.

There was movement in the room—scuffling and clanking—as though someone had tripped on the bottle and sent it scooting back in her direction.

"STAY-WAY...BOOGIE-BITE," the man grumbled again.

"What...?" Alex said, more to herself than to the voice. "Boogie...?" The word...she had heard it last night—but before she could make sense of the deep, shaky voice, there came a threatening growl, and the clicking of nails rushed along the stone floor. Alex realized, too late, that the man had a dog with him.

A hot, gripping sensation suddenly coursed through her buttocks, a tugging that made her almost lose her balance, as the dog held on with powerful jaws. Violently it shook its head, its body swinging in mid air, as though Alex's rear end were a pull-toy.

"Get your dog *off* me!" she yelled, backing up and slamming herself and the dog against the wall until it let go its grip and dropped to its feet. "Orielle!" she hollered. "Get a stick— find a light!"

But Orielle had already slipped in unnoticed, and before Alex could finish her shouting, a wooden match was struck. Orielle held it to a railroad lantern, the yellow flame brightening and gradually lighting the room as Orielle raised the wick.

From a threatening distance Alex saw her attacker: a robust Scottie on short legs, gleaming canines too big for its mouth, and a head that seemed too big for its body. The black dog stood with one paw raised, ready and willing to lunge again at the slightest provocation. "WHERE-MY-MAMA-GO?" it said.

Alex braced herself against the wall, feeling as though she might fall to her knees at any given moment. It wasn't the bite that bothered her so much—she'd been bitten by animals before— but none had ever talked.

"YOU B-B-BAD GIRL," the dog said, and then it bared its teeth and began growling like a normal dog.

Alex looked to Orielle for some sort of help, but Orielle put a finger to her lips, stepping slowly, carefully, over papers and broken glass. "Boogawoog...?" she whispered, when she was within a few feet of the terrier. "It *is* you, *isn't* it?"

The dog looked up at her suspiciously, wondering, perhaps, how it was this stranger knew her name. She stepped quickly back, then slowly edged forward, examining Orielle's outstretched hand with an oversized nose. Then suddenly the terrier stopped and sat, her tail wagging just a bit, as a strange fascination, then recognition, filled her staring eyes.

"Yes...you do remember...." Orielle spoke gently, staring with equal fascination. She reached out and gently cupped the side of the dog's face in her hand. "Boogawoog," she whispered again, "how is it that you still live?"

Alex had nothing to contribute to this conversation. She felt as though seashells were pressed to her ears, the roaring of an illusory ocean muffling the words of Orielle and Boogawoog. Alex braced herself and slid slowly down the wall into a sitting position. The cool floor felt good against her bare legs, and from her lowered perspective she could see objects under the table: bottles, a generator, the lit base of a cordless phone...stems and leaves and orange flower petals. What were they—poppy petals? "Son-of-a-bitch," she said, reaching forward and picking up a fuzzy black ball and a few stray petals. She held them up to the light, the sight of them sending her mind into a whirl of confusion. "It's the poppy thief," she mumbled, "the son-of-a-bitch who's been stealing my poppies...."

❧ 11 ❧
Poisons and Potions

It was a sense of déjà vu—the rush of familiar stimuli—that overwhelmed Orielle: the Scottish terrier, the cauldron and mortars, the medicinal odors escaping from broken bottles. Together, they struck her with memories of another era, another place in time. Even the bottles themselves were old; amber, clear, cobalt blue, all corked and bearing nineteenth-century labels.

With her back toward Alex, and careful not to alarm the dog, Orielle casually reached around and gathered a few unbroken bottles in her hands. Hemlock, heroin, wolf's bane, nightshade...belladonna. "Poisons," she mused aloud, "botanical poisons..." then glanced at others strewn about the floor. "It is her, Alex...it can be no other."

"Who?" Alex groaned.

"The woman you saw hit last night. This is her work, Alex...this is her dog."

Orielle petted the side of the Scottie's face, withdrawing and examining her hand when she came upon a damp and sticky patch of fur. Her palm was smudged with blood. "Oh...dear ... Boogawoog, you've been hurt. Who did this to you?"

"P-PEOPLE."

"People...?"

"BAD!"

"The bad people...Lilah? Was it Lilah who was here?" She asked, gazing around at the chaos.

"NO-SEE-LILAH—BOOGIE-SMELL."

"You smelled her? On the people, you mean. I see..." Orielle's hair appeared strawberry blonde now, her eyes almost sienna in the yellow lantern light. She gently lifted the Scottie's chin, and cupped its head between her hands, talking soothingly. She worked her fingers through the dog's thick, blood-matted fur, trying to determine the extent of Boogawoog's injuries. "So Lilah sent her people, did she? Did they get her, Boogawoog? Did the bad people take your mama?"

"NO—MAMA-GO. MAMA-WALK-WOODS..."

Orielle sighed wearily, piecing the puzzle together. "So Batilda got away...she took the woods to the road. But Lilah was waiting in the car that struck her." Then to Alex she said, "The car, Alex—were you at all able to see the driver?"

"No," Alex mumbled. "Just the kids."

A sense of foreboding washed over Orielle. "*Children?*"

"A bunch of 'em in the back seat."

Orielle turned to look at Alex, but could see nothing of her face; just a full head of curls. Her pathfinder was slumped against the wall, her knees drawn up and her head hanging between them.

"Stay right there," Orielle said to the Scottie, then rose and sidestepped the dog, bending to pick up several more bottles as she made her way across to Alex. "I'm sorry, Alex...let me tend to you."

Alex's head stayed between her legs, but her arm came up like a stop sign. "I'm fine. Really. Just a bout of vertigo—it'll pass when the blood gets back to my head. Give me a minute," she said, without looking up.

Orielle gazed down at her. "I need to see your wound."

"No you don't."

"Yes, I do. Alex..." Orielle began with the expertise of a nurse talking a child into a tetanus shot, "I promise not to hurt you. I am a healer...let me care for you."

"It's only my butt."

Orielle smiled softly. "A part of the anatomy with which I am quite familiar. Please, Alex, let me see."

"It's not necessary."

"I *have* seen buttocks before, you know."

"Not mine, you haven't."

Orielle pursed her lips and waited patiently. "Alex...?"

"Why? Why is it so important? Has that dog got something in its saliva? Am I going to start barking?"

Orielle wanted to smile, but she kept a stern face. "No."

"Then why is it talking? What the hell's making that dog talk?"

"A culinary enchantment—a biscuit recipe. It shouldn't last more than a few hours."

Alex chanced a glance at the black-banged dog. It seemed thoroughly laid back now—not a nervous bone in its body— but belying its extraordinary nonchalance was the fact of its nose wrinkling the moment Alex dared to make eye contact.

"Get him out of here...he's going to bite me again."

"It's a *she*." Orielle glanced at Boogawoog, but the compact dog only lowered her eyes bashfully and wagged her tail. "Oh, Alex, she won't bite again. She thought you were one of Lilah's people—one of the *wicked* ones," she said, stressing the word for Boogawoog's benefit.

"WICKED!"

"No, Boogawoog. Not Alex. Here...come over here and meet Alex...can *you* say Alex?" she cooed.

"Oh, Christ...!" Alex grumbled.

"AL-AL-ALEC...?"

"Alec, yes, good enough," Orielle encouraged, petting the dog's back while it took the liberty of giving Alex the once-over with its oversized nose.

"Alex is nice...Alex is a good girl. She's going to help find your mama."

Boogawoog's eyes lit up beneath her black bangs. "MAMA? ALEC-FIND-MAMA? BOOGIE-GO?"

Alex glared at Orielle. "Don't tell her that, Orielle—her mama's *dead.*"

"Alex...! Don't say that...."

"Why not?" Alex snapped. "Someone said it to *me*...at an age when my intellectual capacity was no more than a dog's."

Orielle nodded. "Ah...I see. So the two of you have suffered a common loss..." she said, then gazed thoughtfully at Alex. There was something wounded, something broken in Alex's eyes; Beyond that gruff and independent demeanor, Orielle now saw something she had only sensed before.

With her head still hung slightly forward, Alex peered up at Orielle. And for an instant, the immediacy of their situation— the anxiety, the questions, the threat of Lilah—paled in comparison to Alex's beauty. Orielle noted the perfect lines of her eyebrows, the strong jaw and Grecian nose. And from where Orielle now stood, Alex's thick and unusually long lashes extended down over her eyes in such a way that her eyes seemed locked behind the bars of a soul cage. "Captives..." Orielle whispered. "We are both captives: I am Lilah's, you your own...."

Alex blinked. "Huh?"

"Nothing..." Orielle said, breathing deeply, then letting out a long exhalation of air. "You needn't worry about the dog. She is simply feeling a terrible sense of loss right now...an awful fear that someone has harmed and taken the one she loves. She is not a mean dog...only loyal."

"Then tell her the truth—don't go making her promises I can't keep."

"Lest you prove *yourself* disloyal?" She patted Alex's knee. "It honors me, Alex, to be in the company of a human as fine and faithful as a dog."

"Yep, that's me—a dog to a tee," Alex said sarcastically. She slid her fingers under her curls and rubbed her forehead. "Ask my ex-lovers—they'll tell you what a dog I am." And then Alex frowned and looked around. "Now what do we do?"

"FIND-MAMA," Boogawoog said, as if the question had been directed to her. "BOOGIE-GO-WITH-ALEC," she said expectantly, as if ready to gladly cooperate with anyone who might have a lead on her mama's whereabouts.

"First," Orielle told the dog, "we're going to Alex's house."

"ALEC-HOUSE? BOOGIE-GO-IN-CAR?"

"No, we will walk."

"GO-FOR-WALK?"

"Yes...to Alex's house."

"Whoa! Uh-uh. This dog isn't coming home with me."

"Well, of course she is, Alex. She's injured...and so are you. I need to examine you both."

Alex rolled her eyes. "Why don't you just step away and let the damned dog have another go at me—put me out of my misery. It would be the kindest thing anyone has done for me all day."

"Well, then, Alex...I will have to make a point of being kinder. And perhaps I should start by insisting you go outside with Boogawoog—away from all this glass—and let me make sense of what I can in here."

Alex looked at the labeled bottles Orielle had set on the stone floor. "Morphia? What *is* this stuff?"

"Morphia—named after Morpheus, the god of sleep. It's what you now call morphine."

Alex reached and took a couple of the rectangular bottles in her hand. "*Laudanum,*" she said, squinting to read the red-skulled label from a Jolly's drug store in Knightstown, Indiana. "Nervine...three grains opium per ounce...twenty-five cents...1906...?"

"Narcotics, Alex. All opium derivatives. The drugs are fresh, though. I suppose she just reuses her old bottles."

"Poppies...." Alex looked around sullenly, pointing here and there to all the withered petals. "They're mine, you know. They came from my field." She looked at Orielle. "She stole my poppies from me—she's been stealing them for years...."

Orielle pursed her lips questioningly, but no sooner did she, than a phone rang somewhere, and she whirled her head,

long waves of hair swishing and whipping against Alex's cheek.
"A telephone?"

"Yep."

"I thought there was no electricity."

"But there's a phone line outside...and a generator down
here," Alex said, gesturing toward the table.

"What should we do?"

"Well, don't look at me—*I'm* not expecting any calls.
Answer it."

☾ ☾ ☾

As soon as Orielle's back was turned the dog's nose began
wrinkling again—just enough so that the tips of her canines became exposed. "Don't start with me," Alex warned. "You bite me
again and you won't set foot in my house—no walks, no
cars...*nothing*! " Her dark eyes narrowed. "I swear I'll leave you
here to starve."

The Scottie listened, its expression grim, its dour demeanor betraying the swiftness and aggressiveness with which it
had first attacked. But now, as if responding to Alex's verbal threat,
Boogawoog calmly trotted over to Orielle, turned to face Alex,
then sat with her squat body pressed against the fairy's leg.

"Benjamin...?" she heard Orielle say into the receiver, "I
can hardly believe I am hearing your voice." Boogawoog became
all ears at the mention of the name. Although her facial expression never changed, she sat up like a black bear cub, temporarily
forgetting her business with Alex. "B-B-BIRD-WHISTLE?"

Alex took the opportunity to ease herself up and shuffle
over to the table—the biggest table she'd ever seen. Her rear end
was throbbing now, and she winced quietly, careful not to put
too much pressure as she sat sideways on a stool and began taking
inventory of the room. There was a black iron pot on the hearth—
a cauldron, if she didn't know better. And on the table were more
hand-labeled vials. Harlequin, Diamondback, Moccasin, Russell—

Snake names, Alex thought. She didn't like this place one bit. It was creepy—the dog included. Everywhere there were broken bottles of poison.

Alex heard her name mentioned then, and she tried to focus her attention on the conversation, as Orielle gave the caller a brief synopsis of the night and morning's events.

"No, Benjamin...Alex says she did not survive the accident...they took her body, apparently." There was a long silence, then, "Hold a moment and I will ask her." She looked at Alex. "Where is the bell?"

"I left it on the table, in my living room."

Orielle relayed the information, her countenance changing like a barometer in response to his reply. She covered the receiver again. "He says to get it into a freezer at once, Alex...it must be kept frozen until he arrives."

Alex's brow shot up. "He's coming? Here?"

"Yes, Benjamin," Orielle continued, "Alex will direct you."

Unable to hear Benjamin's side of the conversation, Alex tried to read Orielle's face. The fairy cradled the receiver against her shoulder now, pulling up her long sweatshirt sleeves as she scanned the room.

"A pharmacopeia? A black one?" Orielle asked. "Yes...yes, I see it," she said, motioning for Alex to pull out what looked like a leatherbound cook book from the clutter.

"Yes, we've got it, Benjamin," Orielle said, then cupped a hand over the phone. "His black cat is here," she said to Alex. "Her name is Sheeky. Benjamin asks that you have a look around. She may come if you call—" And then Orielle stopped, pointing to the doorway with a look of relief.

"She must have heard me saying your name, Benjamin— she is right outside, sitting in the doorway." Then, "Yes, yes...I'll put Alex on," she said, and handed the phone to Alex.

"He's in Manhattan—and terribly upset over Batilda's demise," she said to Alex. "He knows his way here...you need only direct him to your house. He'll need a few hours to order his equipment and pack his bags."

Alex's dark eyes grew wide around as marbles. "What do you mean, *pack*? What for? I thought he's coming to pick you up!"

"No...he'll be coming to stay. Until the solstice."

"But he can't!" It seemed as if someone had thrown a log on the fire, for Alex suddenly felt herself beginning to sweat. "Oh, man," she mumbled, raking her scalp. "I can't *do* this! I'm...I'm expecting company, you see. Yes, that's it...I've got a date Friday and, um...well, you know, she'll probably want to spend the weekend." Alex let out a deep breath and smiled sheepishly.

Orielle seemed confused. "What is your point?"

"That I don't have time to put anyone up for the night...that I'll be too busy to accommodate you." Alex chewed her lip. "I'd like to, really. But..."

"Alex...the situation is far more perilous than you understand it to be. You don't have much of a choice, I'm afraid." And for the first time Alex saw a hint of fear in Orielle's eyes. "Please, Alex, matters are grave...and you are more deeply involved than you might imagine. Benjamin will explain everything when he arrives."

Orielle extended the phone to Alex again, then hesitated one more time. "One more thing, Alex...he cannot continue with his plans until he confers with Batilda...."

"Confers with her? She's dead!"

"He has asked that you arrange for a medium to join us."

Alex wiped her forehead. "A medium? A medium *what*?"

"A *spiritual* medium...a psychic. We will need to hold a seance tonight."

"Why?"

"He needs to reach Batilda's spirit so that he might go about finishing their work in her absence."

"But...I don't know any psychics." But that was a lie, too. Mary Southworth, the Realtor, came to mind. Alex opened her knees again and dropped her head between her legs until her face turned red. She groaned at the thought of what lay ahead.

❧ 12 ❧
Food for Thought

Alex coasted into the parking lot of Grand Union and cut the engine. Grocery shopping hadn't been on her list of things to do today, but what with company coming and all, she had no choice in the matter. Dr. Birdwhistle was scheduled to arrive by nightfall, in time for dinner, she presumed. And Mary Southworth—the Realtor and only rumored psychic Alex could think to call on such short notice—was expected by nine.

Alex wasn't looking forward to any of it. She was glad that Benjamin, knowledgeable and logical as he seemed, was stepping in to take control and relieve Alex of the burden. But his voice was somehow filled with portent, and Alex was struck with the feeling he would come bearing more bad news. As for Mrs. Southworth, Alex wasn't at all convinced of her professed psychic expertise. When Alex telephoned her from the house, Mary had responded with what seemed excessive exuberance—like a caller in a radio station contest. She'd gotten so excited, in fact, that it never dawned on her to inquire about the circumstances of the call. Alex had a hunch Mary was nothing more than a wanna-be.

Alex glanced in her rearview mirror and caught Boogawoog eyeing her. They had left the cat at home, perched atop Alex's refrigerator, but Boogawoog insisted on joining them for a car ride. Ever since Orielle took the liberty of telling Boogawoog that Alex would find her mama, the dog would not let Alex out of her sight. And fearing the Scottie's separation anxiety might result in acting-out behavior and the resultant destruction of her log home, Alex decided it was in her best interest to accommodate the little black hound from hell.

"Is it safe to leave her in the car?" Alex asked.

"I don't see why not," Orielle said. Then to Boogawoog she ordered, "No talking, sweet little girl. We won't be long."

"GO-IN-STORE?"

"Yes, Alex and I, but you stay here. We have to get food."

"HUNGRIES?"

Alex looked at Orielle. "Hungries?"

"That must be what she calls food."

"And how does she know we're at the store?"

Orielle shrugged off the question, as though she couldn't understand Alex's failure to figure out such simple things for herself. "She's obviously well traveled, Alex."

"HUNGRIES—GET-BOOGIE-BONE."

Alex looked in the rearview mirror, then turned to Orielle. "Can you trust her not to talk to strangers while we're gone? She hasn't shut up since she got in the car."

And she hadn't. Boogawoog rode backwards all the way, standing up and staring out the back window. From the front she looked like a little bear, as she had in the cottage. But seeing her from the back, standing up against the seat, she looked like a hefty donkey, a short-legged jackass. Between thick, muscular shoulders, her lean neck seemed incredibly long, her wide skull and big prick ears giving her an equine appearance—minus the mane. And all she did during the ride into town was shout out the names of every passing object she could identify—DOGS, PEOPLES, PUSSY-CATS, the B-BUTCHER and the B-BALL STORE. Alex had even pulled over and made a run into the B-BALL-STORE—the sporting goods shop, that is—hoping a ball would keep her quiet and pacified for a while.

Boogawoog was ecstatic when Alex popped open the can of racquet balls and tossed her a blue one. Her appreciation made

Alex feel oddly ecstatic, too. There was something satisfying about watching someone make such a fuss over a gift. It made you want to go out and buy them more gifts.

But the ball hadn't kept Boogawoog entirely quiet; instead of shouting words, now she happily gnawed on the ball, and for the remainder of the ride it sounded as though someone were in the back seat chewing a mouthful of rubber bands.

"All right then," Alex said, addressing the Scottie as she opened the car door. "You wait here—and *NO* talking. Because if you do—if you talk to *anyone*—next thing you know you'll be interviewed on 'Good Morning America.' Someone will break into this car and steal you, make a fortune exploiting you."

The Scottie listened intently, cocking her head this way and that way until Alex finished her lecture. "BOOGIE-BE-GOOD...GO SLEEPY."

"Yeah, that's the spirit. Take a nap. Take one for me, too. God knows I could use it." Boogawoog curled into the shape of a beach ball, and suddenly a parental-like protectiveness came over Alex. She worried what might happen if Boogawoog *was* stolen. No one would know she owed her voice to the biscuits, and when the spell or enchantment—or whatever the hell it was—wore off, the dog snatcher would be left with a stubborn canine mute. And then what would become of Boogawoog? She'd be abandoned at the wayside or taken to a shelter, left to grieve the loss of her mistress. And Alex had enough dealings with the town's dog control officer to know that adult pedigrees had no better chance than crossbreeds when it came to being abused, abandoned or euthanized.

"Are you sure she'll be all right?" Alex asked for the second time.

Orielle eyed the dog, then studied Alex. "You're growing fond of her, aren't you? I believe it is that feisty terrier spirit—reminds you of yourself, does she not...?"

"And just what would *you* know about my spirit?" Alex

remarked snidely.

Something of a knowing grin came to Orielle's mouth.

"What?" Alex said, narrowing her eyes challengingly. "What are you smiling about?"

But Orielle still declined to answer. "Don't worry, Alex, the creature will be fine...just remind yourself of what she did to the last person who invaded her space."

"I'd rather not," Alex said, stepping out of the white Subaru and shoving her keys in a front pocket. And into her back pocket she pushed her checkbook, prepared to wince as it slid down and over the bandage beneath her clean shorts. But suddenly she realized her wound didn't even hurt anymore. She wasn't quite sure what Orielle had done to the dog bite—what with the medical procedure going on behind Alex's back, as it were—but now there wasn't a bit of pain. When she had first looked at it in her hand-held mirror, the nasty gash looked as if it could use a few stitches. But then Orielle began humming and touching and massaging, and applying strange herbs—verbena, if her memory served her right—and now it wasn't even the slightest bit sore. It was remarkable; she felt wonderful. Her buttocks did, at least.

"I can cook if you like," Orielle offered, as she got out the passenger side.

Alex looked across the car roof. "Fine with me."

"Would you settle for something meatless?"

"Whatever," Alex said. "It doesn't matter." Then she poked her head in the back seat. "Hey, Boogawoog," she whispered.

Boogawoog's head rose up like a snake's face popping out from its coils.

"Do you want meat...do you know what a hamburger is?"

"YEAH-YEAH-YEAH-YEAH-YEAH," the dog answered, almost panting the word, then spontaneously salivated as a wide pink tongue jutted out to lick her lips. "BOOGIE-*LOVE-*BURGERS."

"Good," Alex said, then closed the car door and regarded Orielle. "I, uh...I might throw a couple of hamburgers on the grill. You know—just as a side dish," she added nonchalantly, careful not to insult Orielle.

"A side dish...."

"Sure...why not?"

They walked alongside each other, Orielle nodding in consideration of the idea.

"We'll need herbs, also....and candles, Alex."

"I've got plenty of candles at home."

"Colored ones?"

Alex shrugged. "White, I think. Maybe some green ones."

"We'll need pink and—"

"I definitely don't have anything in *pink*." Alex gave a roll of her eyes. "See what they have in here. If you don't find what you're looking for, there's a small emporium one town over—we can swing by on the way back." Alex looked at Orielle and shook her head in disbelief again. "Should I alert the public? Should I go to the customer service booth and alert them to the fact that there's a fairy slinking around the store?"

Orielle gave a wounded look, and Alex quickly apologized. "Sorry," she said, lifting her brows in resignation. "Why don't you just grab your own cart and go get your vegetables or tofu and whatever else you want."

Orielle nodded. "Could you lend me money until...?"

"Don't worry about the money. Get what you want. Just hurry and catch up with me so we can get out of here as fast as possible."

"As you wish," she said, then she took a basket and was off.

Alex rested her hands on a cart and watched the fairy gliding happily down the vegetable aisle. Alex liked her body; she liked Orielle's long cinnamon hair—her face and her eyes, too. Too bad she was a fairy. If she wasn't, Alex might have thought to ask her out. She stood staring for a long moment, twisting her lips as she entertained the notion. But halfway down the aisle, Orielle, as if sensing Alex's eyes on her, turned and waved.

Alex waved back inanely, then quickly averted her eyes.

(((

Even more than grocery shopping, Alex hated grocery
carts. No matter how new and good they looked, she always wound
up with a defective one—the one whose right front wheel insisted on moving in the opposite direction from the other three.
Growling curses under her breath, Alex forced the cart until it
lurched forward, then forcibly steered it to the meat section.

She picked up a pack of soup bones, thinking to boil them
for Boogawoog. Making friends with the animal didn't figure into
it, she told herself, but the dog *had* suffered somewhat of a tragedy, hadn't she? And she had, after all, specifically *asked* for a
bone. The least Alex could do was indulge her this once. She tossed
a pack of ground sirloin into the cart as well, then went for milk
and hamburger buns, before setting out in search of snacks suitable for the occasion.

What did people serve at seances, anyway, Alex wondered.
Devil Dogs, angel food cake? Maybe she could doctor-up a few
cans of alphabet soup—do something creative with the letters
and call it her Ouija board brew. Mrs. Southworth would love it;
she'd probably hallucinate on the stuff.

Alex found the sesame crackers she liked, then grabbed
two packs of brie, and had just forced the cart to turn down another aisle, when she caught sight of Ana Mae.

"Oh shit...!" Alex swore, fighting with the cart to make a
U-turn. But the one uncooperative wheel didn't want to turn. It
spun and locked, causing the whole cart to skip and make an
attention-getting noise.

"Alex?" Ana Mae called.

Alex looked at her and smiled nervously. "Hey...!" she said.

"Hey, hey!" Ana Mae repeated glibly, "Who's your new
playmate?"

"What are you *talking* about?"

"Your new *friend*—where'd you find her?"

"What friend would that be?"

"The one you walked in here with."

"Oh! Her..." Alex began, feigning innocence and hoping Orielle wouldn't come along just then. "She, uh...she's not a friend, actually. She used to live in my house—before I bought it. Before the people I bought it from bought it." Alex faked a smile. "Can you believe it?"

"Hardly," Ana Mae said.

Alex felt her ears turning red—it was always her damned ears that gave her away and spoiled her otherwise perfect white lies. "I could hardly believe it myself," Alex continued. "She was just passing through...from out of town and...well, she stopped by." She crinkled her nose. "Sentimental reasons, I guess."

"So she got to spend a sentimental moment in her old house, did she?"

"Yeah! We ended up having breakfast and, uh...I had to pick up a few things, and so did she, so we shared a ride—to talk more about the house, you know?" Alex gave a Cheshire-cat grin, but she knew Ana Mae wasn't buying a word of it. She was humoring Alex—making her suffer for fibbing.

"How nice...."

"It is, isn't it?"

"Certainly is...." The corner of Ana Mae's mouth turned up and she nodded. "So why is she wearing your clothes?"

Alex blinked her eyes and opened her mouth, but before she could think up a reason, a cordial smile broke on Ana Mae's face and her eyes shifted away from Alex.

"Hello..." she heard Orielle say.

"Hi, again," Ana Mae greeted.

Alex looked at the fairy beside her, then at Ana Mae with piercing eyes. "Again...?" she said, without moving her lips. Alex wasn't at all comfortable with this situation.

"I saw the two of you come in together," Ana Mae said, her tone so subtly mocking that only Alex could detect it. "But then I couldn't find you, Alex, so I introduced myself to Orielle."

"Yes, we met by the asparagus," Orielle joined in. "Ana Mae invited us for dinner at Raspberries."

Alex glared at Ana Mae. "We're *busy*."

"That's what she told me," Ana Mae said, thoroughly enjoying the fact that she had Alex squirming. "So we made it for tomorrow night."

"Ana Mae said you would teach me how to two-step." Orielle couldn't have been more cheerful.

"I see," Alex said, still glaring at her partner.

Ana Mae sighed, the kind of sigh that follows a good, satisfying meal. "Well, I've got to run," she said. And the rest of her conversation was directed toward Orielle. "Six o'clock, did we say?"

"If it is agreeable with Alex."

Alex flared her nostrils at Ana Mae, but Ana Mae refused to make eye contact. Alex hated when Ana Mae resorted to all that passive-aggressive crap—acting sweet as pie, never raising her voice. Alex would have preferred an honest punch; like the ones Ana Mae gave every time Alex scared her.

"Good. I'm excited!" Ana Mae said to Orielle. With a hand, she flung her frizzy blonde hair over her shoulder. "I'll see you at six tomorrow, then. And come hungry—vegetarian, right?"

"If you please," Orielle said.

"That's what we aim to do," she laughed, then shot a knowing glance at Alex.

As usual, her sweet Southern drawl only added to her charm, and the hospitality she extended to people. "We'll do all we can to make your stay in Halfmoon memorable."

☾ ☾ ☾

Alex buckled her seat belt and pulled out of the parking lot. It was just her luck to meet up with Ana Mae.

"I didn't know you played the violin, Alex."

Alex didn't respond. She was still sulking.

"And the cafe," Orielle went on, "It sounds like a wonderfully charming place...I have not had fun in years."

"Have *fun*...is that what you want to do?" *And why shouldn't she?* Alex thought. Orielle certainly had adequate cause for celebration; there was the reunion with Benjamin tonight, dinner and dancing tomorrow night, and after a hundred years, the solstice would hopefully bring a reversal of Lilah's enchantment. Of course Orielle wanted to have fun, she was overflowing with optimism—that tenuous state we enter when things are going our way. But they weren't going Alex's way.

"I don't want to have to deal with Ana Mae," Alex insisted. "She already caught me in a lie—she knows I'm not telling the truth."

"So tell her the truth. Ana Mae said you were her dear friend *and* partner."

"*Silent* partner," Alex stressed. "Just like I want our business to stay, okay? *Silent.*" Alex gripped the steering wheel hard. "Ana Mae thinks...she thinks I'm sleeping with you. I know that's what she's thinking."

"*Sleeping* with me?"

"You know...like Batilda and Lilah. Women sleep together sometimes. It's not uncommon," she scowled.

"You don't have to school me in the ways of women-loving-women, Alex. The joining of women is quite common amongst fairies."

"Well, it's common in Halfmoon, too." Alex frowned, sneaking a sideways peek at Orielle. The conversation was getting uncomfortable. "Anyway, she thinks we're lovers.

"Is that the way it is supposed to be...?"

"No, it's not the way it's *supposed* to be!" Alex grew flustered. "It's just what she *thinks.*"

"Well, then I will gladly inform her that you gave me your bed, and had a respectable night's sleep on the sofa."

Alex shook her head. "Ana Mae knows better—that's the whole point. The truth is far less believable than any lie. She'd never believe I slept on the sofa."

"Why?"

"Because she thinks I have no scruples, she thinks I sleep around."

"Do you?"

"Sometimes...."

"And scruples?"

"No. None. Just *problems* right now." Alex heaved a sigh, and looked at Boogawoog in the mirror. The Scottie had wagged her tail, woooo-ing at the occasional dog, but she hadn't said a word yet. Alex supposed the biscuits were wearing off. "And here I worried the *dog* would talk to strangers," she complained. "I should've been more concerned about *you* talking to strangers."

"For goodness sake, Alex," Orielle began, seemingly appalled by Alex's lack of etiquette. "Did you expect me to be rude? Ana Mae politely approached me...what would you have had me do?" Orielle gave a patient sigh. "Ana Mae does not know what I am...no one has to know what I am. Alex...if you are that ashamed of keeping my company...ashamed of anyone suspecting we are *sleeping* together...."

"I didn't mean it that way..." She softened her tone and looked over at Orielle. "It's just that...well...how can you expect me to start explaining you to people—especially Ana Mae—when I...when I can't even explain you to myself?" Alex let her head bounce back against the seat as she drove. "I can see it now, we'll get to Raspberries and you'll get everyone doing that dance of death—that water ring stuff, or whatever it is—and spin them into butter or something. Then what? How will I explain you *then?*"

"A fairy ring, Alex...it is called a fairy ring. And it is a dance of *life.*"

Although Alex kept her eyes on the road, she could feel Orielle staring, assessing her. And after a long pause, Orielle spoke again.

"I would not survive in a ring any longer than you, Alex. I am mortal...you forget I have a human body."

"I'm well aware of your human body, thank you." It wasn't the type of body one would easily *forget,* even if Alex had to say so herself. "And if you'd like to buy some clothes to fit it, you can look around the Emporium." She looked at Orielle's bare legs, at the way she wore Alex's shorts. She was adorable, really. And amidst the tiny scratches and mud stains on her knees, Alex could see she'd gotten some sun. "And if you need to dance that badly," she finished, "we can dance at home."

"To what?"

"Country-western music, if it's two-stepping you want to learn. I'll play the fiddle."

"But then you won't be able to dance."

"Sure I will," Alex said, trying to imagine how she might attempt it. She'd have Orielle hold her waist, and she'd hold the fiddle—it would keep them both at a safe arm's distance. Of course, she'd never fiddled and danced at the same time, but considering all she had to do tonight—meet Benjamin, tolerate Mary Southworth, and survive a seance—fiddling and dancing seemed a relatively easy task. She'd made it through the morning, and if she made it through the evening, she'd make it through anything.

⋙ 13 ⋘
Date for a Seance

"**I** didn't know they made brown candles," Alex said.

Orielle strategically placed it in a circle of six pink ones. "Brown is for luck and success," Orielle replied. Striking a match, she reached over the back of a Windsor chair and lit it. "Madam Mimma carries them."

"*Who?*"

"Madam *Mimma*. She runs the crystal shop at the Emporium...didn't you know?"

Alex frowned. "No...I didn't know her name."

Orielle made her lips into an O-shape and brought the wooden match to her mouth, the flame reflecting in her eyes and making them twinkle like diamonds.

She was wearing her white dress again, since Alex had thrown it in the washer for her earlier. And after a hot bubble bath in Alex's tub, she had dried and pulled back her rusty-golden hair, twisting and piling and pinning it so that it now sat loosely on the back of her head. "And the color pink," she said, "is for love...."

"Why do we need pink?" Alex asked nervously. "What's love got to do with it?"

"Why, everything, Alex....everything has to do with love. It is the most powerful force in the universe."

Averting her eyes, Alex glanced around the dining room at the bottles and books they'd dragged back from the cottage in an old potato sack—all at Professor Birdwhistle's request. Alex liked her dining room the way it had been; nothing but the log walls and waxed floors, a huge braided rug and the vase of fresh-cut flowers she always kept on her oak table. Now the damned thing looked like an alter. And to make matters worse, it was getting dark out. The sun had set, Birdwhistle was late, and beyond the open window the last streaks of color quickly faded from the sky.

The temperature would drop soon, too, although for now it was still balmy. The soft breeze blowing in through the screen bent the flames on the candles. It was strange how candles could change an atmosphere, how one too many could make the difference between *romantic* and *spooky*. If Orielle lit one more, Alex was going to start blowing them out.

Maybe she'd do better, she thought, to go sit in the living room where life seemed normal. She had a small fire going in the hearth, and Boogawoog—now an ordinary mute canine—was lying on the carpet, on top of a beach towel, happily gnawing on an after-dinner soup bone. And Sheeky was crouched on the coffee table eating chopped sirloin. Alex had put the cat's bowl up there, figuring the height would give her a vantage point and keep Boogawoog from getting to it.

"I'll be inside," she told Orielle.

"Not yet, Alex. You have to anoint the white candle with me."

"*You* anoint the candle."

"You must be part of this...you *are* part of this," she corrected.

Alex nodded heavily, the muscles in her jaw so tight that she felt a headache coming on.

Orielle seemed to sense her tension, and as Alex gave in and came up to the table, Orielle took her hand and pulled her around so that they stood face to face. "Stop pulling away," she said, pressing her fingers to Alex's temples and cheeks and moving them in a circular motion. "Don't fight me..." she whispered, working her hands and smoothing her thumbs over Alex's forehead.

Alex didn't want to fight—she'd been fighting one thing or another all day long, and now she was tired. But just as she relaxed and gave in to Orielle's healing hands, Boogawoog came trotting in, a low, grumbling growl issuing from her throat. Alex looked down at the Scottie, then heard the sound of tires coming up the gravel drive. "I think he's here," she said.

Slowly, Orielle let her hands drop away from Alex, and straightened her dress.

"You're not even angry at him, are you?" Alex commented. She shook her head, not comprehending the fairy's forgiving disposition. "I'm angry at what he did to you...and I don't even *know* him." He had, after all, enabled Lilah to basically steal Orielle's whole life away from her. "How long has it been?" Alex asked.

"One hundred and three years....he was twenty-six years old when I last saw him," Orielle said.

☾ ☾ ☾

Alex couldn't tell whether Benjamin Birdwhistle had grown into his name, or been born looking like a bird. He arrived in a gray, three-piece suit and hat, a white lily in his lapel, and over his forearm rested a trench coat and the hook of his cane. But what struck Alex the most as she laid eyes on his tall, thin figure, was the odd avian resemblance. He looked like a waterbird in a suit. It wasn't that his features were hooked or sharp or hawk-like in any way; on the contrary, his face was kind, his small blue eyes sincere and wide-set. But his nose was another matter. Long and broad and flattened at the tip, it resembled a bill—a duck's bill—she decided. And when he doffed his hat, the wispy white hair combed back over his scalp gave the impression of goose down.

"Professor Birdwhistle...?" Alex asked.

"At your service, Ms. ..."

"Spherris," Alex said. "Alex Spherris."

"Ms. Alex *Spherris!*" And with an appealing pride and confidence, he courteously held his hat to his chest and bowed with the grace of a flamingo. "But surely we can dispense with formality? Please..." he said, "call me Benjamin."

"Sure," Alex said, pushing open the screen door. "Come on in Bill—*Benjamin*, I mean," she quickly caught herself. She eyed his long legs as he moved past her—just to make sure his knees were bending backwards.

With her back to the hearth, Orielle knelt on the living room carpet, restraining the squealing Scottie until Alex could relieve Benjamin of his coat.

And if eyes could sing, if they could rejoice, Benjamin's did the instant he came within Orielle's view. But the Scottie wasn't about to let any of them engage in pleasantries until Benjamin greeted her first.

Boogawoog pinned her donkey ears back and rushed to him, her long, skinny tail wagging so hard that the back half of her body swayed in time with it.

"Yes...oh yes! Come to your Uncle Benjamin!" he said to the dog, propping his cane against the sofa and holding onto the arm for support as he lowered himself to his knees. "Oh, yes—yes, yes, yes," he cooed, lifting his chin and tightening his lips against her kisses. "I'm *soooo* glad to see you too," he said. "*Soooo* glad." But all the while, Alex noticed, his eyes were locked on Orielle. "And my little Sheeky?" he inquired. "Where *is* daddy's princess...?"

Before anyone could answer, the black cat, having taken to hiding at the commotion, peeked out like an imp from behind Alex's entertainment center, then tiptoed about fifty miles an hour across the green carpet.

In a flash she was climbing up the back of Benjamin's gray suit jacket and curling herself around his neck like those poor glass-eyed foxes women used to wear. Alex looked at Sheeky and she stared back with yellow eyes bigger than any Alex had ever seen on such a small cat. Together, they took up the better part of the "princess's" furry face, not leaving much room for her mouth and nose.

With one hand reaching up to the cat on his shoulder, the other hand reaching down to the Scottie, the professor stroked and petted both animals. "Sheeky's not eating well, I'm afraid. Batilda said that..." He stopped in mid-sentence, sighing sadly at his own mention of Batilda's name. "She said Sheeky hadn't eaten and I...I was thinking she might need a veterinarian if I can't convince her otherwise."

Alex looked down at Benjamin, at the pinkish skin of his scalp and the age spots showing through what was left of his fine hair. Alex felt sorry for him. His fingers were long and slender, almost feminine—the hands of a pianist, Alex thought—his nails well manicured and polished. But his hands were speckled with age spots, too, and showing through his thinning skin were blue veins and the shadows of old bones. There were other marks, also: strange and tiny scars, it seemed.

Until now, Alex had only been feeling sorry for herself, and so for the life of her couldn't understand why Professor Birdwhistle evoked such odd feelings of awe, warmth...and sympathy. Maybe it had to do with the fact of being unfamiliar with old people—she had never really *known* an old person. Everyone in her life, it seemed, had died before they'd had a *chance* to grow old.

"Well, I think you can save yourself a trip," Alex said, shoving her fingers in the pockets of her jeans. "Sheeky just polished off a bowl of sirloin."

"Sirloin!" he gasped, stretching his neck to look up at the cat. "Is that right!" he said, and scratched her under the chin. Then he put one hand on the coffee table, one on the arm of the sofa, and helped himself up.

"Ahh..." he intoned, as though the simple act of getting from his knees to a standing position were an accomplishment. He smoothed his suit, adjusted the withering lily in his lapel, then took Alex's hand in both of his. "Thank you, Alex. Thank you for your hospitality...my little princess thanks you, too."

With the animals now satisfied, he turned his full attention to Orielle.

"My dear maiden," he nodded solemnly. "So beautiful you are...so lovely," he began, as he approached her.

Orielle held her hands out to him, and he took them both, stooping and kissing each one.

"How sorry we are for what we have done to you," he said, his voice heavy with regret. "For an eternity my evil works have consumed my conscience...like worms, those deeds have bored holes in my soul."

He should have thought of that before he wrecked her life, Alex thought.

"Benjamin..." Orielle softly whispered, the sound of her voice causing his blue eyes to glass over.

He let go of one of her hands, cupping the one in both of his, and squeezed it tightly. His hands were nearly trembling now. Again he bowed and kissed it, and as he did, Orielle ran her hand over the top of his head...as a little girl might pet a white duck at the pond, Alex imagined.

"Professor," Alex said, the exchange of sentiments making her a bit uncomfortable. "We saved dinner for you...so why don't you just relax and eat? I'll bring your bags in if you like."

"You *are* a dear," he said, drawing keys from his trouser pocket and handing them to Alex. He stared as Alex took them, his eyes filling with an odd surprise, as though he were seeing Alex—really seeing her—for the first time. "You are as beautiful as Batilda was at your age," he remarked, his eyes curiously taking in Alex's features. "Her hair was black...naturally curled, as is yours. And that olive skin...those lovely eyes and lashes..." he said, his words trailing off so that it seemed he was looking at Alex but seeing someone else.

"So!" Alex said, looking at Orielle in a plea for assistance. "How about that dinner...?"

"Yes, come and settle down," Orielle said, tenderly grasping his elbow and leading him into the dining room.

But the moment he saw Batilda's belongings on the table his bottom lip began quivering and he fell to pieces. "Oh...this is so very terrible," he cried.

Alex quickly pulled out one of chairs from the table, letting Orielle guide him down into it.

"Oh dear...forgive me," he sobbed, "but this is all so *awful*...!" He pulled out a handkerchief and blew his nose.

"I loved her, you know. What I mean to say, is that we spent our lives hating one another...hating ourselves, I suppose, but..." He paused, using the corner of his hanky to dab his eyes. "But now that she's gone I've come to realize how much I loved that witch—*harpy*, I should say. I once turned her into one, you know...never *could* uncross the hex. I don't believe she ever forgave me," he carried on. "It was purely retaliatory, of course, but what was I to do? She buried me alive."

Alex scrunched her face.

"Halloween, 1895. Nearly frightened me to death."

"Geez...." Alex said.

"Oh, but what does it matter, anyway?" He waved his hand as if trying to shoo away the memories. "None of it matters... save for freeing Orielle. That is all that matters."

Orielle patted Benjamin's shoulder, and he turned his watery blue eyes to her, as though waiting for some sort of confirmation. "You do believe I loved her, though...don't you?"

"Sure, Professor. Sure you did." Alex rolled her eyes at Orielle. "How about I go get those bags of yours and—"

"Wait!" he said. "Just...just...*please*, give me a moment to compose myself." He sat there sniffling and shaking his head. The fact that he'd lost his grip on that English reserve seemed to frustrate him. "Just *look* at me, will you? I've fallen *apart*!"

He swiped at his nose again. "But that's life for you. Just when you think you know all there is to know about yourself, something like this happens," he said, gesturing at Batilda's belongings, "and makes you realize there was a part you never knew."

Sheeky held to his neck like glue, licking his ears. Just as Orielle reached to console Benjamin, Boogawoog stood up on his leg and started clicking her teeth.

Absently, he rubbed her ears. "There, there," he said. And then to Orielle, "Were you able to find any biscuits?"

"A few."

"Good," he said, "give her two...we'll need to talk with her as soon as possible. And I'll need to review Batilda's notes," he said, pointing to the papers and black book atop the table. "Meanwhile, Alex, you'll find four metal cases and my computer in the back seat. My clothes are in a suitcase in the boot...what you call the trunk. But you might want to leave them there for now." He glanced at the window. "And you might want to hurry. It's almost dark," he pointed out, "and I don't imagine it will be safe to go out much longer..."

Safe? What did he mean by that? Alex wondered. There'd never been anything *unsafe* about Halfmoon. No one locked their cars—or their houses much, for that matter. When Alex bought the house, in fact, Mrs. Southworth hadn't even been able to locate a key to lock the front door. "How so?" Alex asked, suddenly thinking that maybe she should stop feeling sorry for Benjamin and send him out to fetch his own bags.

"As soon I plug in my equipment I can give you a better idea."

Now that the sun had set, the temperature was quickly dropping, and the breeze moving through the screen suddenly seemed sentient. It was bending the candle flames, causing the wax to melt unevenly. Alex pushed down the sleeves of her long-sleeved tee and scooted around the table to close the window. "Should I lock it," she asked, half jokingly.

"I would if I were you," he said.

Orielle gave a reinforcing nod. "Do as he says, Alex."

Alex looked at Benjamin, then at Orielle, waiting for one of them to acknowledge the joke. But neither did; Orielle seemed as serious and preoccupied as Benjamin now—like his assistant, she was acting...and Alex was the gofer. She looked at Benjamin's keys, then hesitated for a moment. "Boogawoog?" she called nonchalantly, although her voice cracked on her. "Wanna go out?"

"I just gave her a dog biscuit," Orielle said. "Let her eat."

"But she needs to go out," Alex insisted. "She hasn't gone since this afternoon—don't you think it's time?"

Before Orielle could answer, Boogawoog walked in again, crumbs spilling from her mouth as she hurried to finish swallowing the biscuit she was currently eating. Then she shook herself, looked anticipatingly at Alex and burped.

"See, I told you so," Alex said with relief. "She has to go."

Alex turned on the light and she and Boogawoog stepped out onto the porch. The fog was moving in. Moths fluttered about the yellow lightbulb, and out in the poppy field fireflies were lighting. With one paw raised, Boogawoog stood sniffing the air. Alex stood close to the dog, ready to take her cues from the Scottie, and paying careful attention to the night noises.

Up by the road a barn owl hooted, river water trickled off a ways, and above that there were only the echoes of spring peepers and bellowing bullfrogs. The evening seemed well enough—an average June night in the country—but still Alex was fast developing a case of the creeps.

Alex looked at the Scottie, then at the professor's gray Mercedes, wondering how fast she could run to the car and back—and how many trips she'd need to make. "What do you think?" she said. "Is it safe?"

Boogawoog glanced up at her, then responded with a low growl—not a growl of imminent danger, but a comforting, reassuring growl; one which suggested she was alert and on watch and would follow up with further warning if necessary.

Whether they'd been an act of bribery or diplomacy, the b-b-balls, the sirloin, and the soup bones had paid off. Alex had made a new friend...a friend with big teeth and a bad temper.

❧ 14 ❧
Medium Mary

Mary Southworth didn't look like someone in the business of conducting seances. With a patent leather purse dangling from her elbow, she looked more like the president of a women's auxiliary; a fund-raiser, say, or someone who might head a church bazaar committee. She arrived about an hour after the professor, toting an over-stuffed briefcase, and dressed as Alex had remembered her: pleated skirt, loafers, white blouse and pearl-buttoned cardigan. The cardigan was a bit snug, though, and fastened clear to her throat, so that it seemed to serve as something of a girdle in mashing down her large breasts.

And although Alex hated to admit it—lest she seem preoccupied with birds tonight—Mary was, as they say, duck-footed. A perfect match for Benjamin. What with his bill and her feet, there was no telling how far they could go. Alex grimaced, watching Southworth's walk and wondering how it was that the woman managed to move forward when each loafer was pointing in a different direction. But she moved fast, taking quick little steps up the gravel walkway, and only losing her footing once when her leather sole slid across a damp stone. It caused her to momentarily lose traction, and she gave a shout. "*Woooo!* " she hooted.

Run, Mary, run, Alex was tempted to shout, *hurry up before the goblins getcha.* But she didn't. She couldn't. Mary was on *her* team, after all.

By the time Mrs. Southworth climbed the porch steps and reached the door she was out of breath—mostly because of the excitement, Alex presumed.

"I warned you on the phone and I'll warn you again," Alex said, "I've got a fairy, a wizard and a talking dog in here." Mary didn't flinch at all. This was, after all, the night for which she had spent her life waiting.

It looked as if Mary had done her hair for the occasion, too. A light Clairol-brown, it had been teased into a perfect ball and sprayed to stay that way.

And Benjamin, having regained his English reserve, instantly acknowledged her hairdo. The professor may not have been what one would call handsome, but during his heyday, Alex suspected his charm and opulence had earned him the title of lady's man.

"What a pleasure it is, Madam..." he said, extending an arm. "And so gracious of you to oblige us." With his free arm bent behind his back, he leaned and kissed the top of her hand. "I can feel the wisdom, the spiritual energy in your hands, and yet...how strange...how soft and youthful they are—no older than the hands of a maiden."

"Oooh..." Mary cooed. Her cheeks turned a bright and blotchy red, and she fanned her face with her hand and flirtatiously batted her eyelashes. "And you must be Benjamin Birdwhistle. *Professor* Benjamin Birdwhistle." Her voice began to climb and she held the ends of her words as an opera singer holds a note. She looked at Alex and Orielle standing side by side, then back at Benjamin. "And a *wizard,* too. Can you imagine!" she said, teasingly pushing at his shirt. The push nearly bowled the old man over, but he regained his balance and adjusted his tie.

She attempted to pet the cat then, but Sheeky hissed and so Mary quickly turned to Orielle. "And this must be...the fairy princess," she chimed, "...what a *doll* you are."

Mary Southworth was in her glory. Her eyes oscillating between the fairy and the wizard, it was as if she were in the company of movie stars, Alex thought. And of course Orielle and Benjamin, whether they knew it or not, would undoubtedly become far more famous than mere movie stars if word got out.

Boogawoog came around to sniff and inspect her loafers. Mary looked down at Boogawoog and clasped her hands together, her patent leather purse still dangling from her arm. "And the Scottie...I haven't seen a Scottie since President Roosevelt's *Fala*. I don't remember him being quite as big as this one, though. No..." she said to Boogawoog. "You certainly are a big one!"

Boogawoog burped.

"How nice," she said, patting her chest as though she was the one who burped. She cautiously reached to pet the dog, then seemed to think better of it and withdrew her hand. "What a nice doggy...yes. Well!" she said, looking nervously away from Boogawoog and gesturing toward the glow of candlelight coming from the dining room. "Is that where we'll conduct our seance?" she asked, quickly changing the subject.

"Indeed," Benjamin replied.

Mary gave an approving nod. "I'm ready to change now," she said.

Alex glanced at Mrs. Southworth's stuffed briefcase. "What, you have to wear a costume for this?"

Southworth pursed her lips at Orielle, condescendingly, Alex thought, as if silently acknowledging Alex's naivete.

Orielle showed Mrs. Southworth to the bathroom. Five minutes later she was back out wearing a robe over her skirt and blouse; gold-colored moons and stars on a navy background. It had creases in it, as if it had never been worn before, and Alex wondered what other store she had shopped at after leaving the beauty salon. Madam Mimma's, probably.

Mrs. Southworth ran her hands over her breasts and stomach to smooth the fabric, then primped her hair self-consciously and lifted her chin self-importantly.

The professor's flattery had, no doubt, gone straight to her head. And being the astute gentleman that he was, Benjamin quickly responded to her cue, taking hold of her elbow when she held it out, and leading her into the dining room.

☾ ☾ ☾

Benjamin had something plugged into every outlet on his power strip. Sound devices, is all he would say, except for the small machine in front of him. "This will alert us to any anomalies."

"Anomalies?" Alex asked.

"Yes," Orielle answered her. "Deviations in the electromagnetic field. It measures energy levels."

Southworth's giant-sized eyes—bigger than the cat's—lit up and seemed to vibrate. She held up her hand and shook it, as if waiting to be called on to speak. "A *Gauss* meter!" she exclaimed.

"Correct you are," Benjamin answered. Then to Alex he said, "It's basically a negative ion detector. The presence of spirits causes static discharges in the air—discharges which, as Orielle has pointed out, affect electromagnetic properties."

"What the professor means by *anomaly*," Mary explained in her high, singsong voice, "is a concentration of psychic energy in the air—in the *field*. Isn't that right, Professor...?"

"Well put, Ms. Southworth."

Alex narrowed her eyes at Mrs. Southworth, trying to figure out just when it was that Mary had decided to switch teams, leaving Alex to play the game alone. She looked at the medium, but Mary didn't acknowledge her; she was too busy squirming in her seat—the result, no doubt, of Benjamin's ego-stroking.

"Is the front door locked?" Benjamin asked.

"Yes," Alex said. His sudden grimness made her swallow hard.

"Then perhaps it is time to draw the shutters....to keep the night from peeking in on us."

Alex ran her hands through her hair and held her head for a second. "Do I really need to be here for this? I mean, can't I just sit in the kitchen or something? I could *really* use a cup of coffee."

"Alex," he began gently, "Batilda gave *you* the bell...so it *belongs* to you now."

"No, no, no—you don't seem to understand, Benjamin. I don't *want* the bell."

"What you want is not what *is*. The bell is governed by very specific laws, including the way by which it comes to its owner."

"Owner...?"

"You, Alex."

She pointed to herself. "*Me?*"

"You are the rightful owner of the bell now. It is you who owns Orielle. "

Alex looked at Orielle pleadingly, then turned back to Benjamin with a painful, give-me-a-break sort of face. "Let me try this one more time," Alex began evenly, but then her voice broke and climbed an octave. "I don't *want* to own the bell. I don't want to *own* Orielle. I...I..." She threw her hands up. "For Christ's *sake*, Benjamin—I have trouble owning *myself* half the time."

"Let's make that coffee," Orielle suggested. "I believe I'll have a cup of tea." Then to the others she said, "Coffee? Tea?"

"Yes, I suppose a spot of tea wouldn't hurt," Benjamin conceded.

"And you, Mary?"

"The same as the professor, please."

"Some cookies, too," Alex demanded—anything to stall for time. "I want some cookies."

"Whatever you like," Orielle said, accommodatingly. Her tone was so easy, so sweet, that it eased Alex's frustration, lessening her need to break out in a primal scream.

"Why don't you two prepare," Orielle said to Benjamin and Mary. "I'll bring the tea in...Alex will take as *long* as she likes having her cookies and coffee...and then, only when Alex is ready," she stressed, "she and I will anoint the white candle."

⋖ 15 ⋗
Quantum Physics

Alex set a serving tray on the dining room table and sniffed the air suspiciously. "What's burning?"

"Amber and musk," Southworth squeaked. "It keeps the evil spirits away while we attempt to make contact with the...*other* side."

The dining room now looked more like a nineteenth-century parlor. Mary had turned the lights off, so that the green lights on Benjamin's machines and computer now blinked like fireflies along the baseboard. And with Mary's navy-and-gold celestial robe, and all the candles and incense burning, the whole room seemed a strange mingling of hi-tech flair and Victorian ambiance.

Orielle and Alex took their seats across from the two, and Benjamin, holding a strainer over the cups, poured tea. Alex sipped her coffee, then took a cookie from a plate on the tray and bit off a piece. She could chew as slowly and deliberately as she pleased to prolong the inevitable, she reasoned, or she could give the go-ahead and let Southworth get on with her performance.

Orielle looked at Alex, and as soon as Alex nodded, the fairy reached for a little bottle of yellow liquid and unscrewed the cap. "This is anointing oil, Alex...what we refer to as *Van Van.*"

Alex hesitated. "What's in it?"

"Acacia, lily, orange oils. This particular blend is called Spirit's Guide. It is used to clear the pathways and assist in spiritual communications." With that, she pushed the white candle toward Alex and handed her the bottle. "Wet your fingertip with it," she said.

Alex still wasn't happy about having to anoint or stick her finger in anything she couldn't identify, but she had to admit to the calming effect Orielle's presence had on her. And suddenly she realized she had inexplicable trust in the fairy. With a fingertip over the opening, she tilted the bottle and waited.

"In rituals," Orielle explained in a voice that quieted Alex's mind, "the candle represents the principle of fire—willpower." She pointed to the middle of the taper. "You...we...are the center of this candle. Everything above it symbolizes the spiritual plane...all below the center, the physical plane."

Orielle took Alex's hand and gently guided it to the candle. "Place your finger at the center and make a line upward. In doing this we send our wish tonight up to the heavens.

"Now," she instructed, "take another drop...start at the center again...only this time run your finger down the candle. This completes the circuit and asks that our wish on the spiritual plane materialize here, on the physical plane."

Alex wiped her finger clean on her jeans and watched Orielle light the anointed candle. "We'll give it a little time to burn...to let our wish rise up, and by the time it melts past the center, a judgement will be passed."

Benjamin smiled. "You're doing quite well, Alex...I have the utmost confidence in you."

"I'm not sure what you mean by that, but..."

"In you, Alex, I sense a woman of great strength."

Alex tried to make light of her anxiety. "I think you're confusing strength with stubbornness."

"And who are the stubborn, but the strong-willed."

Alex smiled. She liked Benjamin. Southworth might have been in a world all her own, but Benjamin was *connected*. He seemed to maintain a logical relationship to everything around him. And sitting there with his cat draped around his neck—evidence of a more emotional side—he was exactly how she might have imagined a grandfather to be: concerned, humble, omnisciently wise.

Benjamin took the black book retrieved from Batilda's cottage and placed it before him. "It might do us well to begin focusing our thoughts on Batilda."

"Yes," Southworth echoed. "It will do us well to concentrate our energies on the person we wish to summon."

Benjamin patted the book. "This," he explained to both Mary and Alex, "was Batilda's personal *grimoire*—a lifelong collection of recipes, spells, observations...a professional diary, or journal, you might say. Every witch keeps one."

Alex thought of the pink-spotted foxglove she and Orielle had seen in the woods. "Every *witch*? You can't be serious...."

"Apparently not seriously *taken*," he said.

"You can't just expect me to believe in all these—"

"Forgive me for interrupting, but what more will it take to convince you of *any* of this?" His eyes took on an odd shine, as if he were sitting there trying to figure her out. "After your eyewitness account of the real miracle here—namely, Orielle's materialization—it seems the fact of witches would be of minor significance."

"I'm a cynic," Alex defended herself.

"Severely so." He studied her, his eyes softening. "Under the circumstances, however, I must say it's a rather fortunate quality you possess; in fact, it might prove your most powerful resource in the end."

"My cynicism?"

"Precisely."

"Meaning...?"

Benjamin didn't answer. He paused to drink his tea, and Sheeky, bothered by the rising steam, jumped to the floor.

"Alex," he inquired, "do you practice a religion?"

"I don't believe in a God, if that's what you're asking."

He nodded in thoughtful consideration. "Then I may presume you don't believe in spirits, nor ghosts, nor the very purpose of our gathering tonight?"

"No," she said, although her answer wasn't entirely true. She didn't know what she believed anymore.

"Alex," he said, pacing himself. "There is much for you to learn, and little time for me to teach you." He sipped his tea and with a napkin patted his thin lips. "While we give our candle a few more minutes to burn, perhaps you'll allow me to give you a lesson in physics?"

"Physics?"

"Quantum physics."

"Look, Benjamin," Alex said, running her fingers through her curls. "I wouldn't make a good student tonight. I haven't slept in almost twenty-four hours and...truthfully, I don't know *anything* about quantum physics."

Benjamin held a finger to his lips and without another word reached for a box of wooden matches. "This won't take long," he promised. "By the time this match burns you will understand physics." He struck the match, propped his elbow on the table, and held the burning match between them. "What's happening?"

"The match is burning," Alex said, unimpressed.

"Yes...and the burning match...of what is it composed?"

"Wood...?"

"Wood." He nodded. "And might we agree that wood is matter?"

"Matter," she agreed.

"And the fire...what is the fire?"

Alex studied the match flame and gave an uncertain shrug. "Heat, I guess."

"Correct. And heat is a form of—?"

"I don't know...energy?"

"Energy. Yes...!" he said approvingly. "Now, before I burn my fingers, tell us, if you will, what is happening to the matter."

Alex looked at the shrinking matchstick. "It's disappearing, burning."

"And as it burns, what is it being turned into?"

"Energy...?"

"Ah! Very well then. Matter into energy, body into spirit." Satisfied, he blew out the match and dropped it in the tray. "So there you have it—quantum physics in a nutshell. There is no beginning, Alex. No end. Only change and transformation."

Alex felt the hair on her neck prickle.

Benjamin drank his tea. "Fascinating concept—almost religious, wouldn't you say?"

"Yes..." Alex admitted, chewing thoughtfully on her bottom lip. *No end...only change and transformation*, she speculated, wondering if the principle could be applied to her parents, to Fink—to every living thing she had ever loved and lost. It was something Alex had never imagined before.

"Quantum physics...it's the highest branch of science," Benjamin said, his eyes filling with conviction. "And when you climb out on it...you find yourself staring into the eyes of God. And at that moment," he added, "you realize that God and science are one...." He sighed. "Long gone are the days when the two were viewed as an irreconcilable dichotomy...and I a heretic."

Benjamin looked at Orielle and Mary. "Now that I have convinced Alex of the afterlife...of the transformation of body into spirit..." He stopped, leaning into the table, and winked at Alex. "At least I have succeeded in *partially* convincing you... haven't I?"

Alex merely raised a brow at him.

"Good, then," he said. "I needed only to appeal to your sense of logic. I'll keep that in mind." He turned to Southworth, who sat with her mouth open, so utterly amazed by Benjamin's match-burning demonstration that she seemed to have settled into a trance. "Madam Southworth?"

"Here!" she chirped.

"I think we're ready to begin...shall we see if there are any *energies* that wish to speak with us tonight?"

The silver light of the waxing moon glistened through the shutter slats. The owl was somewhere over the house *hooting*

now, and the night breeze had picked up enough to rustle the
wisteria and lilacs outside the window.

Mary squirmed, adjusting herself in her seat, then lifted a
tiny bell Alex hadn't noticed before.

As if sensing Alex's trepidation, Orielle quickly put a hand
over hers. "It's not enchanted."

"Not to worry," Benjamin added. "Bells are a common
part of ceremony. We ring them in churches to summon worship-
pers, no? At weddings to summon angels and well-wishers...and
at   seances to summon the dead."

Mrs. Southworth placed her fingertips on the table top
and waited for everyone to follow suit. Then she shut her eyes
and rolled her neck dramatically.

"Oh, spirits..." she began, but she was quickly interrupted
by the clicking of Boogawoog's nails against the oak floor, and
then the sound of sniffing.

Boogawoog began restlessly pacing. "MAMA!"

At the sound of the dog's voice, Mrs. Southworth's eyes
and mouth popped open, and she stared incredulously, as though
she hadn't *really* believed the Scottie would ever talk. Alex looked
at Mary with one open eye and snickered to herself.

"She senses Batilda," Benjamin said. "Perhaps we're closer
to making contact than we realize."

Boogawoog ran to the front door, then zoomed to the
window, sniffing every crack so hard that she sounded like bel-
lows. Then she hurried over and stood up, her paws on Alex's lap.

"MAMA'S COMING, ALEC."

"Shh..." Alex said, lifting Boogawoog onto her lap. The
Scottie promptly sat up and put her chin on the table. "Sorry,"
Alex apologized to Mary, placing her fingers back on the table.
"Where were you?" she asked flatly.

Mrs. Southworth cleared her throat in acknowledgment
of the silenced dog and took a deep breath. "Oh...! Oh, spirits..."

she began again, "our thoughts are concentrated upon you tonight...as we ask that you might summon for us the spirit of—"

This time it was a *beep* which interrupted Mrs. Southworth, and it was coming from one of Benjamin's machines.

And there it sounded again, a high-pitched beeping similar to that of a radar detector—single beeps spaced seconds apart.

"We've got some activity," Benjamin said.

"Psychic energy?" Mary asked.

"Some, but it's the magameter, not the Gauss meter." He furrowed his brow. "We're picking up something solid."

All three women sat silently as Benjamin went about fiddling with the apparatus, twisting or sliding a knob here and there. Alex strained to hear the night noises outside. The owl had stopped hooting, the silver moonlight shone in lines through the closed shutters, and the rustling out back seemed suddenly louder. Alex listened, thinking it wasn't the breeze anymore, but something moving, skulking through the tall grass.

Mrs. Southworth didn't make another peep, but her pursed lips were quivering, her unblinking blue eyes fixed on what Benjamin was doing. She didn't seem the least bit frightened, though; on the contrary, she seemed to be in a state of delighted shock at having actually managed to summon something up.

"What *is* it?" Orielle asked.

"I'm not quite sure," he said.

"Well, what do you *think* it is?" Alex impatiently whispered.

He stared at the radar a moment longer, the beeps coming in long but steady intervals, then looked up with brows furrowed now to the point of grimness. "In Batilda's cottage," he said, "over the telephone...Orielle mentioned that you saw children last night."

"In the car. Yes...."

Benjamin nodded bleakly. "They weren't children, Alex." He and Orielle looked at one another, nodding in secret agreement.

"Well...?" Alex waited.

"They were imps...Lilah's pets, you might say."

"No," Alex nervously contradicted him. "I know what kids look like—they were *kids!* I'm the one who *saw* them, remember?"

"You saw their faces," Orielle said.

"The *faces* of children." Benjamin nervously cleared his throat. "But not the bodies of children...."

The beeps came in rapid succession now, like a radar detector picking up an approaching police car. *Beep...beep-beep-beep...beep...beep.*

"Just as I feared," Benjamin said to himself. "The bell wasn't put into the freezer soon enough." He looked at Alex. "I'm afraid Lilah was able to track the vibrations."

"But the bell isn't ringing."

"No matter," he said. "Everything vibrates, the earth vibrates—*all* molecules vibrate. And because Lilah is magically connected to the bell, she can feel those vibrations. The only way to halt the vibrations of an object is to *freeze* it."

Alex was scared. And Mrs. Southworth wasn't far behind. Her cheeks, still flushed and blotched from Benjamin's earlier compliments, were quickly losing all their color.

Beep...beep-beep-beep-beep-beep-beep...beep.

Orielle looked at Alex. "It was an imp that tried to claw Boogawoog's throat...but she fought it off."

Alex petted the Scottie's neck where the wounds had been. But it didn't quiet the dog; she growled at the window, mumbling all sorts of inaudible things—curse words, they sounded like. Alex put the dog down and abruptly stood up. "That's it!"

Orielle touched Alex's arm. "Where are you going?"

"To get my rifle."

"It won't help any," Benjamin said. "We'd do better to fend them off with raw meat...if necessary."

At the mention of raw meat, Mary's face turned white.

"They're quite stupid, really; given to impulse and insatiable appetites."

"Lord help us," Mary murmured.

Alex glared at her, then she dashed to the kitchen and came back with leftover sirloin—a patty she'd planned to give Boogawoog in the morning. Alex handed the meat to Benjamin, holding her arm out to block Orielle when the fairy got up from her chair. "You stay right there," Alex said, not quite sure why she felt suddenly protective of Orielle.

"You stay at a safe distance, too," Benjamin said above Boogawoog's voice and the beeping radar. "They're venomous."

Alex swallowed dryly. "Poisonous?"

"And remarkably fast." With his free hand he drew the hanky from his pocket and patted his forehead. Alex noticed his hands shaking slightly.

"But what about the dog? She wasn't *poisoned.*"

"Antivenin," he answered. "Over the years, Batilda injected Boogawoog, Sheeky, and me with serum. We're all immune...." he said, cautiously approaching the door. "This certainly isn't the first time I've dealt with them."

They followed Benjamin halfway until he gestured for them to halt.

"What have I done!" Mary babbled. "What in heaven's name have I called up—"

"Shhh!" Benjamin commanded.

Alex held her breath, her arm still out to keep Orielle behind her.

Boogawoog sat beside Alex, and she could feel the dog begin to tremble. Mrs. Southworth hid behind them all, as Benjamin turned the knob and cautiously opened it just enough to peek out. Instantly, it seemed, the white fog seeped in through the crack. The distant croaking of frogs was the only sound...and then came Benjamin's shout.

"Dear *God!*" he shrieked, stepping back in shock, forgetting to let go of the knob, so that he pulled the door open with him. "We've raised the dead!"

There on the porch, standing in the fog, was the old witch—moths fluttering about her head, her white hair wild and matted, her black eyes glazed over as though she'd gone completely mad. And she was wearing Alex's orange slicker.

⇜ 16 ⇝
Resurrection

"**Son**-of-a-bitch, Birdwhistle—let me in!" Batilda demanded, yelling and jiggling the latched screen door.

"MAMA HERE!" Boogawoog squealed. "MAMA-MAMA-MAMA!" She rushed at the door, clawing at the screen with her paws.

Benjamin stood clutching his chest, too shocked to utter a single word.

"She's alive...!" Alex whispered.

"Surprised, eh?" Batilda pressed her nose to the screen door and sneered at Alex. "And why not? You made off with my bell and left me for dead—stole my little dog, too, I see."

Alex took a step back, so mortified she hardly knew what to say. "But I didn't...I didn't make off with *anything*! I *saved* your dog—I was trying to save *you*. I ran to get help, to call for—"

Orielle stopped Alex with a reassuring squeeze of her arm. "Easy, now...she doesn't mean it."

"*Mean* it—doesn't *mean it*? She's accusing me of—of—" Alex was appalled.

The old witch, or harpy—or whatever the heck she was—looked as though she'd just unearthed herself. Her clothes were still wet from last night's rain, bits of twigs and leaves and mud were stuck in her hair and plastered all over the orange slicker. She looked like the living dead; mean and mad and set to tackle Alex.

"All right, all right!" Her lips peeled back and she bared her teeth. "Calm down, Kiddo! Just lighten up now and let me in, will ya? I'm dyin' a slow death out here."

"ALEC! ALEC! MAMA IN, ALEC! MAMA IN!"

Orielle stepped in front of Alex and unlatched the door, and Batilda limped in. She frowned apologetically, first at Orielle, then at Alex, and then glanced at the professor. "Thanks for crying and saying all those nice things about me, Birdwhistle. I was touched...truly touched." With the back of her hand she gave him a halfhearted swat. "Now either say something or shut your mouth...you look stupid with it hangin' open like that."

Boogawoog was ecstatic, circling Batilda's legs and sniffing at her feet, alternately squealing and shouting out familiar smells. "RIVER (sniff) HORSEY (sniff) RAT, RAT, RAT (sniff, sniff, sniff)."

"Yep, that's mama's little Boogie...mama's little ratter," Batilda said.

"RIVER...BOO-BOO...MORE RAT...RAT, RAT, RAT," Boogawoog grumbled, speaking and sniffing frantically now. "BLOOD, BOO-BOO...MAMA GOT BOO-BOO...RAT, RAT, RAT."

Batilda looked at Alex. "That's the 'possum she smells. But she's a ratter, see? A rat dog. That's her breed. So we use *rat* generically—she calls all her natural prey—foxes, rodents, weasels—rats." Batilda beetled her brow. "Follow?"

Alex nodded, but her face was still frozen. "Opossum?"

"The one in the barn."

"You were in my *barn*?"

"Where the hell else was I gonna go?" she snapped. "You think I *wanted* to keep company with that musky little beast? What a *sorry* excuse for a kangaroo's cousin! Stingy bugger, too—wouldn't give me one lousy bite of his rotten apricots. Even guarded the pits! The pits! As if I might suck on one if he turned his back. I was thirsty enough, let me tell you, but—"

"Shh..." Orielle cut in, taking one of Batilda's knobby-knuckled hands and guiding her to a chair.

"But your *ribs,* your *back....*" Alex said, still trying to fathom how it was that the woman was walking, let alone *living.* "Your bones were protruding...I felt them."

"Wings, sweetie. Those were my goddamned wings! A gift from Benjamin, here," she said, shooting him another piercing glance. "Bet ya never thought they'd end up saving my *life,* did ya!" Then she looked at Orielle and her gruff voice softened. "Maybe you could have a look at 'em darlin'. I think they're busted, but it's hard to tell nowadays. I don't have much feelin' in 'em anymore."

Despite her agitated speech, her bullishness seemed forced, her breathing labored, as if the very act of speaking were consuming what energy she had left.

Alex looked to Orielle, and Orielle nodded in silent confirmation of Alex's thoughts. The two had spent only one day together, but Alex couldn't remember ever having been in such perfect communication with a woman—with anyone.

"Come," Orielle said to Batilda, "you're congested...you've been in the dampness too long. Perhaps Mrs. Southworth can help me bathe you so I can get a better look at your injuries."

But when they turned to Mrs. Southworth, she wasn't in sight. Come to think of it, Alex had neither seen nor heard her since the knock at the door.

"I think our medium is hiding," Alex mumbled to Orielle. "Mrs. Southworth!" she called.

"Yesss?" she answered from the bathroom in her best soprano.

"It's safe to come out now, Mrs. Southworth," Alex said. "Looks like you didn't raise the dead after all." She rolled her eyes, catching Orielle's gaze as she did, and realized the fairy was smiling at her.

"You know where the towels are," Alex moaned, stooping to pick up the sirloin by Benjamin's feet. Boogawoog hadn't even made a move for the meat; her only interest was in keeping her mama in sight.

"Let's get you to the bathroom," Orielle said.

But at the mention of the word *bath*, Boogawoog made an immediate U-turn. "NO BATH—BOOGIE NO LIKE BATH." She pinned back her ears.

"Your *mama*—not you," Alex said. "Relax."

But Boogawoog didn't trust it. The whites of her eyes shone suspiciously through her black bangs, and she looked at Alex with a face that said she was wise to the ways of people tricking dogs into baths. The Scottie followed them halfway down the hall then stopped and sat, deciding to guard her mama at a dry distance from the bathroom.

Alex settled for remaining at a comfortable distance, too. Although she couldn't help but imagine what Batilda's wings looked like, she had no real desire to see them; it was bad enough she'd unknowingly *touched* them last night. And when Orielle called for Alex to bring in the sack of medicinal bottles they'd collected in the cottage, Alex covered her eyes and held it out for Mrs. Southworth to take through the bathroom door.

Alex stood there a moment longer, picturing Batilda soaking in the tub, a beer in her hand, a cigar hanging from the side of her mouth, her wings resting over the edge of the tub like mutant elbows. Quickly she shook the grotesque thought from her head, then headed back down the hallway, leaving the fairy-physician to her healing arts.

"MAMA OKAY?"

"Don't you worry." Alex bent at the waist, her hands resting on her knees, and looked sympathetically into the Scottie's worry-filled, almond-shaped eyes. "Your mama's okay."

"OKAY...MAMA OKAY." And then she sneezed—a happy sneeze. "OKAY, OKAY. ALEC OKAY?"

"I don't know, Boogawoog. I don't know *how* I am. And to tell you the truth, I think I'm better off not thinking about it right now...know what I mean?

"BOOGIE KNOW."

"I thought you would." Alex considered the dog a moment, then patted her thigh. "Let's go see if Benjamin's okay...maybe you can help me close his mouth."

"NO—BOOGIE WAIT FOR MAMA."

"Oh, I see," Alex said. "Well, then you sit here and I'll go check on him." She straightened herself and turned, but then on second thought, turned back to the dog again. "Just one more thing.... Don't ever let it get out that Alex Spherris talked to a dog, okay, because it would definitely destroy my credibility with the women."

Boogawoog cocked her head at the word credibility. It seemed she hadn't the slightest idea what Alex was talking about. But she agreed anyway.

"Thanks, because...as it is," Alex confessed to the Scottie, "my credibility has been waning lately."

⋘ 17 ⋙
The Harping Harpy

"Self-preservation," Batilda was saying, "it's like a shot of adrenaline in the butt. It's amazing what you're capable of doing when you know you're gonna die." She paused, gulping the tealike medicinal concoction she and Orielle had brewed, then smacked her lips. "I heard the car. I knew they'd be swinging back around to search my body, to find the bell—you don't spend your life loving someone not to predict their behavior, you know?" She wiped her mouth with the back of her hand. "Dragged myself across the road, is what I did—rolled right down the river bank and lay by the water until I could move again. Like I said, these here wings took the impact—saved my spine—so I guess I should thank Alex *and* Benjamin." She looked at Alex and Mary. "He gave 'em to me, you know." She sneered at Benjamin from across the table. Did you tell them, Birdwhistle? Huh? Did you tell them you *cursed* me with these goddamned freaking things?"

He looked imploringly at the women, as though they were members of a jury. "As I explained before, it was retaliatory. Why, if she hadn't buried me I—"

"Get over it, Ben." She waved a dismissive hand in his face. "Played a joke on him is all I did. But Mr. Anal-retentive never *could* take a joke."

"Joke? Dear woman...! Can you imagine being buried alive?" He looked at Mary. "Frightful, I tell you! The experience nearly killed me."

Alex's face worked itself into a contortion of disbelief. "They dug you up? You were actually...*buried*?"

"Yes indeed!"

Batilda put her hands up to stop him. "Hold your horses, mister—let's clear this up for the *last* time. I drugged him, see," she said to the others, "gave him just enough to deaden his pulse and put him out for a few hours—long enough for him to wake up at his own wake."

Batilda frowned, as though she had no real interest in rehashing the past. "Back in those days wakes were held in people's houses—smack in the middle of the living room. And the body would stay there until the funeral." She looked at him out of the corners of her beady black eyes and smiled crookedly. "I wanted him to wake up in the middle of the night with the candles burning and see how long it took before he realized he wasn't in bed."

Alex didn't say a word. She just sat there, her forehead still crinkled, trying to decide if Batilda *knew* she was nuts.

"What's wrong?" Batilda said defensively. "Why are you lookin' at *me*? It's not like I poisoned him, or anything. I used soporific chemicals—sleep inducers. How was I supposed to know the man would slip into a coma?" She shook her head, as if the whole thing had been Benjamin's fault. "Who'd think a grown man his size would have such a *weak* system? The stuff had him out cold for...what was it, Birdwhistle...thirty-six hours?"

"And she allowed my family to bury me!" He put a hand to his heart. "My poor, poor mummy...God rest her soul...it nearly *killed* her."

"You're sitting here, Birdwhistle, aren't you? Did I let you die? No. Bought him a Bateson's Belfry, is what I did."

Mrs. Southworth stirred in her seat. "What on earth...?"

"A bell, darlin'," Batilda said. "There was a string on it, see? And the string was fed through a narrow pipe that went down through the ground to the coffin, and into the corpse's hand. So if it turned out the corpse wasn't a corpse—if the hands started twitchin'—the bell would ring and anyone sitting vigil would hear the bell and have the person exhumed."

"That's insane," Alex said.

Benjamin cleared his throat. "Not entirely. In the eighteen hundreds the Society for the Prevention of People Being Buried Alive was established.... In the Victorian era, premature burial was as real a fear as violent crimes are today. Since blood was not drained from the body, and medical technology being rather unsophisticated, well...it was quite possible to confuse a comatose state with clinical death. It sometimes happened that the deceased would miraculously awake at the wake, as it were."

Alex looked at Orielle. "You know about this?"

"It's true," she agreed. "Mr. Bateson himself suffered from such a phobia."

"It prompted Bateson to patent the device," Benjamin said.

"Made a fortune off wealthy families," Batilda joined in. "And then what does the idiot do? Douses himself with linseed oil and sets himself on fire."

Benjamin sighed. "Bateson was so morbidly preoccupied with his phobia that he didn't trust even his own device. Suicide, he decided, was the best prevention against premature burial."

"The irony..." Mrs. Southworth said.

"The fright!" Benjamin emphasized. "I can't begin to describe the dread of regaining consciousness in pitch blackness, of feeling the lid of my own coffin inches from my face...."

"All right, Benjamin, enough—don't start getting melodramatic on us." Batilda shook her head, as if it were all she could do to tolerate him. "I couldn't believe I'd given him an overdose," she said to the women. "The dose I gave him wouldn't affect a *child* the way it affected him. So after they buried him, I rounded up a few of the Magi—Benjamin's friends from an underground guild—and we went to the graveyard and waited with shovels.

"Remember when you woke up and rang it, Ben?" Batilda looked at him hard, her face almost pained, as though she were about to cry. But instead she burst out laughing, and sat there laughing until she'd nearly laughed herself sick. "It was the damned funniest thing I'd ever seen..." she began, when she'd caught her breath. But then she caught sight of Benjamin's solemn, self-pitying face and broke down all over again.

She wiped away the tears, breaking into a momentary coughing fit from the laughter. "Listen to me wheeze, will ya? My lungs sounds like shit." She punched her chest and coughed again. "Anyway, where was I?" she said, calm enough to finish her story. "We waited a day and night for this buzzard to wake up. And then...it rang—and rang-rang-rang-rang. Never stopped until we got down to him. The man was scared stiff, so stiff we thought rigor mortis had set in. Couldn't even bend his arms or knees. Had to slide him out of that hole like a board."

She's crazy, Alex thought to herself. Then, "She's crazy," she whispered to Orielle.

Batilda's hand came down on the table. "I *heard* that!"

"Well it's true," Benjamin said. "It's a wonder I didn't spend the rest of my life in an asylum." He narrowed his eyes accusingly. "And that was what you *wished*, was it not?"

"Knock it off, Birdwhistle, all right? We've been through this five hundred times in the past hundred years. It's getting tired."

"We both know it's what you intended—to get rid of me and have Lilah for yourself." He looked at the others and lifted his chin in a dignified manner. "We loved the same woman," he said. "Batilda couldn't tolerate the thought of it—couldn't tolerate the fact of my very *existence!*"

"And you couldn't stand the *competition*—could you, you ol' bird-faced buzzard!"

"Umph...!" he snorted indignantly. "You're the buzzard...I don't see wings on *my* back you...you old snake-eyed crone."

"A snake-eyed crone, am I? And you're the crone's crony. All you ever were was a crony—the woman's patsy. Patsy, Patsy—"

"Stop it!" Orielle commanded. "Both of you...! I cannot bear this behavior." She stood up, her gray eyes penetrating her captors, and when she spoke again her voice was stern. "The two of you have deprived me of my life. You, Batilda, drugged me...and you, Benjamin, enchanted me...so, yes, I do know what it feels like to hear the hellish ringing...to wake up entombed. That *bell* is my coffin. With it, you have denied me my life."

The room grew silent, and both Benjamin and Batilda lowered their heads in shame. Respectfully, Mary and Alex did the same, so that it seemed the whole table was about to say grace.

Alex sneaked a glance at the fairy beside her. Her hair was coming undone, a few long cinnamon strands falling free, and the tears only made her eyes sparkle more beautifully.

"Despite your common plight," the fairy addressed the witch and the professor, "you have at least known the pleasure of a lover. But I do not know even *that*. I was eighteen when you abducted me...you took me when I was but a *child*! And since that day, it is *I* who serve your *mistress*...your lover born of *devils*. Half the time my consciousness is suspended; I do not know who I am, or even *that* I am. And then I am summoned—Edinburgh, New Orleans, Paris, Manhattan—*wherever* she needs me. *Whenever* she needs me. And there I heal, perform my work...under the *oppression* of her reign. Do you think I do not yearn for freedom...yearn for life and love?"

Alex reached and touched Orielle's waist, tugging gently on the fabric of her white gown. It was strange; strange how the feel of her waist, of her hip had an almost grounding effect on Alex. Last night Orielle hadn't even been solid...and now, right now, she seemed the most solid thing in Alex's life.

"This is just *awful*," Mary said, her fingers pressed against her cheek. "And what a little *doll* she is..."

"Of course it's awful," Batilda muttered. "That's why we've come for the solstice—to uncross the *spell*... *fix* things!"

Mary's lips quivered and she squirmed again in her seat, the way she tended to do whenever anyone mentioned magic.

"Well, then," Orielle said, "maybe the two of you would like to enlighten me...enlighten us," she said, affectionately running her hand over the top of Alex's head.

Orielle paused, looked around at all of them, and touched Alex's curly locks again. "Alex has opened her home to us. She saved you, she saved the bell. She saved me.... But I know little more than she does about this evil web into which she has been woven." She glanced down at Alex, then took her seat again. "The solstice is nearing, but the brighter the moon grows, the darker seems my future."

"No," Benjamin said. "We have waited a century to rectify...to restore the life we stole from you. And we will," he said, "I pledged I would."

"Pledged?" Orielle asked.

"To Steven Rutherford."

"My father..." Orielle murmured. Her gaze dropped then, and for a moment she fell silent, mourning a memory from another lifetime, it seemed. "When did he pass?" she said, shutting her eyes.

Benjamin lowered his own gaze, respectfully. "July 3, 1923...well over seventy years ago."

My birthday, Alex thought. But she didn't say so—didn't want to say anything to steal away Orielle's moment of rightful sorrow.

Orielle drew in a deep breath and nodded, her eyes slowly opening in pained acceptance of the news.

"As I said," Benjamin offered, "we will win back your freedom. Won't we?" he asked, turning to Batilda for support.

The witch nodded wearily. She looked older now than she had last night, Alex thought. In the candlelight, the black circles shone beneath her eyes like half-moons—the same size as the ones decorating the mystic robe she'd borrowed from Mary—and with her wings piled beneath the robe, she appeared exceedingly hunched. "We're going to kill her," she said, quite matter-of-factly.

Alex looked at her askance. "Murder...?"

"If we have to use our bare hands."

Orielle seemed suddenly confused. "Wait a minute...Do you not have a *plan*?"

"We had one...and still do," Benjamin assured her. "I suffered a misfortune, is all. My apartment in Manhattan was broken into the night before last. Certain belongings were stolen...but I should be able to manage with my notes."

He gave a tired sigh, trying his best to keep an optimistic face. "Don't you worry, Orielle. It took us decades to acquire the bell...but we succeeded. We'll succeed on the solstice, too."

"You can count on us," Batilda said. Then she turned to Benjamin. "Truce?"

"He raised a brow skeptically. "Truce," he finally agreed. "And sincere apologies for our misconduct," he said to the others, then addressed Batilda again. "I take it back...I was *jealous*. Quite truthfully," he confessed, "I never understood what it was Lilah ever saw in me next to your Mediterranean beauty."

Batilda waved a hand at him. "Oh, go on, Birdwhistle." She frowned, seeming to have second thoughts. "Well...all right, maybe I was beautiful—looked a lot like Alex, didn't I?—But you had the class, Birdwhistle. You sure were a dapper fella."

"Truly?" He cocked his head, pleasantly surprised by the compliment.

"Oh yeah...a *dapper* fella, you were—dapper to a fault." She looked at Mary. "Always wore the best suits...a fresh flower in that lapel of his...." she said, pointing to his withered lily. "He had money and manners and brains. They even inducted him into the Royal Academy of Science. Of course...they threw him out later."

"My association with the Magi," he explained, "forced me into underground societies. A man before my time, I was. And still am. But in Victorian England I was an outcast, viewed as a heretic. And really," he said humbly, "I was simply a genius."

"Well," Orielle suggested, "perhaps the two of you will find a way to get along if you keep focused on the *fonder* memories of one another. It just might make for a more productive collaboration."

Benjamin and Batilda both nodded again.

Orielle waited. "What exactly will you do when the moon is full?"

The professor glanced at Batilda, gesturing for her to do the talking.

"In a nutshell?" Batilda gave a slightly crooked smile. "We're going to let her beat herself to death. Right, Ben?" Then she broke into a maniacal cackle.

"Beat herself..." he repeated, his face grim, "...with the sound of her own heart."

☾ ☾ ☾

No one said a word for a long time, and it wasn't until Alex saw that Mrs. Southworth was holding a hand over her heart—as if pledging allegiance—that Alex realized she was doing the same.

"Her own heart? With magic?" Southworth anxiously asked.

"A bit of magic," Benjamin offered. "Combined with drugs and sound waves."

The volumes were all turned down on Benjamin's machines, but the buttons were flickering like a disco ball, and Alex began to think about imps—whatever imps were—slinking around her yard. "Benjamin," she warned, pointing at all his lit-up gadgets.

"It's all right, Alex. We're picking up a bit of activity in the area...but nothing dangerously close." He scratched the tip of his bill-like nose and it moved back and forth like a piece of rubber. "Lilah's here...probably in the cave...and no doubt her legions are sniffing about. But I don't believe she knows where the bell is. I'd say you froze it in the nick of time."

"I don't like this," Alex admitted. "Bells and imps and—"

"Bears, oh, my!" Batilda snickered, widening her eyes for Alex's amusement. "Relax, Kiddo...it'll come together. Just think what a difference a day makes, huh? Little more than twenty-four hours ago you had no idea how interesting your life would become." She grinned, exposing her crooked teeth.

Alex felt Orielle's presence beside her, and she looked at the rest of them—the haggard and toothy harpy, the bird-faced professor...and Mrs. Southworth, who looked as though she should be singing in a church choir right now and not sitting there at all. She rolled her eyes. *What a motley crew,* she thought.

"She's right," Benjamin said. "We will teach you all you need to know—in good time, Alex, in good time. For now, I believe you've a bellyful to digest. Take a day to process and assimilate...and most importantly, take time to rest."

Rest. Yes, she wanted to sleep, needed to sleep, but how was she supposed to rest with *them* around? Go to a hotel is what she had half a mind to do—simply abandon her house and everyone in it—and go rent a quiet room. She might even go to Ana Mae's. But it wouldn't be quiet there. Ana Mae would keep her awake all night, asking the million questions she probably had by now. But before Alex could respond to Benjamin, *he* made the offer.

"We'll be better off in a hotel," he said. "I must work in peace and quiet—mostly peace," he said, narrowing his eyes at Batilda, "if I'm to duplicate my work in time." He glanced at his watch calendar. "Thursday," he muttered. "Tomorrow is Friday, the solstice is Sunday. That gives us three full days to work."

"Two!" Batilda corrected. "We need to spend at least a day prepping Alex."

"Prepping?" Alex asked. "You make it sound as though I'm some sort of entrée to be offered up to this...Lilah...this..."

"Sorceress," Benjamin supplied. "Lilah is a sorceress, with powers matching, if not surpassing, our own."

"Praise the power! The power of magic," Mary mused. She held her hands up and closed her blue bug-eyes, working herself into a trancelike state.

Benjamin looked at Southworth sideways. "Not *her* power. Please...let us *never* bow to *her* God...."

Alex twisted her mouth nervously. Benjamin still hadn't explained what *prepping* meant. But just as she thought to ask him again, Boogawoog's gruff voice startled them all.

"YOU DIRTY RAT...YOU FILTHY MOUSE...BOOGIE KILL YOU."

Alex looked at Batilda and Batilda leaned over, peering under the table. "Awh...she's just dreaming," Batilda said in a harsh whisper.

Alex followed suit and took a peek at the dreaming Scottie. She was sprawled out between Alex and Batilda. Her paws twitched as though she were running, her hind feet moving like a locomotive, and strange little tongue-clucking sounds issued from her throat.

"BOOGIE KILL YOU...KILL, KILL, *KILL* YOU...."

Batilda sucked her teeth like a proud parent. "Will you look at that? There she goes again, killing things in her sleep... ain't she just the sweetest little thing?"

"Real sweet," Alex said with a roll of her eyes, wanting, but deciding it best not to disagree, or insult the harpy.

"As I was saying," Benjamin went on, "take tomorrow to rest, Alex. On Saturday morning Batilda will meet with you—"

"I'll pick you up at ten," the harpy butted in.

"And I'll see you in the early afternoon," he finished. "We'll explain everything then."

"So now what, Birdwhistle? You're gonna go off to some hotel and not take me with you?"

Alex took a deep breath, feeling guilty for not insisting that they stay. "Look," she said, "if you really need a place..."

"Oh, no," Mrs. Southworth chimed. "I wouldn't hear of it— they can stay with me!"

God bless Mrs. Southworth, Alex thought with relief. Finally, the psychic was coming through with something *real.*

"We couldn't possibly consider such an imposition," Benjamin started to say.

"It's no imposition at all, Professor." She pursed her lips and batted her eyes. "Why, it's just me in that big old lonesome house."

"What about your husband?" Benjamin asked.

"Arthur? Oh, Arthur's passed on...nearly seven years now."

"Good. Arthur's dead," Batilda said impatiently. "So it's settled. Pack up your crap, Birdwhistle, we're going to Mary's."

This time it was Alex, not Mary, who squirmed anxiously in her chair. "Orielle can stay with me if she wants to," Alex said, making the offer, but trying to feign indifference.

"All right," Batilda said, directing everyone. "Alex wants Orielle to stay, so—"

"I didn't say I *wanted* her to stay," Alex argued, "I said she *could* stay if she *wanted* to."

"I accept Alex's invitation," Orielle said. "Alex and I have plans for tomorrow night...we're going to dance," she happily announced, "and Alex has promised to play her fiddle for me."

Batilda elbowed Alex in the ribs teasingly, but Alex just pulled away and ignored her.

"You can let Boogawoog sleep here with us, too," Alex said.

But the Scottie was awake now and stretching like a seesaw; forward, backward, then forward again with a yawn.

Batilda looked at Alex as if to say *watch this*, then looked down at Boogawoog. "You wanna stay here with Alex?"

"NO...."

Batilda grinned. "Don't take it personally, Kiddo."

"I won't," Alex said. "It's nice that she's so loyal."

"Well, what do you expect? We've been together a hundred years."

The thought, the possibility, boggled Alex's mind. She couldn't fathom spending one *week* with the same woman, let alone a hundred years with the same *dog*.

❬ ❬ ❬

Within the hour the four of them, Boogawoog included, were set to go. Benjamin's Mercedes was packed, and he and Batilda would follow Mary's car. But just as they said their goodbyes, Boogawoog pawed at Alex's jeans, then crept into the living room to have one last peek at the beach towel full of crumbs and bone bits. Then she looked back, pinned her ears submissively, and seemed to shyly smile.

"What?" Alex questioned, trying to figure out what it was Boogawoog didn't know how to say.

Batilda nodded at the dog and winked at Alex. "She's thanking you. It's just like me, isn't it, not to teach my dog how to say thank you? So I guess I should say it for us both."

Batilda stared at Alex, nodding appraisingly. "Thanks, Kiddo," she said, heading for the door, then stopped and looked up at Alex's coatrack. "Mind if I borrow this?" she asked, lifting Alex's black cowboy hat from a hook.

Before Alex could refuse her, Batilda had the hat on her head, her shaggy white-and-gray-streaked hair hanging down along the rim.

"I guess..." Alex shrugged.

"Do look after yourselves," Benjamin broke in, as he stepped out the door, his cat wrapped around and clinging to his neck again. "I don't suspect you'll be in any danger tomorrow evening, but," he said, regarding both Alex and Orielle, "better safe than sorry. Please make certain you're home by midnight."

❧ 18 ☙
Rat Fink and the Family Tree

All night long Alex had talked and whimpered in her sleep. Even from the bedroom Orielle could hear Alex stirring on the sofa, but she hadn't dared to wake her. Alex needed the rest...she needed the dreams.... So when the first hint of the melon-colored sun appeared, and the sound of stirring birds replaced the bellowing of night frogs, Orielle crept quietly about the house, and went outdoors to luxuriate in the soft mood of morning.

And now she was back, settling beside Alex on the edge of the sofa and gently stroking her sleeping pathfinder's head.

Wearing only a white T-shirt and underwear, Alex had tossed and turned herself out from under her sheet, so that both it and the cotton blanket were twisted about her waist, her bare and already tanning legs hanging over the edge of the sofa.

Orielle gazed adoringly at Alex's face. She loved her. She'd known that yesterday morning when Alex had first come into the bedroom. And she was sure Alex would come to love her, too...in her own time. It was hard to explain how fairies knew these things—how they knew, upon that first meeting, the one with whom they were to share a predestined love. For humans, courtships seemed such complicated matters; dating, deliberating, and still, quite often, making the wrong choice. Perhaps humans had never quite learned to trust their instincts; or perhaps it was that their instincts were simply poor.

Orielle brushed aside Alex's shiny curls and smoothed her fingers across the sleeping woman's forehead, tracing her eyebrows ever so lightly. They were wise brows, seeming to guard an as-yet undiscovered spirit. And from some deep sorrow within, night-time tears had dampened her long, black eyelashes.

Alex whimpered, turned her head back and forth. Her nose twitched and suddenly her hand came up as though swatting a fly from her face, but then she opened her eyes and jolted.

"Easy," Orielle said as Alex attempted to pull herself up into a sitting position. "It's not good to jump out of bed so fast. You'll forget your dreams that way."

"Dreams..." Alex murmured, self-consciously tugging at the blanket and covering her loins. She looked at Orielle, then took a deep breath, relaxing her muscles and settling back again.

"You've been talking in your sleep," Orielle whispered.

"Nothing too interesting, I hope...."

Alex was losing her resistance. Even her sarcasm was half-hearted now; no more than a weak attempt to hide from Orielle...to hide from herself. "Tell me," Orielle said.

Alex stared up at the ceiling, puffing her cheeks, and lay there silently until her eyes welled up. "I don't know...I was with Boogawoog," she finally said. "You were gone and we were searching for you in some...some strange house."

"And...?" Orielle encouraged, "Did you find me?"

"I could hear you...hear you talking to people, familiar people, but the house was dark...except for one candle burning on the wall. So I took it—took it from the sconce—and started walking with the dog, only...only when I looked down, Booga-woog wasn't a dog anymore...she was a white rat, a pet I had when I was little." She glanced at Orielle, then looked back up at the ceiling. "And then I heard you call me, and when I opened the next door there you were...sitting with Benjamin and Batilda and...and my parents. My *parents*..." Alex whispered. "And they weren't even surprised to see me. I mean, they were happy and everything, but it was as if they'd never been away, as if they'd been part of my life all along."

"Spectral visitors," Orielle mused.

Alex sniffled. "What?"

"Your parents...your pet...they came to visit you in the night...."

Alex's eyes welled up. "Don't say things like that...it was a dream...that's all. Just a stupid dream."

With the back of her fingers Orielle stroked Alex's cheek. "Dreams are never stupid...especially when visitors bring you messages...."

"What do you mean? Messages from where?"

"The other side...the life beyond this life."

"When did I tell you my parents were dead?"

"At the cottage. But you didn't have to, Alex. I have sensed your loss is very great...and very old." She held a hand a few inches over Alex's chest and moved it in circles. "Something broke your spirit...I can feel it...a wound that has never quite healed, and which has left a gap that divides your soul...."

"A gap? Wonderful," Alex moaned. "Remind me to pick up a bucket of cement filler at the hardware store—that'll do the trick."

Orielle smiled. "Drink," she said, handing Alex a cup from the coffee table.

"What is it?"

"Coffee."

Alex paused for a moment, then propped herself up on an elbow. "You made coffee?"

"My first pot ever."

Eyeing Orielle sideways, Alex took the cup and brought it hesitantly to her lips, sipping and involuntarily cringing as she swallowed.

"It's too strong," Orielle said disappointedly.

"A little. It's good, though...really," Alex managed politely, swallowing again as if to swallow away the aftertaste. She settled back again. "Will you please let me get up now?"

"The dream, Alex...finish the dream."

"Why don't you go outside and pick flowers or something," Alex whined.

"I already did. I brought a bouquet of white lilacs back for the kitchen," she said, playing with one of Alex's curls that caught a shaft of morning sunlight coming through the open shutters. "You were standing in the doorway...saw your parents...and?"

Alex draped a forearm across her face again. "I wanted to run over to them, you know? To bend down to Fink—my rat," she said, peeking out from under her forearm. "I wanted to pick him up and walk over to my parents, but...but I couldn't find anything to set the candle in. It was starting to drip all over me...all over the floor, but I couldn't blow it out because it was the only light in the room. So I...I..." She paused, puffing her cheeks again. "I started to look around the room—for a candle holder—and all of you kept saying, 'Join us, Alex...come sit with us...' and I kept saying, 'Wait, let me find a holder for this'—meaning the candle, you know?"

"This candle is good, Alex...the dream is a good sign. It means things are coming together...*melting* together."

Alex sighed. "And then...then you reached out and offered to hold it for me...." she said, heaving a still deeper sigh.

Orielle couldn't let her get up now...not now. Alex was regressing, still caught in those before-and-after moments of sleep, when the watchmen—keepers of the psyche—drop their guard and leave it to commune with itself.

Once Alex was fully awake, so would her defenses be. And they were strong, too strong to be penetrated in Alex's typically guarded state. But now, in the early hours, they were still weak. And Orielle needed to break through them, for then and only then could she help Alex to rebuild those defenses. And if she could, if she could help Alex integrate her broken pieces, maybe she would emerge whole enough—conscious enough—to win the battle for Orielle when the moon grew full.

"And you handed me your candle...?" Orielle prompted.

Alex nodded from under her forearm. "And then I scooped up Fink in my hands and sat between my parents and just...just started crying, apologizing for causing them all to die."

"By what fault of your own...?"

"That's what my Aunt Sophie told me—my father's sister. I hated her...hated her *so much*. She never liked my mother—hated me. And hated the fact that I brought Fink to live with me in her house after my parents died. She knew the rat was in the car with us when we crashed...and she used to tell me that my playing with Fink in the car had distracted my father...that he didn't see the other car coming because he was looking in the rearview mirror, paying attention to Fink and me...." Alex stopped, sniffling, then tried to continue, her voice growing shaky. "A few months after the accident—when she was given legal custody of me—she killed Fink. Beat him to death right in front of me. I was only five, you know...only five...."

Orielle couldn't see Alex's eyes, only a few stray tears finding their freedom and running down the side of her face.

"Oh, Christ," Alex said, forced to expose her face in order to angrily wipe away her tears. "I'm sorry—this is so stupid," she complained. "So *stupid*.... I never cry and here I am...crying over things that happened twenty-five years ago...crying over a goddam *rat...*!"

Orielle stroked her, absorbing the negative energy, sending Alex's spirit a positive one. "Love is not stupid, Alex. And why should it matter what form it chooses? Whether love comes to us on two legs, four legs or on wings...it is a gift...love is always a gift."

"Fink *was* a gift...an Easter present from my aunt."

Orielle looked at her, not quite understanding. "She gave you a pet and then killed it...?"

"No...it was a gift from my other aunt—my great aunt, really...Aunt Tilly." Alex laughed, despite her tears. "Can you believe somebody *actually* had an Aunt *Tilly*?"

Orielle smiled sweetly.

"I only met her once, though...when I was three," Alex said, wiping both her eyes then her nose with the back of her hand.

Orielle thought to retrieve a box of tissues from the bathroom, but she knew Alex wouldn't wait for her on the sofa. She'd be up and about when Orielle returned, defensively playing down the emotional interaction and employing the sarcastic humor that was, Orielle was learning, an illusory armor. Orielle simply wouldn't give her an opportunity to put it on.

"I don't remember much, except seeing this little blue ball of fur curled fast asleep in a pink and yellow Easter basket." Alex seemed to forget her tears for a moment, caught now by a wondrous moment in her childhood.

"Blue?" Orielle asked, perplexed.

Alex nodded, managing a faint smile. "Blue," she said. "He was *dyed* blue for Easter—you know, just like they used to dye chicks and bunnies...only...only she told me he was blue because he had fallen asleep in a blueberry patch."

Orielle smiled at the thought.

He was as smart as a cat or dog...my parents taught him all sorts of tricks. And then a couple of years later, after the accident, we went to live with my aunt."

"He was all I had," Alex went on. All I had left of my parents, my life. Just Fink...Fink and my fiddle." Alex paused, collected now, and ran a hand through her black hair. "And Aunt Sophie couldn't stand either of them. She hated the rat and hated the sound of me practicing the violin. So she got rid of them both in one night."

"How?"

"She smashed the violin to bits...smashed it in the process of beating Fink to death. I used to take him out of the cage...you know, to play with him before I went to sleep. And one night, I guess I just fell asleep...forgot to put him in his cage...and he wandered into the kitchen."

Orielle searched Alex's dark and glassy eyes, eyes so rich with opposing emotions, and watched Alex's jaw muscle stiffen.

"The next thing I knew there was this big commotion—Aunt Sophie yelling, chairs moving, violin strings popping and...and, um...." Alex stopped to bite her bottom lip. "...And then Fink squealing. I ran in, screaming for her to stop, but she kept on...beating, bashing him...and he kept squealing and screaming and squealing and..." Alex put her hands to her head as though still hearing the animal's death cry. "...I wanted to stop her. I was so little, though, and she seemed larger than life. So I just stood there holding my ears, watching the blood gush from his nose, crying until I hyperventilated....

"And then you know what that sick bastard did?" Alex said. "Marched me right outside in my pajamas and bare feet—wouldn't even let me bury him—and made me throw him in the trash can. I'll never forget," Alex said, her voice quavering again, "...how cold the cement was against my feet, how warm his broken body was in my hands. And then she made me go back to bed—like nothing had happened."

"How very sorry I am for that child," Orielle whispered. Then, "Alex," she said, cupping the side of Alex's turned and hidden face. "It is time for you to mourn."

"Mourn? What do you think I've been doing the past twenty-five years?"

"For your parents, for your beloved pet, for the life you lost...but not for that little girl. You've never let yourself cry for that little girl who once was you."

Alex rolled her head again, hiding her face from Orielle, and lay there silently for a long while, Orielle's hand touching her...always touching her...until Alex's body began to yield and she heaved a bit.

"Grieve, Alex, cry for the past that is present with you."

And with that, Alex began to sob, her face shamefully covered from Orielle's view.

"Sweet woman," Orielle whispered, "I can almost touch your pain. And I am happy for that...so happy to be here with you."

"I'd be happy too," Alex mumbled, "if you'd let me get up."

But Orielle would not. She kept her hands on Alex, taking the pain that released itself. She felt the flesh of Alex's arm...the warmth of her thigh, her body...and knew the *rightness* of this bond. She smiled down upon Alex, wanting to give herself; wanting to lay her body along the length of Alex's own.

But Alex did not need her that way. Now, right now, Alex needed a mother. Maybe tonight she would need a lover.

☾ ☾ ☾

Orielle was working in the kitchen by the time Alex was showered and dressed. A mixture of fragrances wafted through the room and Alex's kitchen table had been transformed into a florist's delight. Lilacs and lilies and wild flowers lay scattered on the table, and what looked like syrup filled the bottom of Alex's mortar.

"I need to run into town," she said to Orielle as she tucked a sleeveless shirt into her shorts.

"Go," Orielle answered. "I'll be here...working."

Alex nodded, peering into the mortar. "What is it?"

"Poppy tar," she said sheepishly. "Batilda made it from your poppy heads, and asked me finish some of her work. It's a good incense base."

Alex looked at her, frowning, but then her countenance changed to a more soft and serious one. "Thanks, by the way...."

"For...?" Orielle asked, almost cheerfully.

"You know," Alex said, awkwardly averting her eyes. "For before...."

Orielle only smiled.

Alex had an urge to close the distance and hug her, thank her somehow, but simply nodded instead. "You won't tell anyone...right?"

"About...?"

Alex shrugged. "You know—about before. I've never told anyone about my rat and all that."

"Then I am honored by your trust...and you can trust me never to tell."

Alex just stared at her, nodding a second time, then watched as Orielle moved about the sun-filled kitchen. She needed to buy Orielle a cowboy hat; a new one for herself, too, Alex decided. She didn't have high hopes of Batilda ever returning her black one. "Can I get you anything while I'm out?"

"No...but maybe something before you go...?"

"Anything," Alex said.

"Wisteria? I need the oil...but I can't get near the flowers."

"The bees are busy?"

"Yes...I saw your white bee boxes out there."

"The bees aren't mine—I just have connections with their *keeper*." Alex smiled. "I borrow the bee boxes every year when the wisteria blooms, then bring them back and have a jar of honey made. It's hard to buy wisteria honey this far north," she added.

"Come to the porch," she added. "I'll pick you as much wisteria as you want—as long as you'll pull the stingers out of me."

"I thought I just finished pulling one out."

"You did," Alex said, sighing in understanding. "I guess you did..."

Orielle gave a knowing smile.

Alex grinned back, impulsively giving Orielle's body the once-over and imagining what she'd look like in a hat, tailored shirt, and the jeans she'd purchased at the Emporium. "So six o'clock? You told Ana Mae we'd be there by six?"

Orielle looked puzzled. "I thought you wanted to stay here."

"I thought you wanted to go there."

"But you said you'd rather dance with me *here*."

"But you *really* want to go *there*."

"Only because Ana Mae invited—"

"So it's settled, then. We'll go. Okay? We'll go.... The least I can do is take you out dancing."

"You will have to lead me, though...."

Alex considered the idea. "It's a date," she said, then motioned for Orielle to follow and headed out to fight the bees.

⋖ 19 ⋗
Two-Stepping

"**DO** I look like a cowgirl...or a fairy?" Orielle asked, coming up behind Alex in the mirror.

Alex regarded Orielle's image as she adjusted her own new black hat, then turned and looked Orielle up and down with an assessing smirk. "Fairy...but I've got the perfect disguise," she said, ducking out of the hallway and reappearing with a hat.

Orielle took it appreciatively. "You bought this for me?"

"I never saw it before," Alex teased. "It was waiting for you on the porch when I came home."

"Do you suppose I have a secret admirer?"

"You never know..." Alex took the hat from Orielle's hands. She placed it strategically on the fairy's head, then stepped back to eye Orielle appraisingly. In western boots, jeans and a green silk shirt, Orielle was striking. The stone-colored hat complemented her auburn hair the way Alex had imagined it would when she'd first spotted it in the store. She came up close again, giving the hat a final tilt, then looked down at Orielle's feet. "How do they feel?" Alex asked.

Orielle looked down at the light brown boots she'd selected from Alex's closet. "Fine," she said.

"You sure?" Bending down, Alex squeezed the boots. "They're not too big?"

"They fit...as perfectly as we do," she coyly remarked.

Alex straightened up, briefly locking eyes with Orielle, but didn't say a word.

☾ ☾ ☾

Dinner at Raspberries went more smoothly than Alex had expected. Ana Mae made a point of exuding her Southern charm in Orielle's presence, but with Alex she remained aloof. Alex didn't mind, though; she much preferred being ignored to being inter- rogated. Only once did Ana Mae voice her suspicions. "Are you all right? Is something going on in your house?" she had asked when they'd first arrived. But upon Alex's reassurance, Ana Mae dropped the subject completely, never once addressing the matter of how or *why* the two women were spending so much time to- gether. In fact, Ana Mae seemed oddly content in the knowledge that they *were* together.

Equally impressed by one another, Orielle and Ana Mae couldn't have gotten along better. Throughout dinner and even now, over dessert, they talked away, exchanging tips on growing, harvesting and preserving every fruit, herb or vegetable that grew from the earth. Alex could have joined in the conversation—she knew enough to hold her own—but she wasn't much in the mood for garden chitchat. She sat there watching Orielle eat fried ice cream dipped in hot raspberry sauce, and absently picked at her own, stirring the melting ice cream with a fork.

The band members, Annie and the Oakleys, were assem- bling themselves in the bar room now, and Alex's dark eyes moved back and forth between them and the fairy.

"I'm so sorry Laurie isn't here to meet you," Alex heard Ana Mae say to Orielle. "She'd just love to show you the rasp- berry fields out back."

"Laurie...?" Orielle asked.

"Her lover," Alex offered.

"She's a regional sales manager—had to fly to Boston for a few days. She'll be back Sunday night, though," Ana Mae said, glancing at Alex, but addressing only Orielle. "If you'll still be in town Monday, maybe the four of us could have dinner...?"

Alex shot her eyes at Orielle, and Orielle, put on the spot, simply shrugged at Ana Mae. Hesitantly, she replied, "I could let you know over the weekend...my plans are rather tenuous right now..."

That's right, Alex wanted to say, *tenuous. It all depends, Ana Mae, on whether I succeed in slaying the sorceress on the solstice. If I don't...well...Orielle will have to go back into her bell...in which case dinner on Monday is out of the question.*

"HOW YA'LL DOIN' TONIGHT?" shouted Pokey, the lead singer.

Through the large archway Alex could see the woman. She'd slept with her—how long ago? Alex couldn't remember. She'd slept with the drummer, too. And the harmonica player, come to think of it.

"ANY SHARP SHOOTERS HERE TONIGHT?" Pokey yelled to the crowd.

All the women at the bar clapped.

"NO *STRAIGHT* SHOOTERS, I HOPE!" This got the crowd to whistling and clapping even more.

"WELL, THEN...IF YOUR HEART AIN'T BUSY TO-NIGHT," Pokey went on, "GRAB YOURSELF A GAL AND LET'S DANCE TO SOME TANYA TUCKER!"

"I better get up there," Ana Mae said. She winked at Orielle and looked over at Alex. "You better ask this lady to dance before someone else does." She rose then, gesturing for one of their waitresses. "We need a round of drinks here, hon—another raspberry margarita for Orielle and a..." She stopped. "What are you drinking, Alex?"

"Bourbon and ginger," Alex said, without looking up.

"A blackjack with a ginger back for Alex," Ana Mae called.

Alex shot her eyes at Orielle when Ana Mae left the table. "Have you ever drunk tequila before?"

"No.... Wine, once," Orielle casually answered.

Alex frowned, not at all eager to find out what a drunken fairy might be capable of doing. Orielle had never danced, never in a women's club...she'd never even slept with anyone. And there were plenty of women, Alex knew, who'd flip a coin to be part of that first experience. Alex rubbed her ears, thinking that if anyone tried to take advantage of the tipsy fairy she'd have to throw a punch. "Want to learn a two-step?" she offered.

And when Orielle nodded, Alex smiled and took her by the hand. She stopped to greet the Oakleys, introducing Orielle as a matter of courtesy. Ginger was on lead guitar, and Mary Ellen on bass. Kathy, who was on keyboards, was talking with Ana Mae and the others.

Orielle was full of social grace. She seemed thoroughly relaxed, comfortable, talkative. Almost intuitively, she seemed able to zero in on people's attributes in such a way that the women experienced her compliments as revelations.

"Ready for that dance?" Alex asked, thinking it might be best to help Orielle work off her margarita before the tequila reached concentrated levels. She led Orielle on to the floor and took hold of her.

"Now...just follow me," Alex said, squaring her shoulders and pulling Orielle close as the music started.

"Put your left hand in mine, okay? Like this," she instructed. "Now reach around and hang your right thumb in my loop."

Orielle smiled cheerfully. "Your *loop*?"

"My *belt* loop—right above my back pocket."

Orielle giggled, as though Alex were playing some sort of trick. "And where does *your* thumb go?"

Alex grinned. "In *your* loop...see? Like this," she demonstrated. "Now, when I step forward with my left foot...you're going to step back with your right...and you're going to keep moving back in steps of two, like this: one...two...one, two. One...two... one, two. Got it?"

"Got it," Orielle mimicked her.

"Ready to try?"

"Ready, Alex."

"Set?"

"Go," Orielle said smiling ear to ear.

Easily following Alex's lead, Orielle proved exceptionally light on her feet. And she insisted on dancing to four or five songs before finally agreeing to return to her margarita.

"I liked the song before last," she said when they were back at their table alone. "What was it called?"

"I've Got Tears in My Ears From Lying on My Back in My Bed Crying Over You."

"No..." Orielle said, propping her elbows on the table and pursing her lips. "You're teasing me, Alex...."

Alex widened her eyes and she laughed. "I swear I'm not. Ask Ana Mae if you don't believe me—hey, Ana Mae!" she called. "What was the name of that Hank Williams song?"

Flinging her mound of blonde hair, Ana Mae did a dance-walk over to them. "I've Got Tears In My Ears." She peered at Alex. "And don't I *know* it, honey."

"See!" Alex said, turning back to Orielle with a grin. "See? I wouldn't lie to you."

Orielle looked deep into Alex's sable eyes, her chagrin instantly dissolving. "No," she said, "you'd sooner lie to yourself, wouldn't you...?"

Alex narrowed her eyes. "You think you've got me all figured out, don't you?"

Orielle countered Alex's stare but didn't answer, and Alex had a feeling she wouldn't have answered, even if Ana Mae hadn't come to the table to spoil Alex's fun.

"The gals want you out there," Ana Mae said. "I brought your fiddle up."

Alex grimaced. "Ana Mae, not tonight...please? I'm really not up for—"

"Oh, Alex...please *do* play," Orielle pleaded, coaxing Alex, with gray eyes that sparkled with anticipation. "...For me...."

Ana Mae nudged Alex. "Go on," she coaxed. Then to Orielle, said, "How about a dance?"

Alex headed for the band, watching as Orielle walked off arm in arm with Ana Mae. She opened her case, put on a shoulder rest, then tightened her bow and tuned her violin.

"Something fast?" Pokey asked.

"Yearwood?" Alex suggested. "Something new?—'If I Ain't Got You'?"

Pokey conferred with the Oakleys then nodded to Alex. "So how are ya?"

"Good," Alex said.

Pokey leaned into her. "My cat's been asking for you."

"Oh, yeah?" Alex chuckled. "I'll have to grow some catnip and send it to her."

"Why don't ya hand deliver it....?"

Alex chuckled again. "I'll think about it...while the catnip's growing."

"You do that." Pokey winked at her. "ONE-TWO-THREE-FOUR..." she shouted to the band. And on the count of four they began to play.

It felt good to fiddle—Alex hadn't played in the past few days—and it amused her to watch Ana Mae teaching Orielle how to dance. Orielle wasn't paying complete attention, though. It was proving difficult to keep her eyes on Alex and Ana Mae's feet at the same time. Soon the two were laughing more than they were dancing, and Alex turned away, walking across to fiddle in front of the woman on bass. But when the song was over and she turned back, Orielle and Ana Mae were gone.

Suddenly edgy, worried really, that Ana Mae—sly as she was—might take this private opportunity to question Orielle, Alex put her fiddle down and quickly excused herself. She snaked her way through the crowd, smiling back at the familiar and strange faces smiling at her, and found Orielle and Ana Mae waiting back at the table.

To Alex's relief, the two weren't talking much at all. Ana Mae's forearm, with her denim sleeve rolled up above the elbow, was resting on the table, and Orielle appeared to be doing something—massaging, palpating it.

"This is incredible," Ana Mae commented, as Alex slid into her seat. "I was just telling Orielle about my carpal-tunnel syndrome—it's been bothering me."

"Close your hand...now open it," Orielle instructed.

"It feels like acupuncture," Ana Mae commented. "I'm getting the strangest feeling...a tingling sensation," she said to Alex, "like...oh, what's that thing...*ultrasound*, they use in my doctor's office."

Alex tensed at the mention of sound; Orielle was playing with those waves again...healing Ana Mae, she supposed, and she glared at the fairy. "It's ten o'clock," she said to Orielle, her words even, deliberate. "Didn't you say you had to be somewhere?"

"Yes...yes I do," she went along, picking up on Alex's cue.

"Well, how about that!" Ana Mae declared, flexing her hand and rotating her wrist, too preoccupied with her own spontaneous recovery to notice the exchange between Alex and Orielle. But then Ana Mae looked at Orielle, her face reflecting fascination mixed with gratitude. "What did you say you were?"

"Dance with me!" Alex blurted, jumping up and grabbing Orielle's hand. "Please? This is my favorite song," she begged.

"Excuse us," Orielle said, shrugging, smiling politely at Ana Mae. Then, "Alex...!" she said when they were far enough away. "How rude."

"Rude? How could you do that?" Alex scolded. "You can't just go around healing people—especially not Ana Mae. She's on to you—she knows now."

"What does she know, Alex?"

"That you're a fairy."

"She didn't say that—"

"You heard her—she asked what you are!"

"I'm sure she was referring to my occupation. Now please, Alex, relax and tell me where to put my feet...or should I just stand on top of yours and let you lead?"

"We're waltzing," Alex said, moving with Orielle. "One big step, two little steps. ONE-two-three, ONE-two-three. And don't do that anymore. Please!"

Orielle looked at Alex in wry amusement. "Do what?"

"Heal people, play with those sound waves—whatever it is you do. I'm going to have to answer to Ana Mae. I know her— she'll be telling everyone here for years to come about how this woman Alex knew came in one night and cured her, just like that."

"Oh, dear...such an awful predicament I've put you in."

Alex sensed Orielle was humoring her, and so she didn't say any more.

"So what is this favorite song of yours, Alex?"

"Trisha Yearwood...'Thinking About You,'" Alex grumbled.

"And exactly what *do* you think about me...?"

Alex smiled in resignation as Orielle slipped her hand inside Alex's back pocket.

"I *think* you're getting drunk...and I *think* we should go. Benjamin warned us to be in by midnight...remember?"

"It can't be midnight."

"It's ten."

"If we leave now," Orielle negotiated, "will you promise to swing with me on the porch?"

Alex stared curiously at her. "You'll only swing yourself to sleep—and I'll have to carry you to bed."

"Just like you carried me the first night..." Orielle murmured.

The first night.... Alex thought. Only two days and two nights ago...but suddenly it seemed so long ago. Alex couldn't remember the last time she'd spent forty-eight consecutive hours with the same woman.

And later, when Ana Mae passed by, making a comment in Alex's ear about how Alex hadn't given any other women a second glance tonight, it made Alex start to worry about herself. Here she was, her interest in new women, in indiscriminate sex gone. She was going home with Orielle, with a fairy, and the worst part was that she was looking forward to it!

⤙ 20 ⤚
Laws of the Heart

A peach moon loomed in the black sky like a primeval timepiece. It was nearly full, unusually large tonight, and Alex could only imagine that the steady squeaking of the porch swing wasn't the swing at all, but the taunting ticking of the lunar clock.

"If you put your arm around me we'll have more room," Orielle said innocently.

Alex gave the fairy beside her a sidelong glance. It was a tight squeeze; tight enough, at least, so that their shoulders were pressed together, and the heat emanating from Orielle made the rest of Alex's body feel chilled. Hesitating, she nervously obliged Orielle, sliding her arm along the back of the swing so that the fairy's head came to rest against her chest and shoulder.

"I could sit here like this every evening," Orielle mused. "Out in the night...free...with my beloved," she murmured.

"Well, first we have to free you—*then* you can go off to find a beloved." Alex looked down at the top of Orielle's head and smirked. "And since you can dance a two-step and look so damn good in country-western clothes, maybe you should head out to Texas or Tennessee." Alex paused. "You said you were raised by your father...where was that?"

"Saratoga."

"Sara—" Alex's face startled with surprise. "Sara*toga*?" It seemed so American, so ordinary, so right-around-the-corner.

"Yes," Orielle said. "It was by a waterfall on my father's estate that my mother first appeared to him one spring equinox. He was a lawyer by profession...a poet by passion, and used to spend his leisure time writing in the gardens."

With one finger Orielle made imaginary designs on Alex's thigh as she spoke, and Alex wondered whether Orielle had any idea how that touch was affecting her.

"It was there, by the waterfall," the fairy continued, "that they met and fell in love...there that they *consummated* that love. But my mother was bound to a world beyond the mists. Only while she carried his human child could she stay with him in this world. And she did...until their child was born."

"You...." Alex whispered.

"Mmm. But upon my birth she had no choice but to return to her own kind, and left my father to raise me. And he raised me well...gave me more than I could ever ask for. But as I grew, I developed my mother's healing powers. I bore such a striking resemblance to her that sometimes...when my father looked at me...his eyes would well with joy. But in that joy was a deeper sorrow, a longing for the woman with whom he could not be."

Alex was silent for a moment. "He never married or—?"

"Oh, no...there were always ladies, of course—ladies who, upon learning his young wife had died in childbirth (that is what he told everyone), were more than willing to fill the void. But it was my mother who filled his heart."

"What became of her—you never saw her again?"

"Every solstice and every equinox. It's strange, Alex," she said, looking up from where her head lay on Alex's shoulder, "but for all my father's fortune, for all his accomplishments, he seemed only to live for those four precious nights. Sometimes it was as if the other days of the year were but time to be bided until again he might see her.... I remember the hours he spent," Orielle mused, "writing in the moonlit gardens. And when my mother visited he would gift her with those writings, and she would hold them tightly to her breast...for they were the only part of him she could keep.

"I remember, too, the times she led us to the pool in the cave to watch the fairies dance. And when we returned, my mother would come inside and sing me to sleep. In the morning she was always gone. And for weeks afterwards, my father was left somehow changed; seeing but not really seeing, hearing without listening...smiling without feeling."

Alex drew in a breath and sat quietly. Before this moment, the fact of the fairy having a geographical history, a biological family, had never occurred to her. And as Orielle snuggled closer to ward off the night's damp chill, Alex found herself responding in kind; holding the fairy tightly to her, as though offering sympathy or understanding.

"And you, Alex? Where were you raised?"

"Here in Halfmoon," she said, "until the accident. Then I was taken to the city." Alex regarded the peach moon. "When I turned eighteen I came back...back to find...." Alex stopped herself and shrugged, thinking that her life didn't deserve attention right now. Orielle had endured more losses than she had, it seemed...the loss of her mother, of her father...of her very life. "I don't know," Alex finished. "I'm not sure what I thought I'd find."

"All that you once lost...."

"I suppose." Alex shrugged. "But I didn't...so I learned to find other things."

"Lovers?"

"Sometimes...." Orielle glanced up at her and she frowned. "A lot of the time," Alex confessed.

The barn owl was back, hooting in one of the maple trees, courting another whose distant voice issued from the fog. Alex and Orielle sat silently for a while, listening to the owls, the creaking swing, and breathing in the fragrant breath of the wisteria blooming around the porch.

"And which one do you love the most?" Orielle inquired.

Alex regarded the fairy as though she were speaking a foreign language. "Huh?"

"Of all the women you love...which one do you love the most?"

Alex couldn't help being amused by Orielle's frankness. And it was precisely that—her innocence, her disarming guilelessness—that drew Alex to her. "If I loved any *one* of them, I wouldn't love the rest, now *would* I?"

Orielle appeared baffled by Alex's line of reasoning. "How is it that you make love without loving?"

"I love oxymorons."

"How profane."

Alex stopped swinging. "Oxymorons?"

"No, that you should come to possess carnal knowledge of so many women."

"Carnal knowledge? Geez, you make sex sound so... religious."

"It is a sacrament, Alex."

"Sex? You mean all this time I've been running around committing sacred acts on Saturday nights?"

Orielle played idly with the silver button covers on Alex's white shirt. "If we had met tonight...would you have made love to me?"

"No," Alex said flatly, without even stopping to consider the possibility.

"You wouldn't have taken me home with you?"

"You're here, aren't you?"

"I mean if we had been strangers, Alex...would you have taken me home?"

Alex only shook her head. "No..."

Orielle pushed herself up, turning a little in her seat to challenge Alex's deep and murky eyes. "You don't find me attractive?"

"Sure you're attractive."

"But to *you*, Alex...am I attractive to *you*?"

Orielle's gray eyes were washed with moonlight, and staring into them made Alex nervous. "What...what do you want me to say?" she stammered.

"Say what you feel."

"Yes—okay? Yes..." she confessed, "I *do* think you're

attractive."

"But you would not make love with me?"

"No, I—I couldn't. Not that."

"Should I take this as a compliment...?" Orielle murmured, contentedly snuggling up to Alex again.

"Yes—I mean, no—I don't know!" Alex said, stumbling over her words. She was acutely aware of the fairy; of Orielle's fingers on her buttons, her head on Alex's shoulder, the thigh of the fairy's crossed leg pressed up against her knee. And her arousal suddenly caused her to panic. "I can't think about sex right now—I've got *imps* on my mind!" Alex nearly snapped. It's almost midnight...you know what Benjamin said about—"

"Shh...." Orielle reached up, bringing a soft finger to Alex's lips. "Listen to the night songs, Alex...there is no danger yet."

Orielle was right; the owls, the frogs, the insects would all fall silent at the slightest hint of an intruder. She thought of all the times she'd tried to sneak past a chirping cricket on her porch, without it ceasing to sing.... But now there was a new noise.

Alex turned her head, listening to a rustling in the poppy field, a stirring in the brush beyond the barn. They were familiar sounds, though; sounds that joined the other noises...became part of the pattern. "It's just Susie and Stewart," she said, leaning forward and grabbing the handle of the lantern on the Adirondack table. Alex held the light just above her head. "Yep," she said, "my garden bandits."

"Raccoons?" Orielle asked, getting up from the swing and peering over the porch railing to watch the animals pushing through the poppy field. Their eyes glowed in the light of the moon and the lantern.

"Stewart is a raccoon and Susie is 'possum."

"You've named them," Orielle said, a hint of amusement in her voice.

"Stewart came with a name. He was raised at a wildlife rehabilitation center outside of Albany. The director's a friend...I released him here as a favor to her."

"And Susie...?"

Alex grinned. "I named her that because she reminded me of a woman I dated, when I first spotted her by the barn one night."

"The woman or the 'possum?" Orielle asked.

"The 'possum. Anyway, Susie had these tiny eyes and a pointy kind of face," Alex said, putting her fingers to her face and drawing them forward to illustrate."

"The woman or the—"

"Both," Alex laughed.

"And which of the two do you have a date with this weekend?"

"Date?"

"Yes. When we were in Batilda's cottage you said you had a date for the weekend...remember?"

"Oh...that," Alex said, thinking she'd need to make a more concerted effort to remember her lies, although lying wasn't what she'd meant to do—an excuse was all she'd intended it to be. "No..." she said, feebly, "...not Susie." She cleared her throat.

Orielle pointed, tracing the movement of the animals with a finger. "They're coming."

"Throw them a donut," Alex said, gesturing toward the fruit basket with her chin. "There's a stale one in there."

But before Orielle could react, the raccoon waddled up the porch steps.

"Hey," Alex said to him.

But in another instant he was on the porch, curiously waddling over to the fairy. He sniffed her, inspected her, as though the fairy were different and he knew it.

Alex's body tensed, and she stood and reached for the broom, ready to sweep him right off the porch the moment he growled or snapped at Orielle. The animals knew Alex—knew her well enough to take food from her hand—but never had they invited themselves on the porch. "It's not like them to behave this way..." Alex commented, a bit uneasy with the situation. "Why don't you just step back...slowly," she said, calling the animals to distract them.

But Orielle paid her no mind. "If you're worried about rabies, you needn't be. They are healthy," she said. "I can tell." Orielle bent then, the donut in her hand.

Agile, animated, Susie joined Stewart, and they pranced over one another, then leaned back on their haunches and reached up with their little hands. Alex watched, not sure whether they were reaching for the donut or reaching to hug Orielle.

Lips parted in wonderment, Alex stood there watching. "They know you're not...they know what you are, don't they...?"

"Yes," Orielle whispered, smiling up at Alex and breaking the donut in two.

"Lucky me," Alex mumbled, "I get to sleep with St. Francis tonight."

"I was hoping you would agree."

"To what?"

"Sleeping with me."

"I didn't mean in my *bed*...I meant in my *house*."

"You need your bed, Alex...you're not sleeping well on the sofa."

"The sofa's fine...it's great."

"Then *I'll* sleep on it, Alex."

"No. It's not *that* great. I lied. It's lumpy, actually." Alex heaved a sigh. "I really should buy one of those goose-down comforters for the—"

"Alex...!"

"Huh?"

"We can both sleep comfortably in your bed...we'll fit just fine."

That was Alex's fear—that they'd fit just fine. Too fine. She let her eyes fall along the length of Orielle's body. "Why don't you go on ahead, then. I need some tea first...I um, I usually drink a cup before bed."

"What would you like?"

"Lipton."

"I think you're a bit overstimulated as it is...."

"Who's overstimulated?"

Orielle smiled. "I will make herbal tea from your garden...and have a cup with you."

"Tea from *my* garden?"

"I collected wonderful things while you were away today." She leaned back against the railing, a faint smile coming to her lips. Alex felt seduced, manipulated somehow, and although she tried to smile back, her own lips were too taut.

Orielle stepped toward Alex, her voice soft, her movements breezy. "Come...we'll have tea and then we'll sleep," she coaxed, amused, it seemed, by her hostess's apprehension.

Alex's eyes roamed the length of Orielle's petite white jeans as she contemplated the new sleeping arrangements.

"You needn't be afraid Alex...I promise not to let you touch me...."

☾ ☾ ☾

It felt good to be back in her own bed, except that now Alex didn't feel tired anymore. On her back, she stretched, folded her hands behind her head, and gazed up at the moonbeams on the ceiling. Then she sighed again, deeper this time.

"What is it, Alex?" Orielle whispered in the dark.

"Nothing...why?"

"You keep sighing...."

Alex shrugged, even though she knew Orielle couldn't see her "I...I just can't seem to get a deep enough breath," she said. Alex rolled her head on the pillow and looked at the shadowy figure beside her. "You're not an *incubus*...or *succubus*...or whatever those life-suckers are called, are you?"

"No...but it's nice to know I take your breath away."

"Not that way—I didn't mean it that way. I was just—" But before Alex could finish speaking, Orielle had slipped out of her half of the covers and was crawling on top of her.

"Hey!" Alex laughed, flinching and pressing her arms to her sides as Orielle's fingers found her ribs. "Quit tickling me," she said, warding off the fairy's advances.

"It's the least decadent way I can think of to take your breath away."

"Tickle me to death and you'll lose your freedom all over again—they'll lock you up."

"Such harsh punishment for what would seem like a misdemeanor?"

"*Miss DeMeanor's* the one they send in to carry out the punishment."

Orielle giggled, her fingers finding Alex's rib cage again.

"Cut it out!" Alex mockingly warned, groping and finally managing to restrain the fairy's wrists. "You better stop before I pin your wings to the headboard."

"I don't *have* wings, Alex."

"No, you don't...I've been wondering about that. You're *supposed* to have wings...and you're supposed to be tiny."

"How tiny would you have me be?"

"Tiny enough to keep in a jar with holes poked in the top."

"You're confusing me with a sprite, Alex. And a sprite wouldn't want to be kept in a jar—she'd wither away in captivity."

Suddenly Alex was aware of Orielle's weight pressing down on her pelvis, aware of her wrists in her hands. She desperately wanted to pull Orielle down to her. "And why haven't *you* withered in captivity? How is it that you've stayed so beautiful for so long...?" she asked, her voice trailing off.

Orielle bent forward, her hair as fine as corn silk, her lips soft as a feather. And the moment those lips fell upon hers, Alex was unable to resist. She kissed Orielle slowly, sweetly, her hands dropping to Orielle's hips, her head rising from the pillow to reach Orielle's mouth and deepen their kiss. Just one kiss, and she felt herself falling so hard. She stopped suddenly, her head dropping back to the pillow, her hands releasing the fairy and falling to the sheets. "Orielle..." she said hoarsely.

"I did not know kisses made magic...." Orielle said. "How is it that when you touched my lips you touched me in other places as well?"

Alex lay still, struggling with the magic of her own physiology. "I don't know," she finally said softly.

"Do kisses always do that to everyone?"

Alex shook her head on her pillow. "No," she said, her breathing heavy. "Not all the time...usually not...almost never," she concluded.

"You could win the heart of a maiden with such a kiss."

"Win you?" Alex teased, trying to ease the sexual tension.

"I've already won you. I own you. Isn't that what Benjamin said—that I own you?"

"Only by default..."

"Default? Well, it won't be *my* fault if anything should happen in this bed...you promised not to let me touch you."

"Then I will keep that promise."

"It's too late now," Alex began to say. But before she could get the words out Orielle had climbed off just as smoothly as she had climbed on, leaving Alex to regret the fairy's integrity.

Her thoughts racing, her body aching, Alex didn't understand her own reluctance. It was a perfect setup, after all; the kind of arrangement on which Alex normally thrived—a woman in her bed, a woman who wanted her, who would gladly give herself, and in two more days she'd be gone—never to be seen again, probably. So why, Alex wondered, was she lying here...passive, paralyzed, somehow?

Frustrated, Alex folded her hands behind her head again and groaned. "Why couldn't I have found a lamp instead of a bell?"

"Pardon?"

"A genie's lamp...you know, one that would have granted me three wishes."

" I am your three wishes, Alex...."

"Alex turned away, fluffing and punching the feather pillow, then buried her face in it and groaned again.

❧ 21 ❧
Mushroom Madness

Batilda honked the horn at 9:45 and didn't stop honking until Alex came dashing out. She sat behind the wheel of Mary Southworth's Plymouth, Alex's black cowboy hat on her head, her black dog hanging out the window of the back seat.

" 'Morning, Kiddo," she greeted, "get a move on it!"

Alex had expected they would walk—drive down the road maybe, then park and make their way around the creek—but Batilda made a right at the corner and headed into town instead.

"Now where?" Alex asked, rolling up the sleeves of the denim shirt she'd thrown over her T-shirt and white shorts. "Why are we heading toward town?"

"Because the best way to *get* to town is to head *toward* it."

Clenching her teeth, Alex regarded Batilda, then turned her attention to the Scottie who had wedged her way between the two front seats, waiting to be noticed. "Hey, Boog—how ya doing?" Alex asked, scratching the Scottie's head and suddenly bracing both herself and the dog as Batilda, for no apparent reason, began swerving like a sidewinder slithering through the desert.

"Hey! Take it easy—what are you doing?"

"Relax, will ya? I'm just gettin' this bastard off my ass!"

Alex glanced in the side mirror. "He's half a mile behind you."

"Not 'til I swerved—that's what ya gotta do to get these idiots off your ass. Makes 'em think you're drunk. They get out of your way and give ya the whole damn road."

Alex shook her head. "You really are nuts."

"Sure—call me nuts, invalidate me, side with the enemy." She glared at Alex. "And while you're at it, maybe you'd like to snack on a juicy apple, huh?" With a gnarled thumb she gestured behind her. "They're fresh...injected 'em just this morning."

Alex waved off the crone's words. "Just tell me where we're going."

"Church," Batilda said, pointing to what looked like a miniature cathedral up the road a ways.

"Uh-uh. No way. I'm not going to church."

"Did I say *you* were goin'?" The Plymouth jumped the curb as Batilda pulled up alongside a meter. The wheel came down with a bang. "There's a turkey baster and an empty bottle behind my seat, Alex. Hand 'em to me."

Alex looked behind the seat. "What for?" she asked, hesitating before reaching her arm around.

"I gotta pick up something." Batilda reached into the pocket of a black cardigan she'd obviously borrowed from Mary, and handed Alex a twenty-dollar bill. "Be a sport and run into that smoke shop, will ya? I need a box of clove cigarettes and snuff."

"Snuff?"

"Yeah. Tell 'em Tilly sent ya."

Alex startled at the name. "Tilly?" she asked uncertainly.

Batilda raised a bushy eyebrow. "Yeah, why? You got a problem with that?"

"No..." Alex shook her head thoughtfully, "...no."

"Then, would ya stop at the candy store," Batilda went on, "and get me a bag of Twizzlers, some Tootsie Rolls, a water gun...a vanilla dixie cup for the dog, and whatever you want for yourself."

About to say something, Alex pinched the bridge of her nose instead, resigning herself to keeping peace with the wacky witch. She watched Batilda grunt as she climbed out of the car and stomped like a bulldog toward the church. Then Alex got out herself, sprinting across the street to run Batilda's errands. In a few minutes she was back, sitting with the car door open while Boogawoog ate her ice cream by the curb. But just as Alex bent down to clean up the remains, shouts issued from the church, and Alex looked up to see a priest shaking his fist at Batilda.

"Step on it!" Batilda yelled, scuttling toward the car.

Alex didn't hesitate. She scooped up the Scottie, slid to the driver's side and started the engine.

"STOP!" ordered the priest. "I COMMAND YOU IN THE NAME OF—"

But Batilda didn't hear in whose name he commanded her to stop. She was climbing in the car and slamming the door by then. "Go!" she huffed.

Responding mechanically, Alex made a quick U-turn and sped down the main road. "What's going on? What the hell did you do?"

"Borrowed some holy water, is all."

"Borrowed?" Alex glanced at the bottle, then at Batilda. "You *stole* it, didn't you? What a hypocrite—you went to church to steal holy water?"

"*Borrowed.*"

"Just like you *borrowed* my poppies, I suppose." She looked at the witch disapprovingly as she drove. "I've been trying to catch you for three years, do you know that?"

"And it'd be another three before you catch anything with that stupid trap."

"And just *what* was wrong with it?" Alex asked, insulted.

"It didn't work—that's what's wrong. A tin pail shining up there on your roof? And all that fishing line glowing in the damn moonlight like a spider web?" She nudged Alex's arm. "You've got spunk, though, kid—I'll give you that much. I like a woman with spunk."

"It's all I'll have left after you steal everything else from me—my poppies and my hat included."

"What?" Batilda said, pointing to herself in feigned surprise. "You think I meant to steal your hat? I'm hurt, Alex. Here," she said, removing it and leaning over to plop it on Alex's head.

But Alex pushed her off with a raised elbow, the car swerving as she did. "Keep it. I don't want it now—it's all greasy!"

"Greasy? My hair ain't greasy!" She grabbed a handful of the white stuff, holding it in front of Alex's face. "Feel it. Go on...*feel* it! Then her voice dropped and she playfully nudged Alex again. "*Mary-Mary-Quite-Contrary* washed it for me this morning."

"Oh, yeah?" Alex frowned. "And how does *her* garden grow?"

"Wish I knew," she said, smoothing a gnarled hand over her head before putting the black hat back on. "Maybe tonight I'll blow some as-you-please powder in her face and get her to wash the rest of me."

"You'd do that, wouldn't you...drug someone to make them want you...."

Batilda smiled slyly. "Hey, that powder's great stuff— makes your woman desire to please you at any cost."

"She's not *your* woman—and she's straight."

"You picked up on that, huh? You noticed those little flirtations there—between her and my friend the buzzard, eh? Well, let me tell you, one night with me and she'd never look at the birdman again," Batilda said, invading Alex's personal space again with a nudge, as though about to confide a secret. "I mean, not for nothing, but when it comes time for sex...I don't know if Benjamin would even think to take his suit off."

Alex couldn't believe she was having this conversation. *Is history repeating itself?* she wondered. Aggravated, she lifted a hand from the wheel. "What is it with you two, anyway? The reason you're in this mess—the reason Orielle's in it—is because you and Benjamin just had to insist on competing for the same woman. And now here you go again with Mary! If Orielle could hear you now she'd be sick!"

"Don't start preaching—I hate preachy types."

They waved each other off at the same time.

"Whatever," Alex said, "but just forget about Mary. She wouldn't approve of your sexual orientation, anyway."

"You kiddin'? She's fine with it—her sister Maude is a dyke. Lived in Boston with her *roommate* for thirty-five years... until the woman went west."

"Went *west?*"

"Yeah..*west.* She died—went where the sun sets. Mary says Maude took it hard."

Alex slowed down, driving along the shoulder of the road. "Where is it you want to stop?"

"Up near the caves."

"The openings aren't big enough to get in. And, besides, they're not the best place to be this time of year—there's mothers with young in them."

"We're not going inside. It's just cooler up there. A good place for us to sit and talk."

Alex looked at her. "You know the area well."

"Yeah, well, I've been coming here off and on for a hundred years."

"To that cottage?"

"Used to. Then me and Birdwhistle had to go underground for a few years—spent some time in Greece, Egypt. Then I headed for New Orleans and Birdwhistle went home to London...until last year when he took an apartment—pardon me, a *flat*—in Manhattan, so we could be close enough to *collaborate*, as he likes to call it."

Batilda fell silent, but Alex could feel the old woman's beady eyes on her. "What?" Alex said.

"Nothin'."

"Why are you staring?"

"I'm not staring."

Alex picked up speed and continued along the road, driving parallel to the river until they reached the creek.

☾ ☾ ☾

For the duration of their walk, Batilda did nothing but complain—about her wings, her knees, her arthritis—so that by the time they'd climbed above the creek Batilda plopped to the ground, her back against the trunk of a tree, and stretched her legs. "Whew," she said, fanning herself, "is it hot out here...or is it just me?"

"It's warming up," Alex said. She shoved her hands in her shorts pockets and stood leaning against the next tree.

"I should be lying in a hammock now," Batilda complained again, "with a cold glass of lemonade on one side and Mary-Quite-Contrary fanning me on the other side."

"Don't start," Alex warned. "Let's not mention Mary again."

With a twisted grin, Batilda looked up from where she sat on the ground. "Well, then how about Orielle...you sure have a thing for that fairy."

Alex swatted an insect, then folded her arms and looked away. "I don't know what you're talking about."

"You know exactly what I'm talking about." Batilda cackled to herself. "Takes one to know one, Alex."

"What, you're saying I'm a dyke?"

"I know you're a dyke."

"So? What does that have to do with it? You think I like the fairy because I'm a *dyke*?"

"No," Batilda said nonchalantly. "You like the fairy because you like the fairy—period."

"Well, I don't!"

"Sure you do. You'd like to get in her pants."

"It's not about that," Alex answered huffily. "I have more women than I know what to do with, okay? So please, spare me."

"Whoa!" Batilda held her hands up. "Excuse me. The *she-stud* of Halfmoon has spoken."

"Why do you have to be so *difficult*?"

"I'm not difficult," Batilda snapped. "I'm *honest*."

"Just make your point."

"I did. You got the hots for the fairy. That's my point."

"You're wrong," Alex said, unnerved by the presumption.

"Yeah? Well you just better watch yourself, because you don't know the first thing about Orielle. Strange breed, fairies are."

Alex put a foot up against the tree. "How so?" she asked, trying to make her inquiry as casual as possible.

"They only fall in love once. And once they do, they love for life—ain't no gettin' rid of 'em." She looked up at Alex with a self-deprecating frown. "Too bad Lilah wasn't a fairy."

Batilda leaned forward, wiggling her arms out of the black cardigan, and as she did, Alex avoided the sight of her lumpy avian appendages protruding from the back of her flowered house dress. Like flesh-colored bat wings they were, and just as Batilda stuck a hand in one of her sleeves to adjust them, Alex spotted what looked like a blue glass eye pinned to the strap of the harpy's bra.

"Is that an *evil eye?*"

"Yeah...blue and evil like Lilah's."

Alex studied her. "What are you—Greek? Spanish?"

"Who wants to know?"

"Me."

"Why, what are you?"

"I asked you first."

"None of your business."

"Well, then it's none of yours, either," Alex said snootily. "So there."

"Fine...!"

"You sure are a moody one!" Batilda remarked.

"You're the moody one. All I asked was—"

"What's your sign? Wait, don't tell me. You gotta be a Cancer—such moody little crabs they are—moody, moody—"

"I'm...*not*...moody!" Benjamin was right, Alex thought. Batilda *did* have snake eyes, and she shot them at Alex just then.

"But you *are* a Cancer. Come on now, Alex...don't lie to me."

"So what if I am?" she admitted, hating to give the witch the satisfaction.

"I need to know 'cause I've gotta make you an ouanga bag. Why do you think we're spending this *quality* time together; I can't make the bag until I know what I need to put in it. So let's see...you're a Cancer, Orielle's a Capricorn..." The witch stuck her chin out, considering and nodding at the possibilities. "Could work...could work well."

"Will you stop harping about Orielle and me."

"So I harp, I'm a harpy—it's what I do."

"You're nuts," Alex said under her breath.

"But you like me, don't you? Tell the truth."

"What's to like about a poppy-picking thief? We're not even getting along," Alex added.

"We're gettin' along just fine." Batilda reached for a thermos she'd brought along and patted the ground. "Sit. Have a cup of tea with me."

"What for?"

"I need to read your tea leaves."

"My fortune?" Alex regarded her disdainfully. "You'll probably get that wrong, too."

"Have some faith," she grumbled, pouring the tea into paper cups.

Alex picked a fairy wand, twirling it in her fingers. Strange as it seemed, she missed Orielle. She'd only known her a few days, had only been away a few hours, but suddenly Alex wanted to be home with her.

The bushes rustled just then, and Boogawoog, who'd been out scouting the area, came out. Her nose was dirt-brown, and from her mouth hung a lifeless mole. Alex looked away in disgust. "Does she have to kill rodents like that?"

"She's a ratter! It's in her blood. Foxes, badgers—Scotties used to hunt all sorts of fierce critters. Somewhere along the line, though—probably because they wouldn't come when they were called—they were demoted to killin' rats on ships."

Boogawoog dropped the mole at Alex's feet.

"Gee, thanks, Boogawoog," she said, looking away with distaste.

"Show your teeth to Alex. Come on now," Batilda coaxed, "show 'em to her."

The Scottie curled her lips, grinning devilishly.

"Ain't they somethin'?" Batilda pressed. "Big as a Rottweiler's—lots of power in those jaws."

"Believe me, I know...she bit me."

"No!" Batilda said, as though shocked to hear the news.

"Yes."

"*My* dog? My dog *bit* you? I think you're fibbin', Alex."

"Fib—" Alex looked at her incredulously. "Why would I lie? Your damn *ratter* bit me in the butt. I could've used a couple of stitches."

"Oh, this I've *gotta* see."

"You want to see my butt?"

"If you wouldn't mind."

Nostrils flaring, Alex angrily got to her feet, unbuttoned her waistband, and was just about to pull down one side of her shorts, when suddenly she remembered and stopped. "It's not there anymore..." Alex said, sheepishly. "...Orielle healed it."

"How convenient," Batilda said, sniffling from the snuff as though she'd snorted cocaine. "And such a darn convenient spot, too." She grinned at Alex, her nose wiggling and twitching. "Must've felt real good having your butt rubbed by a fairy. Those sound waves have a nice tickle to 'em, eh?"

"Don't *start*," Alex warned.

Edging the brim of her cowboy hat down over her eyes, Batilda snickered. "You should get a dog, Alex...."

"Why? So I can become attached, then have to watch it die of old age in a few years?"

Batilda tilted her head back to peer at Alex from under the hat, and as she did, Alex could have sworn she saw genuine concern in the witch's black eyes. "You're really scared shitless about loving anything, aren't you?"

Alex declined to comment. Instead, she blew furiously in her teacup, then downed half of it.

"Sorry, Kiddo. Here I'm pokin' fun and teasin' you about Orielle and all.... I didn't realize I was really hitting such a deep chord."

"Let's just drop it, okay?"

Batilda glanced curiously at her, a glint of mischief shining in her eyes. "You finished with that tea yet?"

"I'm working on it."

"Clove cigarette?" Batilda asked.

"No."

"Tootsie roll?"

"Not now."

"Tell you what, then," the witch said, grunting and groaning as she got to her feet. "You keep sipping on that tea...I see some nice mushrooms over there you can eat with it."

"I'm not eating any wild mushrooms."

"Why not?"

"Because I'm not a mycologist."

"But you're with one. I'm an herbalist, chemist and a *damn good* mycologist."

"Really?" Picking mushrooms was a tricky business, and Alex was decidedly impressed.

"Nothin' like fresh mushrooms." Batilda wandered off into the shade and came back brushing off a light-colored mushroom on her black cardigan. "Taste it...it's a chanterelle."

Alex took it, inspecting the fungus in her hand. "Are you positive?"

"You think I'd poison you? I'm not your enemy. We need you...Orielle needs you." She gestured with her chin. "Go ahead, now...*trust* me."

Alex bit cautiously—a tiny bite, then a slightly bigger one, chewing deliberately, slow at first and wincing when she swallowed.

Batilda grinned. "Loaded with vitamin B—not bad, huh?"

Alex shook her head. "No," she agreed. "It's pretty good."

With a sweep of her arm the harpy gestured toward the woods and valley and water below. "Yep...nature's one big pharmacy." She smacked her lips. "If only I had a few years left...."

Heck, if the druids discovered aspirin, I know I could find the cure for cancer. It's gotta be growin' around here somewhere," she said, looking down around her feet as though she might very well have been stepping on it. "But when I was young and in love with Lilah...what'd I know? I walked right past the good plants and picked the bad ones—like I did just now. Walked right past the *chanterelle* and picked the *death cap*."

Alex's face lit with confused horror. "What ?"

Batilda only shrugged. "I don't know *what* the hell comes over me sometimes."

Alex felt her mouth watering, but she wouldn't swallow. She got to her feet, struggling to process what she was hearing. "You...you've *poisoned* me?"

"A Jekyll and Hyde, ain't I? Can you believe it?" Batilda broke out in a toothy grin, then burst into a maddening, high-pitched cackle.

Alex put a hand across her stomach. She'd run somewhere, make herself vomit, then with Mary's keys still in her pocket, she'd speed home to Orielle.

"Better fight the nausea, Alex. Throwin' up will only worsen the pain, speed up the hypoglycemia. You're already feelin' a little light-headed, are ya?"

She *was* nauseous. Dizzy, too, come to think of it.

"Any sharp pains in your gut yet?"

A forearm against the tree, her head hanging down and her curls damp with perspiration, Alex glared up at Batilda. "You son-of-a-bitch," she cursed, spitting, wiping her mushroom-tainted lips, then tightening an arm around her stomach. Cramps were coming on now. On the count of three she'd bolt—before the pain doubled her over—and drive straight to the hospital. She could always have the nurse call Orielle.

"All right, all right...get a grip," Batilda said, waving her hand disgustedly. "Joke's over. Now sit down and finish your tea— you've gotta meet Birdwhistle in an hour."

"Huh?" Alex said, trying to focus.

"You ate a *chanterelle* ! Not a death cap...."

"A chanter...?" Almost instantly the pain subsided. Alex let go of her stomach, her breathing now becoming labored with rage. "Take me home," she demanded. "*Now!*"

"What, like we're on our first date and I put the move on you too soon? Sit down."

Batilda's mocking tone was gone, and an unmistakable disappointment replaced the mischief in her eyes. "Drink," she said, coaxing Alex to take the cup. "And for the record..." she commented, her bones creaking as she squatted opposite Alex, "throwin' up *is* the best remedy. The problem with mushrooms, though, is that symptoms don't appear for hours...sometimes days. So by the time you started feelin' sick, well, your liver and kidneys would've been shot to hell."

Alex didn't say a word. Feeling somehow foolish, she finished the last of the herbal tea, staring cross-eyed into the cup to avoid swallowing the leaves, then handed over the cup.

Batilda swished around what little tea was left in the cup, then turned it over to let it drain out. "Yep...I've taken out a lot people with salads."

"Mushrooms...?""

"Sometimes. Zoological toxins, other times—snake juice in the bloodstream. Mostly botanicals, though. I always fancied the pretty poisons. Like lily of the valley...so fragrant and feminine with all those dainty, virgin-white bells—but that shit'll stop your heart like that!" she said with a snap of her fingers. "Why, even the water from a vase of cut flowers will damn-near kill ya. Ha!" Batilda grinned. "That's why Lilah was attracted to me. If somethin' was beautiful and deadly, she loved it. Had to have it. For her enemies, of course. I travelled the world with her, you know...the lover posing as the private *parfumeur.*"

Batilda stuck out her bottom lip and nodded, as though still proud of the position she had held in Lilah's life. "Beautiful and deadly," she murmured. "I think I still love her, Alex. I'm gonna kill her tomorrow...but I still love her."

"But how? How could you love someone so...so evil?"

"Wait 'til you meet her...then ask me that again." Batilda's chest was rising and falling fast; she seemed to have forgotten the teacup in her hand for now, and was staring out at the hills. She seemed sad and agitated at once; so agitated, in fact, that Alex didn't say anything for fear the old witch might unintentionally deck her.

"God, was she beautiful. Wealthy, beautiful...classy gal. Do you know she was on the McAllister's social register in the 1890s? And there were only four hundred on it—that was all Mrs. Aster's ballroom could hold. What a dancer Lilah was...what a lover."

Batilda was still staring off, slowly nodding to herself, as though in a trancelike state. "Yep...all those parties with the Delmonicos, the Vanderbilts and Carnegies...Scott Joplin and that ragtime music...and then there were the social seasons in Saratoga and Newport. We used to ride around in Lilah's Duryea. Imagine...America's first gasoline car. I'd be behind the wheel with Lilah next to me...always dressed in black, laughing and smoking her Cameo cigarettes in that gold holder of hers. Course, the bird-man always tagged along in the back seat."

"The *bird*man?"

"Benjamin. He never could drive—too scared. Drivin' was dangerous back then. But me? Loved it! I even gave Diamond Jim Brady a ride once. He wanted to finance some of Benjamin's work, but Lilah kept Birdwhistle too busy with her own work. Yep...Ol' Diamond Jim...I took Lillian Russell for a ride once, too. What an actress...what a *time* we had! And that was just in the States."

Alex looked at her, trying to imagine the harpy in her heyday...trying to imagine her tooling along in a car with Lillian Russell. "Where did all Lilah's wealth come from?"

"Opium...heroin."

Alex shook her head, not quite following.

Batilda kept nodding, but then her nods turned to shakes, until finally she seemed to shake herself away from the past and back to the teacup held limply in her hand.

Alex studied the witch's ravaged face as she turned the cup clockwise in her crooked fingers, her face contorting into a series of grim expressions. Then suddenly, she mumbled something, snorted, and simply tossed the cup aside.

"What's wrong?"

"Bad news," Batilda said. "You got a pig, a rat and a pair of scissors...not good, Alex. Not a pretty picture."

A lump grew in Alex's throat. "Why? What's wrong with it?"

"Well, the *pig's* good—pigs mean money. But what good is money if you won't be around to spend it? And the rat? A bad omen. The rat warns of a thief."

Alex shot her a vengeful look. "Does her name start with the letter *B*?"

"Very funny—HA!" she shouted in Alex's face. But Alex had the feeling Batilda wasn't at all amused. Her breath smelled of cloves. And it was hot—like dragon's breath. And as they sat there, the witch's cave-black eyes locked on hers. She suddenly appeared as a wise crone to Alex...a sage, mountain-dwelling seer.

"*Lilah* is your thief, Alex...the thief of hearts. She stole mine, she stole Benjamin's, and she'll break yours when she steals Orielle's soul—if you let her play with your mind the way I just did."

By now, Alex had recuperated from the mushroom scare, but the thought of losing Orielle—of seeing Orielle lose her freedom to Lilah again—made another wave of nausea pass through her. "But how...how do you expect *me* to fight her? I don't have any *powers*."

"Ah, but you do. And between today and tomorrow night your homework assignment is to figure out what they are—figure out who *you* are. Know what you loathe, what you love, what you fear. And most of all, know the past from the present, the *real* from the *unreal*...otherwise, Lilah'll poison your ass with an imaginary mushroom. Now won't *that* be a laugh!" But Batilda still wasn't laughing. She leaned in, piercing Alex with those reptilian eyes.

Alex countered her stare. "And the scissors...?"

"Separation. Scissors sever ties."

A quiet panic rose in Alex. She wasn't ready to cut her ties with Orielle—no matter that they hadn't known each other long enough to tie much of anything. "Couldn't the scissors represent Orielle breaking free from Lilah?"

"With the rat smack next to them? Doesn't look good."

"So how...how do you expect me to fight this woman?"

"Lilah? She won't *fight* you—she's too classy for that. She'll simply ask you for the bell, Alex. Maybe you'll give it to her, maybe you won't."

"Well of course I won't, I *wouldn't*, I—"

"You don't know *what* you'll do 'til she asks...and Lilah has a way of seducing anyone into givin' her anything she wants. Too bad you're not straight—the fact that you love women doesn't help any."

Self-doubt began weighing down upon Alex. "But you'll be there...with me, right? To poison her...?"

"She'd never let me that close to her. *You're* gonna do it."

"Me—*ME?* No...."

Batilda sniffled, wiped the back of her hand across her nose. "We have no choice," she said, standing and rubbing her hip as if to work out a kink. "There's a bottle of wine in that cave. Lilah brought two last time. She drank one and saved the other for her return a century later when she would come for her final bath in the waters of immortality. My plan was to get down there early in the week—inject the wine through the cork before she arrived, but," she shrugged tiredly, "what is it the philosopher said about life being what happens in between the plans we've made....?" Batilda faked a toothy smile, but it only made her look more haggard, the circles beneath her eyes more pronounced.

"I've never killed..." Alex said.

"And you won't—the poison will do it for ya. *Atropa belladonna, Digitalis purpurea...Convallaria.*"

"Huh?"

"Nightshade, foxglove, lily of the valley...all Lilah's favorites. You know, her mother was named *Atropos*, after the eldest of the three fates—the one whose job it is to sever the thread of life."

Alex thought of the scissors.

"Atropos..." Batilda mused. She cocked her head, her brow furrowing. "I think she didn't have a last name before she hooked up with Lilah's father...I don't suppose demons do."

Batilda stared up at the leafy tree tops. She seemed to be mentally wandering, free associating again. "Lilah used to have me fetch her nightshade leaves for her eyes—just like women did during the Renaissance—laid 'em right on their eyes—just like cucumbers—'cause it made their pupils dilate, made their eyes look bigger, more beautiful. That's how it came to be called *belladonna.*"

"Then it can't be strong enough to kill...."

"Nightshade ain't so bad in small doses, neither is fox-glove; we wouldn't have atropine or digitalis without 'em. But in lethal doses—twenty drops of extract, say? Lilah's heart is gonna beat so fast, Alex...so damn loud that you'll hear it—the whole damn cave will hear it!" Batilda stopped to wipe spittle from the corner of her mouth. "*Great* stuff!"

Alex didn't want to meet Lilah, let alone listen to her heart-beat. "So now what? You're telling me I have to inject her?"

"Nah...reaction time would take too long. You gotta get it in her mouth—that way it gets absorbed into the bloodstream very quickly."

"How am I gonna do that?"

"The water gun."

"The water—"

"I know, I know, it's so unprofessional. But trust me, that water gun is gonna pack more power than a nine-millimeter gun."

Alex shook her head. "I can't do this..."

"Sure ya can. Ever been to a carnival—ever seen those plastic clown heads with open mouths and water balloons poking out of their heads? Well, just make believe she's one of them. Just wait 'til you're close enough. Make a little conversation, enjoy a glass of that priceless wine with her and when she laughs—Lilah

loves to laugh—you start pumping that poison like you're tryin'
to win Orielle a stuffed teddy bear!"

"Drink *wine* with her? Oh, for Christ's—this is insane!
This is—you're turning this into a blind date! I'm being set up on
a blind date with a murderess!"

"*Sorceress*," Batilda corrected. "*I'm* the murderess. And
you're my sidekick." And with that, she put her fingers in her
mouth and whistled for the dog. "Darned bugger hears me whistling, don't you know it. But it'll take her ten minutes to react."
Finally, she ordered, "Shake a leg, Alex. The birdman's probably
waitin' for ya."

Alex stood, brushing her legs and the cuffs of her long
shorts. She felt a headache coming on and only hoped it wasn't
the chanterelle she'd eaten.

"Don't worry about the technical stuff—don't even think
about shootin' that water gun or playin' your fiddle."

"My violin? I have to bring my *violin*?"

"I *SAID* don't worry—that's my job. *Your* job is to enjoy
the company of your houseguest." She winked knowingly.

"I don't get any of this! You drag me up here to teach me
something—the lesson of my life, I suppose—and now you tell
me to go home and—"

"*Life* is your lesson," Batilda tapped her temple with a
crooked finger. "Get it? So review your notes, Alex, 'cause like I
said, Lilah's connected to you now. You have her bell. And when
you enter her cave...she's gonna enter your mind."

❦ 22 ❦
Violets and Violins

In a meadow just beyond the poppy field, Benjamin waited for Alex. In summer-white trousers and matching vest, he sat on a sun-dried log, his little black cat crouched there beside him.

"Did you bring your violin?" he called, flagging Alex with a waving arm.

She lifted her violin in answer as she strolled toward him through the clover. Her eyes were drawn to the violets blowing about his black-and-white saddle shoes. She had left the case at home, so that now, as she held the violin up to the breeze like an aeolian harp, its maple wood gleamed in the afternoon sun.

"Ah...Alex," he said, rising to greet her, "with all our misfortune I was feeling bereft of good luck. But seeing you, with youth on your side and that violin in hand...my faith is restored."

Alex shook his hand, regarded both the black cat and his metal briefcase, then laid her fiddle and bow in the grass and settled down beside him. "I don't feel so young today."

"Batilda gave you a workout, did she?"

"A workout? *Whew*...I feel like I've been in a *war!*"

"Speaking as one soldier to another, I understand completely." He patted her knee sympathetically. "Did you pass her mushroom test?"

"No...." she said, embarrassed by the admission.

"There you are then!" He smiled easily. "Better you fail today than tomorrow."

"She must think I'm some kind of impressionable—"

"Quite the contrary! I haven't seen her so impressed by someone in years."

Surprise creased itself in Alex's forehead. "Impressed?"

"Indeed. She praised you incessantly," he said, addressing Alex with amused curiosity. "The woman's a hard nut to crack— I'll give you that—but trust her, Alex. She's competent, purposeful, the last of the true witches...even if I *did* turn her into a nasty old bird."

Alex chuckled softly. After having been antagonized all morning, keeping company with Benjamin was tranquilizing, revitalizing.

Benjamin rolled the sleeves of his starched shirt to the elbow, then from his briefcase took a white legal-size envelope so stuffed the flap couldn't be sealed. "Before we begin I want to take care of an important matter. Please take this envelope," he said. "In it you'll find the deed to Orielle's property."

"In Saratoga...?"

"Yes. Her father, Steven Rutherford, remained ever hopeful that I, one day, would uncross the spell that held his daughter captive. Of course, for nearly twenty years he refused to speak with us. But on his deathbed he sent for me. You see, he couldn't possibly will his estate to a daughter in 1923, then expect that daughter, still a young woman, to surface as his heiress seventy-five years later. So he transferred his properties to me under the agreement that I, in turn, would transfer them to Orielle at the appropriate time." He looked at the sky as though looking up to the man to whom he'd made his promise. "There are a few blue chip stocks as well," he added. "You'll find the name and number of an attorney inside...Orielle can do with it as she pleases."

Alex held the envelope between them, not sure whether to hand it back or take it. "Why not give it to her yourself?"

"I don't expect I'll be here after the solstice."

"Why? Where are you going?"

Benjamin cocked his head almost whimsically. "Alex... Batilda and I—Boogawoog, especially—are on borrowed time. Why, if not for an accidental splashing on the night of original enchantment, we would have expired a good many years ago." He patted her on the back as he spoke casually of his demise—as if dying were but a minor event in one's life.

Alex sat with a hand pressed lightly to her mouth, not knowing what to say, how to feel. "So that's *IT?*" You're gonna crawl in that cave like a lamb off to slaughter and just...just DIE?" she sputtered, startled when she heard herself. For a moment she'd sounded like Batilda. She'd spent too much time with Batilda this morning—that was it; the harpy was rubbing off on her. Alex combed her curls with rigid fingers, until her forehead came to rest in the palm of her hand. "So then what? I ...I have to bury all of you—have funerals and—"

Benjamin let out a heartier laugh than Alex imagined him capable of. "Such an inconvenience! Surely not," he smiled. "I don't expect we'll amount to more than a pile of ashes and dust. Just step over us and get on with your life, Alex...help Orielle get on with hers. And if it be destiny's will, then it is *my* wish that those two lives become commingled into one."

Saddened, Alex looked away. She hadn't even wanted to let any of them into her life—not the dog, the witch, the wizard, nor the fairy. And now she'd have to say goodbye to them all— the fairy included, once Orielle sold her estate and went off in search of her own kind. But it was the story of her life, wasn't it? The *forces* thrust people into her life, then kicked them out without giving Alex a say in the matter.

"Cheer up, child...this is hardly a time to grieve. It is a time of joy and celebration. Why, if we hadn't lived to see this solstice, Orielle could never hope to be free," he comforted her. "Our jobs are almost done, we are ready to move on," he said.

Then, with a chipper clap of his hands, he opened his arms to the meadow. "What a magnificent concert hall!" He shifted his gaze to the violin lying in the windswept clover. "May I call upon the concert master to tune her heart strings?" he asked, tipping an imaginary hat.

Alex smiled in spite of herself. "I could use some fine-tuning, Benjamin. After the last few days," she said, pointing to her head, "I could stand to have these strings tuned."

Benjamin chuckled. "I'll entrust that to your fairy...." he said, with a wink of a sage blue eye. And before Alex could think to respond, he had eased himself off the log to a softer seat in the timothy grass.

Halfheartedly, Alex leaned forward, dragging the fiddle toward her by its scroll. She tightened the bow, then pulled a mute from her shorts pocket.

"No," he said, before she could put the mute on the bridge. "I want the meadow to tremble with the power of that instrument." And with that he withdrew what appeared to be a cellular telephone from his briefcase. The bottom half was encased in black plastic, while the top half was made of a metal resembling mother-of-pearl. A white, tubular antenna protruded from the top. Without explanation he proceeded to punch in a series of numbers, as though he had suddenly remembered to call someone.

"What is that?" Alex asked, watching as the antenna began to glow like a fluorescent bulb.

"My sound accelerator. And now," he instructed, "if you'll just walk out a few yards...we can *both* play."

Alex looked at the device suspiciously, but quietly obliged the professor. "Any requests?" she asked, moving out into the open.

"Mozart? No, no...." He changed his mind with a wave of his hand. "Something high, fanciful. Can you play Paganini?"

"Not like Paganini," she said, tucking the violin under her chin.

Benjamin smiled. "Then Paganini it is—a caprice, perhaps?"

"Sure," Alex agreed, although she wasn't at all in the mood to play; the witch had exhausted her, Benjamin had depressed her...and the fairy? Alex didn't even know where she was. She hadn't been home when Alex stopped in to retrieve her fiddle, and she only guessed that Orielle was probably by the river, basking in the sun, playing hopscotch with the dragonflies.

Alex inhaled deeply and brought her bow down, pausing just before it touched the strings...*heart strings,* she thought. Maybe her song would summon Orielle to the meadow.

"Ready when you are," Benjamin signaled. After another moment of meditative silence, Alex brought the bow down and began filling the meadow with music for the fairy on her mind.

"Lovely!" the professor called, extending his arm and passing the antenna from left to right, as though it were some sort of tracking device. Then he held it at nose-length, inspecting the digital reading. "Wonderful! Just *wonderful*," he said, busily punching in another series of numbers, then pointing the antenna at her again. "Simply marvelous...!"

Alex didn't know whether Benjamin was referring to her music or his sound accelerator, but as he spoke Alex could see the antenna beginning to glow with an energy almost too bright for her eyes.

Benjamin was conducting her now, his free hand waving in time with the music. Then, "Wait!" he instructed. "What was that? A double stop—a triple stop? Play it again. Yes...yes!" he exclaimed. "And again. Hold it while I take a few measurements, will you?" Then, "Hit your highest note? What would that be, Alex?"

"...G...E...?" Alex said, bowing single notes with one long draw. "...open G."

"That's it, by golly...that's it!" He looked up, his face shining like that of a little boy operating a remote-control airplane. "Once more!"

With an upstroke, then a downstroke, Alex held her highest note, the sun burning down on her head and shoulders, and reflecting off the polished maple wood.

"I do believe we're in *business,* Alex. Now, let's hear that caprice again—from the top, shall we?"

Alex played beautifully, the frequencies tickling her ear-drums. But as she played, the music began to change strangely; it sounded as though she were playing an electric violin. Suddenly, it seemed a string had popped. She kept bowing, staring sideways at the bridge, counting all four intact strings, but the E string wasn't emitting any sound. Then a second later it came back, full force, and the G string fell silent.

Benjamin let out a high-pitched giggle. "Don't stop, Alex!"

Cautiously, Alex continued to bow, trying all the while to make sense of what was happening. It sounded as though her music was coming out of speakers, as though someone was playing with the volume control. One moment she could only hear her music from one ear, the next moment from the other, until suddenly it seemed the music was coming from another fiddler beyond the hills.

"Don't be alarmed," he reassured her. "I'm just throwing your sound. And now...now...." he said, his voice trailing off in concentration as he fiddled with his device, "I'm going to...*send* it!"

And as he said the word, the frequency of the notes in-creased beyond Alex's control, climbing to an inaudible pitch and instantly reminding her of the bell. Alex kept bowing—franti-cally she bowed—but her fiddle made no noise. The strings vibrated, Alex could *see* them vibrating—but the only sound in the meadow was of the cardinals and blue jays and Birdwhistle's ecstatic giggling.

"We've done it! By golly, we've *done it*! If it were night-time," he shouted, "if it were dark now, you'd see what you no longer hear; the *colors* of your caprice...your music moving at the speed of light." He turned a knob then, and as he laid the device to rest in the clover, the sound came screeching back to Alex's violin, causing her whole body to jolt.

"Bravo!" he applauded with quick claps of his hands. "Bravo!"

The fiddle in one hand, the bow in the other, Alex stood with her arms hanging at her sides. Dumbfoundedly, she stared at him.

"Science and magic...such *fun!*" Benjamin fairly glowed. A bit woozy, Alex strolled back to the log and sat, inspecting her instrument, stroking the maple wood, strumming the strings with her thumb. Benjamin rose to his feet, his arms held open to the sky, his face to the blue heavens. "Did you see that, Rutherford? Am I a man of my word, or am I a *man of my word?*" he cried. "Not to worry, Steven, old chap...your little girl is almost free!"

He looked at Alex then, a mystical shine in his ancient eyes, as they filled with a tearful pride. "Thank you, Alex," he said, grabbing and heartily shaking her hand. "Thank you...!"

But Alex regarded him blankly, her hand limp in his.

"I know what you're thinking, Alex...you're thinking that I've defied the law of relativity, aren't you? Of course, Einstein was busy failing math at the time I was putting my most extraordinary theories to work."

Alex nodded, although that hadn't been what she was thinking at all. Her mind was too jumbled for a coherent thought—let alone a *scientific* one.

"But let's take it to be true," he went on, "that nothing can travel faster than light—the reason being, of course, that the faster an object moves, the more its mass increases, so that the object, upon reaching infinite mass, would require an infinite amount of energy—all the energy in the universe—to move it that fast." He paused, narrowing his eyes at her. "Are you following me?"

Alex nodded, although the gesture was a lie; she'd lost Benjamin a while ago.

" But let's assume that—through the application of magic to science—I could *reduce* your mass as I increased your speed, and by doing so could actually move an object—your body, say— at the speed of light. Now, if I can do that, and yet *still* have it hold true that nothing travels *faster* than light...then in theory, your body would have to *become* light the moment you achieved the *speed* of light."

"But it's not theory," Alex said. "It's what you just did to my music...it's what the bell does to Orielle."

Benjamin gave a modest giggle. "Precisely. The bell, Alex, is a mystical vortex. It accelerates sound, and in doing so, opens a pathway by which the sound and any object bound to it are reduced in mass and transported at the speed of light.

"You see," he continued, "unlike light, sound is dependent on matter. If there were no air—if we were having this conversation on the moon, for instance—we wouldn't hear each other speaking. It might help if you picture sound as a strand of pearls. The strand itself is the vibration, the sound wave, and each pearl a quantum, a particle of matter which passes that sound on to the next pearl. Without the pearls—without air or water, without matter, sound cannot carry."

Alex stood there, visualizing the pearls, except that in her mind they were delicately draped around the fairy's neck, and it struck her that she missed Orielle terribly.

"I'm sure you're familiar with the use of ultrasonic devices in the medical arts," Benjamin went on. "Low frequencies heal tissue, high frequencies destroy. And at speeds I've managed to achieve, well, the frequencies create a molecular instability which allows for the reduction of mass and...*Alex?*" he questioned.

"Huh?" she said, realizing she was fantasizing about the fairy and not paying attention to a single word of what the professor was saying. "I'm sorry...?" she said.

Benjamin sighed good-naturedly. "It's not important," he said. "Batilda warned me not to waste your time with my encyclopedic gibberish—she thinks I'm an absolute bore." He peeked at the pocket watch in his vest, then propped his cat on his shoulder and lifted his briefcase. "Allow me to escort you home," he said. "Mary should be here for me shortly."

Absentmindedly, her brow deeply furrowed, Alex collected her fiddle, the bow and the white envelope, and walked alongside Benjamin. "I don't get it...."

"What part?"

"The poison part...what's the connection?"

"With my sound accelerator?" Benjamin's face lit with anticipation, as though he'd been wishing she'd ask. "The botanicals Batilda has selected affect heart rate—nightshade, especially. When a lethal level of toxicity is achieved, Lilah's heartbeat will become so fast, so strong, that it will be audible at a distance of several feet. And when it is, when we hear it...I will do with it as I did with your music—make her heart beat at the speed of light and send her through the vortex and into oblivion.

"Proper timing with the eclipse and with the arrival of the fairies is crucial, though... and that's where you and your violin come in, Alex. You must play while I work, for it is your music I will use to intercept the pathways. Otherwise...Orielle and all the fairies will be sent with her."

"So I'm on the front line?"

He regarded her with a comforting wink. "The experts will be standing right behind you."

Alex frowned as they walked past the barn. The daisies and pink hollyhocks were coming into bloom, and the peppermint plants were dappled with tiny purple flowers. But overnight, it seemed, the poppy petals had fallen, the lilacs had faded, and it all made her think of the grim tea-leaf reading.

Benjamin pointed to the other side of the barn. "That rowboat," he said, "I noticed it on my way out to the field earlier. How many will it hold?" he asked.

"Three...four."

"Could we take it up the river tomorrow night?"

Alex shrugged. "I suppose so. Why?"

"The less we travel on foot, the better. The woods won't be safe tomorrow night."

As they came up along the cabin Alex glanced hesitantly from Benjamin to a jar of sun tea Orielle had left to brew by the porch. "Iced tea?" Alex offered, eyeing the jar's contents, but unable to identify all the leaves and sprigs floating in it. "We could talk more," she said. "I still have questions."

"The answers you most need are those to the questions you must ask yourself," Benjamin said kindly.

Alex nodded, then reached to pet the black cat on his shoulder, but the cat hissed and Alex quickly pulled her hand back.

"She can't help it—she's a Scorpio," he said, astrologically rationalizing the cat's actions—blaming her behavior on the zodiac.

Alex chewed the corner of her lip as she regarded the cat, then looked at Benjamin. "What about Batilda?" she asked. "What sign is she?"

"A Cancer...just an old cranky crab," he said, "with claws too big for her own good."

Smiling to herself, Alex nodded thoughtfully, but didn't comment.

❦ 23 ❦
The Art of Seduction

Alex set the jar of sun-brewed tea on the kitchen counter, then turned back to the vase of lilacs on the table. She was disappointed in a way; disappointed that Orielle wasn't here to greet her. It's not that she *missed* the fairy, Alex told herself. She had simply *expected* her; expected Orielle to hear her music in the meadow and—what?—Come running home, she supposed.

Wearily, Alex rubbed her temples, and as she did was suddenly struck with the horrible thought that maybe Orielle *couldn't* come home; that someone had snuck in while Alex was gone and stolen her—stolen the bell. Gripped by a sudden fear, Alex panicked and lunged at the refrigerator. But the bell was there; cold, frosty, frozen in silence, as it were.

With an exhalation of relief, Alex stuck her head in the freezer, closed her eyes against the refreshing frost, then reached past the bell and scooped up a few ice cubes. A cold glass of Orielle's herbal tea was what she needed; that and a cool shower. And by then, she surmised, the fairy would be back.

But an hour later Orielle still wasn't home. In underwear and a sleeveless denim shirt, Alex paced the bedroom, towel drying her hair and wondering where Orielle might possibly have gone. Maybe to Mary's to visit with Benjamin and Batilda? No, Alex thought; Orielle didn't know where Mary lived. And besides, Benjamin and Batilda seemed intent on having Alex and

Orielle spend the evening alone together. The Emporium, she speculated. Orielle liked the Emporium, liked Madam Mimma—hadn't she said that to Alex?

Alex's nostrils flared at the prospect of her fairy visiting with some crystal-wielding soothsayer; sharing mystical experiences, while swapping herbs and spells and God knew what else. But the Emporium, Alex calmed herself, was several miles away. Too far for Orielle to go on foot. Or was it? And as Alex absentmindedly paced, she caught sight of a bare hanger on the doorknob; the hanger that had held a black silk shirt she'd ironed only yesterday. Raspberries, she thought. *Orielle had dressed up and gone to Raspberries.*

Tossing her damp towel on the bed, Alex picked up the phone and dialed the cafe. "It's me," she said when Ana Mae answered.

"Hi, Alex," she greeted, disinterestedly, as if she'd been expecting Alex to call. "What's doing?"

"Is Orielle there?"

"Yep. She's here, why?"

"How'd she *get* there?"

"I drove by earlier, but you weren't home. She said you had plans all day. Plans for tonight, too—a date with a Susie?— And so I figured I'd bring her back here with me and keep her company. Who the heck is Susie, anyway?"

Ana Mae's coy Southern drawl was irritating Alex. "There *is* no Susie."

"Well, that's who Orielle said you'd be with—Susie."

"Susie's a *'possum...!"* Alex hissed.

"Oh...." There was a pause, then, "Well...personally, I wouldn't eat a 'possum unless it was in a stew, but...whatever floats your boat," Ana Mae said, sounding already bored by the conversation.

"I'm coming to pick her up."

"She's not ready to leave, Alex—she just met someone."

"Someone? Who the hell is *someone?*" Alex demanded. The thought of someone—*anyone*—taking advantage of Orielle's good nature made Alex's head pound.

"What's her name—Ellen, I think."

"Ellen the slut?"

"Yep, that's right...your friend's taken quite a fancy to her." Ana Mae may as well have snickered as she said this.

"Well, just tell Orielle I'm coming to get her," Alex said.

"You make it sound like you own her."

As a matter of fact, Alex thought to say, *I do own her.* "See you soon," she said instead, and hung up. She wrestled into a pair of baggy denim shorts, then stormed down the hallway to find her car keys. But midway into the living room she stopped in her tracks, her breathing quick and heavy, and wondered just what it was she planned to do when she did get there. Order Orielle home? What if Orielle didn't want to come home? Then what?

"Shit...!" Alex scowled, looking toward the kitchen, thinking of other options. But when only one came to mind she marched into the kitchen in a jealous rage, flung open the freezer door and eyed the bell.

(((

"Maybe I shouldn't have lied to her," Ana Mae was saying to Orielle. "I didn't realize she was so possessive of you."

"Possessive?" Orielle said. "Alex has no desire to possess me."

"Could've fooled me." Ana Mae took a breath, ready to speak again, but then hesitated. "Forgive me for prying, but...you two aren't...romantically involved?"

"Alex and I? I wish we were, but...Alex hardly shows any interest at all."

"She doesn't?" Ana Mae's face was a puzzle waiting to be solved. "So you're...you're not sleeping together?"

"Alex is too respectable for that."

"Alex? Respectable? Are we talking about the same woman? I was sure she'd have charmed the socks off you by now."

"Oh, no...Alex isn't at all charming."

"She's not?" Ana Mae asked, perplexed. "Well, you know, charming in a playful way. Alex has a very playful sense of humor...women usually like that about her."

"I suppose I've seen only her serious side."

Ana Mae regarded her strangely. "And you're not sleeping together..." she repeated under her breath, as if struggling to convince herself of the fact.

Orielle shook her head. "Alex sleeps on the sofa, mostly."

Ana Mae's brow beetled suspiciously. She leaned back in her chair, rubbing her chin, taking a moment to study Orielle. "Well I'll be darned," she said with sudden conviction, "Alex is falling in love...."

The sound of those words sent a twinge of excitement through Orielle. "Oh, Ana Mae, do you really think so?" she asked, smiling as she sipped from her glass. But as she swallowed, the sudden ringing in her ears caught her by surprise and she gasped, nearly choking on her margarita.

"You okay, honey?"

Orielle nodded and reached for a raspberry-colored napkin with which to pat her mouth. "Yes, I'm...I'm fine," she said.

"Pardon?" Ana Mae said.

"...fine," Orielle said, but her voice was already fading to a whisper. "May I use the ladies' room?" she asked, forcing out the words and a smile along with them. But her mind was spinning, and the room right along with it, it seemed.

"Of course—right over there, Orielle," Ana Mae said, pointing to a door covered in the same fabric as the raspberry-patterned tablecloths. "Are you sure you're okay?"

"Yes..." she said, fighting the weightless sensation and inconspicuously using the table for support as she got up and excused herself. She kept smiling at Ana Mae, knowing her voice was gone and no sound would come if she tried to speak again.

Panic set in. Orielle could barely feel her legs now. Waves of vertigo blurred her vision. She focused all her remaining energy on walking straight, on reaching the bathroom. And when she had, she locked the door and leaned over the sink, giving in to the dizziness as she sank to her knees and lost consciousness.

❨ ❨ ❨

"Well, it's about time!" Alex said, tapping both her foot and her watch. She stared as the colors arranged themselves, quickly collecting in the outline of Orielle's body—the black silk shirt, fair skin, dark and fiery waves of hair. *She is beautiful, isn't she,* Alex thought—*even now in a blurred and half-composed state.*

But as Orielle's gray eyes grew sharp and clear, Alex saw she wasn't smiling. Fear filled her—not like the first night, not a fear of Orielle, but of Orielle's reaction to what she'd just done. Dashing out of the kitchen, Alex ran into the hallway, then stopped, turned and cautiously peeked back in.

The fairy was furious; Alex could see that now. Probably physically upset, too, from the sudden commute and all. There was a spark—a flare—of disapproval in those crystal eyes, and Alex suddenly regretted what she had done.

"How *could* you...?" Orielle said, her voice stern and even.

Alex shrugged.

"Were your intentions to thaw the bell so that Lilah could track us before the solstice?"

"No! It's in the freezer—I swear!" Alex guiltily shifted her eyes. "I put it back as soon as I rang it."

"I see... So maybe you simply wanted me to put on a magic show...a disappearing act...for Ana Mae...?"

Alex stood speechless, like a child being reprimanded, her dark eyes as blank as they were wide.

"I'm sorry," she finally blurted defensively. "But...well... what about *me*?"

"Yes, Alex...what *about* you?"

Alex flailed an arm, gesturing nervously at the front door. "I've been out there all day....preparing to save your life and...and all you can think about is running off to bed with the first woman you meet!"

"To bed? With the first woman I *meet?*"

"That's right—Ana Mae said you were with some other woman."

"I was with Ana Mae, Alex...talking about you, mostly."

"Well then...then she lied. Why did she lie?"

"Maybe she has to lie in order to get *you* to tell the *truth*."

"So you...you weren't with Ellen?"

Orielle stared at Alex, her lips twitching with slight amusement. "Is that what this is all about?" She gave Alex a curious, sidelong glance. "Are you jealous, Alex...?"

"Me? Why would I be jealous?"

"Why did you ring for me?"

"Because I...I couldn't find my black silk shirt. That's why," Alex feebly said.

Orielle tilted her head sideways. "Your *shirt...?*"

"The one you're wearing," Alex said sheepishly. "It was gone from the hanger, so I...I didn't know what happened to it."

"Your *shirt...!*" Orielle repeated, thoroughly amazed that Alex could even muster such a poor excuse. But she shrugged concedingly, and began to slowly unbutton the shirt.

"Wait!" Alex panicked. "What are you doing?"

"Giving you your shirt...so you can keep your *date*."

"I don't need it now—it's too late. I couldn't find it and didn't have time to iron another because...because, well, I was out all day, you know, so...so I just canceled my date," Alex said, all in one breath. But she knew Orielle wasn't buying a word of it.

"I see." Orielle nodded, pretending to go along with the story, but it didn't stop her from unbuttoning the shirt. She held Alex's eyes with her own as she let the black silk slide off her shoulders and down her arms.

Alex stood there, helpless, unable to turn her eyes from the fairy's breasts, from the nipples that she had only seen as shadows beneath Orielle's white dress...until now.

"Maybe you can still keep your date after all," she suggested, handing the shirt to Alex.

"Please," Alex said, her voice unsteady, and turned her head in refusal. "Put it back on...I'll take you back to Raspberries."

"No, Alex. I'm not going back. You rang for me...I came to you....now tell me what it is you want."

Alex swallowed dryly, trying not to look at Orielle. It wasn't just her breasts—wasn't the fact of her standing there half naked—it was something about all of her: the way her hair caught the light and streaked her shoulders, the way her lips softly shaped themselves into a subtle, almost sultry smile. There was something about her eyes, too—an agenda in them.

"I don't feel so well," Alex blurted.

"What seems to be the trouble?"

"I don't know..." Alex shrugged stupidly, her head still turned away. "I feel sort of...sort of *weak*," she squeaked.

Orielle's smile broadened just a bit. "And if you were never weak...however would I know the joy of comforting you?" She took Alex's face in her hand. "Look at me...."

Alex hesitated, suppressing a desire to kiss Orielle again, to put her hand over the hand that so gently, lovingly, stroked her face. She tried to smile, but a quavering sigh was all she achieved.

"Take me to bed...." Orielle began again, "and take what you really want from me."

"I can't," Alex said, lowering both her voice and her eyes.

"But you can...."

Alex realized her hands were shaking. She hid them behind her back and leaned against the wall, staring up at the ceiling and away from Orielle. "Really, I can't."

"*Yes*, Alex...you *can*. Tell me you do not want to, or that you will not let yourself...but don't tell me you *can't*."

"No..." Alex said. "Honestly, I can't because...." She paused, her eyes welling. "Because I don't know what I'd do if I ever...ever fell in love with you," she said, daring to meet Orielle's eyes again.

With the back of her hand, Orielle stroked Alex's face, affectionately searching her sable eyes and seeming to understand the mixture of fear and desire which tore Alex from within. "You already love me, Alex...you loved me long before you ever met me."

"Orielle, I..."

"Alex," she whispered, taking and pressing Alex's hand to her breast. "Come inside my heart tonight...and in it you will find your own again."

"But I—I'm afraid I'm just not good at this."

Orielle smiled sweetly. "With all the companions you keep? I'm expecting you to be *exceptionally* good."

"I meant at loving, Orielle. I'm not good at loving."

"Then you will learn... I will teach you to teach yourself."

"Oh, sure," Alex complained. "So I'll get good at that, too, and...and then you'll go. Something will happen."

Stepping closer, Orielle reached up and softly kissed her cheek. "I'm not going anywhere, Alex...only to bed with you." Without waiting for a response, Orielle turned in the hallway.

"Wait..." Alex said, reaching in desperation and catching Orielle by the waist. But when Orielle turned and Alex found the fairy in her arms, she wasn't quite sure what to do next.

"Yes...?" Orielle asked expectantly.

But Alex could only stare, thinking that the fairy's eyes looked like stars, lighting the way, as it were—compelling Alex to follow her. "Just...just...*wait!* Please," Alex begged, loosening the hold she had on Orielle's waist.

"No, Alex..." Orielle whispered, "I do not want to wait."

Alex rubbed the perspiration from her brow. "You don't?"

"No, I don't...and neither do you." Slowly then, Orielle backed up and extended her arms, taking hold of Alex's hands and gently pulling, urging her toward the bedroom.

But once Alex reached the doorway to the room, she couldn't move. She stood there paralyzed, her hands slipping from the fairy's waistband as Orielle moved toward the poster bed, shedding her remaining clothes in the subdued afternoon light.

Alex wondered why it was that she, and not Orielle, felt so inexperienced, so virginal. And despite the fresh air moving through the open window, it seemed there wasn't nearly enough oxygen in the room. Alex thought to run out, to go to the kitchen and breathe into a paper bag until she could collect her thoughts. But although it was only a thought, she must have thought it aloud because Orielle quickly responded.

"Forget the bag, Alex. You do not *need* to breathe in...you need to breathe *out*," she said, not the least bit alarmed—even a bit entertained, in fact—by the sight of Alex nervously breathing through her mouth. "Just let it out, Alex...you *need* to let it all go."

Quite nonchalantly then, Orielle climbed upon the bed, tucking her legs beneath her. A balmy breeze wafted through the open windows, stirring the warm colors in Orielle's hair and sending the soft scent of her skin toward Alex.

Alex regarded the beautiful outline of Orielle's figure, thinking that the room might just as well have been an enchanted pond, the bed itself a lilypad on which the fairy was floating.

"Give me your hand..." Orielle persisted, extending her arm once more and looking upon Alex with such tenderness that, for a moment, Alex had to shut her eyes against the surge of emotion she felt.

"You don't understand," she said, "it's not that easy. When you take my hand, Orielle, it's like you're taking my...my life."

"Then put your life in my hands...so that on the solstice I may do the same." And again she offered her hand.

Hesitantly, Alex moved toward the bed, stopping inches away, and held on to a post for support.

Kneeling on the bed, Orielle moved close and reached for Alex, slipping her fingers inside Alex's waistband and pulling her close so that Alex's legs butted up against the mattress.

She was being charmed, seduced, she knew; her poorly planned scheme to make Orielle come home had backfired—blown up in her face, really. She knew this. Orielle knew it, too. And if Alex didn't know better, she'd have sworn Orielle was enjoying the advantage.

"Make me a woman, Alex...I want to know how it feels to be a woman," she whispered. Slowing then, she began stealing through what little clothes Alex wore, unbuttoning one article, unzippering another, until Alex felt both her shirt and shorts slip to the floor. She stood frozen, her heart pounding with fear, her body throbbing with such desire that her whole being was beginning to hurt. And as Orielle tenderly touched her arms, her shoulders, her breasts, Alex's chest heaved, her nipples growing erect.

"I want you, Alex," she said, "...you rang the bell because it was the only way of telling me you want me, too," she whispered, her lips brushing against Alex's, her body pressing against her still-standing lover.

Alex parted her lips to answer, but she was afraid that if she tried—if she tried to utter a single word—something else might happen; she might cry or flee or—or lose control of everything she fought to contain right now.

But Orielle's mouth quickly took advantage of Alex's parted lips. And Alex lost herself in the gentleness, the warmth of Orielle's kisses, felt herself begin to helplessly yield until, all at once, something inside—her emotions perhaps—seemed to give way and collapse on themselves, forcing the breath from Alex as they did. "I do..." Alex hoarsely whispered, her words coming in short gasps, "I do want...I want to love you...." And Alex did. She'd known that all along, hadn't she? And now, staring into Orielle's starry eyes, glimpsing her naked beauty, she wanted to be to her what no other woman could be to her.

Alex paused, hesitating for an instant, but then she abandoned herself, crawled on the bed, over the sheets, her mouth hungrily following Orielle's mouth as the fairy lay back and drew Alex to her. "Take me, Alex..." she whispered, "take me and heal yourself."

And as Orielle received her, Alex slowly lowered her weight onto Orielle's naked body, her leg grazing Orielle's wet invitation as she did. Alex wanted to touch it, to discover it for Orielle. But she didn't; she would make this last...last until she could no longer bear the fire that now burned in her veins.

✥ 24 ✥
The Heart of the Matter

"Alex?"

"Hmm?"

"Are you asleep?" Orielle whispered.

"Mmm...."

"It's almost nine."

Sleepily, Alex lifted her head from the warmth of Orielle's breast and gazed at the window. The room was set in shadows, cooler air moving in on the breeze, and outside the trees were darkening, all silhouetted against a pale rose sky. "It's chilly," she said, pulling the soft cotton blanket up around them both, their bodies still damp from love making.

"Are you hungry?"

"Starving," Alex whispered, snuggling close to Orielle's breast again.

"Let me make us something...."

"Let's go out," Alex said. "Somewhere quiet and cozy and...." Then she spied the flashing light on her answering machine and added, "...somewhere Ana Mae won't find us."

Orielle brushed away the unruly black locks which fell across Alex's forehead and kissed her. And kissed her again. "I don't want to get dressed, Alex. I want to stay with you...like this...all night."

Alex smiled at her. "Then I'll just have to ring for room service—where'd I put that bell, anyway?" she teased.

"That's hardly funny," Orielle reprimanded.

But Alex laughed anyway, rolling on her back, and pulled Orielle on top of her.

"You've had occasion to ring that bell two times...and look what trouble it has gotten you into," Orielle murmured, trying to roll herself off Alex.

But Alex only held tighter and rolled with her, so that they both came to rest face to face on their sides. "Then I'll have to serve you in bed," Alex said.

"Serve me?"

"You've played the enchanted servant too long. It's time you played master, don't you think?"

"Mistress," Orielle corrected.

"That too." Alex paused, kissing her neck then running her lips up to Orielle's ear. "And I *would* be your servant, you know...you have that power over me," Alex confessed, teasing Orielle's earlobe with her lips.

"I don't imagine you'd make a good servant," Orielle good-humoredly pondered.

"Me? Sure..." Alex argued, her face still buried in Orielle's neck, "I'd even peel grapes for you."

Against her cheek Alex felt the crease of Orielle's smile, and she pulled back then, propping herself up on an elbow to study her fairy's face.

Adoringly, Orielle gazed back at the face above her.

Alex winked, smiled just a bit, but just as quickly her smile vanished and, once more, she was sensitive to the feel of their damp and tangled bodies. What little light was left in the room now seemed to concentrate itself in Orielle's eyes, so that for a moment, in the shadows, they appeared a silver-gray, her hair as dark and richly colored as the bark of a redwood tree. And for an instant Orielle's primordial beauty took Alex's breath away.

"Let me light a candle," Alex whispered, "...so I can see all of you." Stretching across the fairy's body, Alex opened the night-table drawer on Orielle's side of the bed, and fumbled around inside it. She pulled out a cigarette lighter first, then a beeswax candle which she lit, using it to light the drawer for further inspection. "I thought I had a candle holder in here," she commented, handing Orielle the lighted candle and climbing out of bed.

"Are you certain you want to?"

Spying a candle stick on the dresser, Alex slipped into her robe, tilting her head in question as she did. "What do you mean?"

"If you put your candle in a holder," Orielle whispered, "however will you burn it at both ends...?"

Alex stood over the bed, taking the burning taper from her, and taking a moment to revel in the ethereal sight of her lover in the candle light. "I suppose I'll just have to change my no-good, candle-burning ways...won't I?"

"Yes, you will, Alex...if it is me with whom you desire to be."

Whether that was a warning or an ultimatum, Alex wasn't sure; but she *did* want to be with Orielle...again and again and again. That's what scared her to death, wasn't it? But for the first time in years—maybe in her whole life—she felt ready to cope with the emotional confusion. Maybe it was okay, she told herself, to be in love and afraid of losing that love...to want something as much as you fear it. "Don't go anywhere," she said, tying her sash. "I'll be right back."

(((

Alex set a glass of Zinfandel on either night stand, a tray of bread, hummus and fruit on the mattress between them, then slipped out of her robe and crawled back into bed. "Well...at least the hard part is over..." Alex mused, after she was settled again.

"The hard part...?"

"Letting myself make love to you..." Alex said. "Now I just have to face Lilah and slay the dragon," she joked, trying to make light of what lay ahead.

"You just slew your dragon," Orielle said, kissing her with wine-coated lips.

Alex didn't answer. She gazed knowingly upon Orielle.

"Perhaps I can convince you to do it again," the fairy said softly.

"Again...?"

"Yes...I want more of that."

"That...?" Alex smiled.

"What you did to my body, my senses. I want to feel that again...."

Alex pushed a grape between Orielle's lips, then leaned over the tray and kissed her. Alex's heart, her mind, her senses stirred to arousal by Orielle's verbal request. "I want to give you something first," Alex said, gesturing at the white envelope on the tray between them.

Orielle took it and peeked inside. "For me?" she asked, taking out the bulk of folded papers.

"From Benjamin," Alex said. "You don't have to sort through it now...but he wanted you to have it. He said you'd find the deed to your father's property in it."

"In Saratoga?" There was an edge of shock in her voice.

Alex nodded. "Your father's grave is there, too." She hesitated for a moment, reaching for something slipping out from the papers. "Is this a photograph?"

Orielle looked on as Alex held the snapshot up for her to see—a close- up, it appeared, of the epitaph on Steven Rutherford's headstone. "It says something..." Alex said.

Orielle took it, holding it up to catch the candlelight, and slowly read. "'Time...is too slow for those who wait, too swift for those who fear, too long for those who grieve, too short for those who rejoice...but for those who love...time is eternity.'"

"Van Dyke," Alex said, identifying the poet.

Orielle nodded appreciatively, her eyes glassy as she lowered the photo and turned to Alex. "He was a friend...one of my father's favorite poets."

"Mine, too...." Alex said, suddenly feeling a strange affinity with the departed Mr. Rutherford. It seemed he and Alex had quite a bit in common—poets and fairies, at least—and it occurred to Alex that they would have gotten on well; sipping brandy in the library of his estate and complaining—affectionately, of course—about Orielle and her mother.

"*Fairies...*" Alex would say to Mr. Rutherford. "*Yes...fairies...*" would come his reply. "Can't live with them, can't live without them." And then they'd discuss poetry and the like—maybe she'd even have gotten to meet Henry Van Dyke. Entertaining the notion filled Alex with a sense of loss, of regret that she'd never have that opportunity. She looked over at his daughter, instead, trailing a finger down Orielle's cheek and stopping under her chin. "I'll take you if you like...."

Orielle looked perplexed. "Take me?"

"Tomorrow. We could drive up there for a few hours...if you'd like to visit his grave...."

"In Saratoga?"

"Why not?"

"You would do that for me?"

"Of course I would," she said, surprised that Orielle should seem surprised. "I'll take you anywhere you like. It's *your* day."

Orielle touched her softly. "It may be my last day, Alex."

"I know," Alex said with a heavy sigh, although in truth, her heart couldn't bear the thought of it. "So we'll go, okay? If that's where you want to be."

"I want to be where you are, Alex...and if we could go there...together...that would make me very happy."

"Then it will be my pleasure to make you happy." She smiled tenderly. "We'll drive up in the morning...stop along the way."

"You *do* make me happy...*tonight* you have made me happy...in a way so wonderful and new."

Their eyes locked in the candlelight and desire mounted in Alex. And as they stared at one another in the shared silence, Alex took the photo and envelope from Orielle, laid them on the night stand, then took the tray that separated them and lowered it to the carpeted floor.

"Come close to me," Alex said.

And without another word Orielle moved close beneath the sheets, seeking the comfort of her lover and climbing atop Alex's body with a soft sigh of pleasure.

✦ 25 ✦
Belladonna and the Devil

There had been periods in Alex's life when time had been a prison. But now, now that she would have wanted time to stand still, the hours seemed to spill away like water through her fingers.

Upon their arrival at the Rutherford estate, Alex had suppressed her anxiety at entering the cemetery. But Orielle, sensitive to Alex's secret uneasiness, had quietly taken her hand and kept her close. And in a short time, the comfort of Orielle's hand, the fragrance of her nearness—even the reassurance in her eyes, the warm shine of the sun on her hair—made the fear dissipate. Strangely, this place, the gravesite of Mr. Rutherford, no longer seemed the unhappy and inevitable conclusion to all of life, but a place of transfiguration—a sort of celestial airport, Alex imagined. And it made her think of her own father...of the beloved few who had departed so abruptly from her own life.

The two wandered about for a while, Orielle leading Alex through a blooming botanical maze, to the waterfall where her parents had fallen in love, to the gardens where the fairy had played as a child.

Dogbane and bluebells blossomed, roses and mountain laurel splashing the entire estate in a blissful array of whites and pastels. From the elms and sweetgum trees came songs so heavenly that they might not have been coming from birds at all, but from a chorus of angels and fairies. All of it overwhelmed Alex's senses, filling her with a haunting, yet indefinable sense of peace. And she suddenly felt they weren't alone. There was something about this place, an energy reaching almost palpable proportions. It was more than memories...there was an undying love which lingered and still lived here.

"You feel it...don't you..." Orielle asked.

Alex only gazed at her and swallowed.

"You feel it in your heart...."

Alex swallowed again. "Yes..." she finally answered.

Orielle smiled lovingly, placed her hand on Alex's chest. "I'm glad that you do, Alex...glad that you are *able* to." She looked up, seeing the leaves moving against the blue sky. "It's the powers waking," she said. "The energies are rising."

Alex swallowed but said nothing, realizing the significance of Orielle's words. It reminded her of their urgent need to be getting home soon.

As if reading her mind again, Orielle said, "Can we say goodbye to my father before we go?"

"Of course," Alex replied softly, thinking how quickly their time in Saratoga, like their tender night together, had flown. How she wished she could have slowed time's flight.

◖ ◖ ◖

They arrived home at 3:30 p.m., mere minutes before the official arrival of the summer solstice. And no sooner had Alex closed the door behind her than Benjamin, Batilda and Booga-woog made their appearance. Impatiently, Batilda rapped on the screen door, letting herself in before Alex could even get to it.

Benjamin, as anyone might have guessed, came dressed in a black suit. His countenance grim, a white carnation fixed to his lapel, he looked something like a funeral director, which did nothing to help Alex's nerves. He wore white tennis sneakers, though—a gift from Mary, who, he said, had insisted he wear them lest he slip on the slimy floors of the cave and smash both his head and the sound accelerator. Mary had purchased matching sneakers for Batilda, but aside from that, the harpy, too, was clad in black—the familiar black house dress and the black western hat.

"You two going on safari or something?" Batilda said by way of greeting as she walked in. Alex realized she was poking fun at what Alex liked to think of as her outdoor preparedness.

Yes, Alex wanted to say, *we'll have our elephant drop you and Benjamin at the Halloween party on our way.* But she didn't. She had neither the energy nor the inclination to bicker with Batilda. Instead, she looked at the blending of olive green and khaki colors she and Orielle wore, and at their hiking shoes, cotton trousers and fishing vests over long-sleeved shirts. "I see your point," she said tersely.

"And what's that awful smell?" Batilda asked, sniffing the air like a dog and waving her hand in displeasure. "You making poisons in here?"

"It's insect repellent," Alex said. "And I'd advise the two of you to spray some on...put some on the dog, too." She gestured toward the table where her Jansport knapsack lay, ready to go, the scroll of her fiddle sticking out from the unzipped top.

"You want repellent," Batilda pressed, I'll give ya repellent," she said, taking out a clear round bottle from her own sack. The bottle was full, a small, waterlogged cross resting at the bottom.

"Is that the holy water?" Alex asked.

Batilda crookedly grinned, flashing her equally crooked teeth. "This stuff'll repel worse things than skeeters, Kiddo."

Alex braced herself, wincing as Batilda unplugged the bottle and spread the water across her forehead with a rough and calloused thumb.

"There came a time," Benjamin interjected, "when we couldn't touch it."

Alex shook her head. "Touch what?"

"The holy water," Batilda butted in. "Made our flesh burn. Honest to God. Ask Birdwhistle."

Benjamin looked shamefully down at his hands, and Alex's eyes followed his line of vision to the tiny scars she'd noticed earlier. "After the Fountain was found, the bell crafted and Orielle enslaved...after we had unknowingly served our purpose...Lilah decided we'd overstayed our welcome," Benjamin began.

"She asked us to run a little errand," Batilda finished.

"It was the time of the Samhain ceremonies and feasts. We were instructed to fetch an urn of holy water from a little white church up on the hill." Batilda pointed in the direction of the living room windows. "It's not there anymore, but it was then, and we had to walk past the marsh to get to it."

"It was the night of the new moon," Benjamin added, "and so we couldn't see the imps coming until they came within the glow of the lantern we carried."

"We heard them, though," Batilda chimed in. "You could hear the slap-slap-slapping of their wet feet against the ground. They have feet like frogs, you know," she said, widening her black eyes in Alex's face, "big heads on tiny bodies, and faces like kids...until they smile and you see the rotten meat of carcasses hanging between their pointy teeth. And then—"

"Do I need to hear this?" Alex snapped. "I don't *need* to hear this," she said to Orielle.

"Alex doesn't need to hear this," Orielle said.

"Spare me," Alex angrily complained.

"Don't get smart with me," Batilda warned, waggling a bony finger in Alex's face.

"Please," Benjamin intervened. "We're all a tad on edge," he said, apologizing for Batilda's deportment. "But *we*, not the imps, are the point of the story," he reminded Batilda.

"Anyway," Batilda said, "we panicked when they surrounded us. Turned to run and bumped right into each other. Nearly knocked ourselves out. Lilah'd set us up to be killed—"

"Eaten alive by the blasted creatures!" Benjamin agreed.

"We almost dropped the urn," she said. "The top flew off and, not knowing what else to do, we went wild, splashing those abominations with the holy water. And they hopped back into the marsh, hissing as their skins sizzled."

"Needless to say," Benjamin said, "we escaped...only to discover that our own hands were covered with second degree burns." He lowered his eyes with the confession. "We had become evil, Alex...as evil as any creature who has crawled up from the depths of hell. And that revelation, the sight of our melted flesh—coupled with Lilah's harsh rejection, of course—"

"To put it mildly," Batilda pointed out.

"Yes...to put it mildly," he agreed. "That's what prompted us to take moral inventory of ourselves."

The four spent the next few hours discussing details and trying to force down some food, although only the dog seemed to have anything of an appetite. And before they left—when all of them, Boogawoog included, had been anointed with holy water, then anointed again with insect repellent—Batilda presented Alex with the ouanga bag she'd custom made.

On a black leather string the talisman hung like a sachet around Alex's neck. "Custom made," Batilda said, tucking the small bundle inside her shirt. "Your body heat will release the aroma. Smell it, touch it when you need to...and if anything goes wrong, if you accidentally get poisoned...*suck on it*!"

☾ ☾ ☾

A rose-colored sun sank low in the lavender sky as the four travellers picked their way through the tall grasses and golden club, finally sliding the rowboat into the creek. Everyone stuffed their belongings into the bow of the rowboat—save for Benjamin who refused to let go of his attaché case. He insisted on keeping it in his lap, so that it seemed he was sitting on a train, rushing off to the office, say, instead of a cave.

Cattails and pickerelweed grew high along the shore. The air was cooling, the sky darkening as Alex pushed off shore.

Rippling the water, the flat-bottomed rowboat glided quietly through swamp pinks and duckweed and pond lilies, until finally the water grew clear and deep, allowing Alex to settle back and begin paddling up river.

In no time the night sky turned black, the constellations became visible and a strawberry ring encircled the full solstice moon. But although the sky was clear, a heavy fog was forming on the river, enveloping the travellers as if with an invisible cloak. The beam of the flashlight Orielle held picked up pairs of glowing orange eyes here and there along the shoreline.

"Beaver," Alex answered, in response to Orielle's questioning eyes. But just as she said it, something hit the water with such force that everyone in the rowboat flinched.

"Beaver tails," Alex said, calming them. "There's a big beaver lodge over there on our right." She gestured with a paddle. Through the swirling mist the sticks and branches of the rounded structure were faintly visible as they passed—as faintly visible as Batilda and Benjamin seated directly opposite her. The fog made them look as though they were in a cloud and it saddened Alex to think that the two of them would die tonight. Even Boogawoog, sniffing the water, and with her paws hanging over the side— happy to be along for the ride—had her hours numbered.

And now the moon, Alex would have sworn, was developing facial features; it looked like a skull, dark depressions lending it a hollow-eyed and sinister aspect.

Alex pressed on, breathing in rhythm with the movement of her paddles, concentrating on keeping her thoughts at bay, her mood even. The crew, especially Batilda, was unusually quiet, and the eerie silence wasn't helping Alex's nerves one bit. The only comfort was in knowing Orielle was by her side, the flashlight held in one hand, the thumb of the other tucked in the loop of Alex's pants, as if to remind Alex, simply, that she was there.

☾ ☾ ☾

Ghostly tendrils of mist curled up like swamp gas to meet the light of the bone white moon. The river fog was nearly impenetrable by the time they reached their destination. Alex paddled slowly now, the rowboat gliding soundlessly along the shore as she steered into the mouth of a little creek. Silently, they got out. The ground was spongy, the vegetation dense at first. An assortment of bellowing, peeping and ribbeting frogs fell away behind them as they gathered their gear and worked their way to higher ground. Boogawoog, after Batilda had given her a couple of biscuits and a drink, took the lead, sniffing and grunting incoherent obscenities.

"Look," Benjamin said, pointing up to the full moon.

The lunar sphere was slightly lopsided.

"It's here," Orielle said. "The eclipse is beginning."

Involuntarily, Alex gripped the fairy's hand tighter, as though doing so might help to hang on to all the night threatened to steal. But then there was an unfamiliar sound—a heavy hopping over stones and sticks, as though something from the river were stalking them. Alex spun around. Boogawoog pivoted along with her, the dog's sniffs turning to snorts, the tips of her canines flashing as she formed syllables. "K-KILL..." she snarled, back legs planted apart in an aggressive stance. "BOOGIE K-K-KILL...."

At once, the others enclosed Alex. "The meat," Benjamin said. "Quick!"

But Batilda already had her sack open and was rummaging through it. "This will hold them," she jeered, holding up a large Ziploc freezer bag.

Alex couldn't identify its contents, but whatever was in it was raw, bloody and chopped beyond recognition. And when Batilda opened it, the stench made her turn away. "What the hell did you put in there?"

"Raw meat."

"What did you do to it?"

Batilda grinned menacingly. "We...how should I say... *marinated* it."

"In poison?"

"Laxatives." She held up her hand. "I know—I know," she said, "It's not my style. But considering I was hit by a car this week, had my cottage broken into, my work destroyed...I think it's a pretty damn *ingenious* idea if I do say so *myself.*"

"What's it going to do?"

"This stuff'll dissolve their guts as fast as spider venom." Then, "Stay!" she ordered Boogawoog, holding the bag and heaving the rancid meat into the brush.

The woods were quiet for a moment, and then, all at once bloodcurdling screams ripped through the silence. The impish creatures, ravenous as jackals, rushed from the shadows, yowling and yipping, as they fought for bits of the flesh.

"Leave them," Benjamin instructed. "We must hurry."

"Dig, Boogie-girl," Batilda whispered harshly. "Take us to Lilah's hole."

"YEAH, YEAH, B-B-B-BOOGIE FIND HOLE...."

"That's what I thought you'd say." Batilda bent, her bones creaking, and gave the dog's side a hearty pat. "That's my good Scot. Now go to it—go dig for mama!"

With her nose to the ground, as if tracking a fox to its hole, Boogawoog went enthusiastically about her business. "DIG IT, DIG IT," she snorted, moving wildly about in figure eights.

"There are entrances up on the hill, you know," Alex said.

"Why drag our asses up those hills...?" Batilda said. "We're going in the back door."

And before Alex could think of more reasonable alternatives to accessing the caves, Boogawoog let out a rolling howl.

"She's found it," Orielle said, an unmistakable dread in her voice.

Through the trees and against a pile of rocks, the Scottish terrier's body was silhouetted in the moonlight, her head poking down into something.

"The cover has been removed," Benjamin said, as the others caught up to the manhole-sized opening over which Boogawoog growled. "I suppose we can assume it's an open invitation...."

Alex peered down at what seemed a wooden staircase to a cellar. It was dark, but a faint blue haze emanated from somewhere within. "Has this always been here?"

"At least a century," Batilda said.

Alex's stomach sank at the prospect of journeying down into the bowels of Lilah's lair.

Benjamin checked his watch. "Thirty minutes and the eclipse will be full...another thirty until it's over...."

Batilda nodded. "Well, Kiddo," she said to Alex, "you best go first...it's *you* my lethal lover waits for."

Benjamin lifted his head, peering haughtily down his nose at Batilda. "Need I remind you she was *my* lover, too?"

"She was mine first, Birdwhistle! All mine until you came along and—"

"Stop it...!" Orielle ordered.

Batilda frowned. "Aah..." she said, abruptly giving up the fight and stepping close to straighten Benjamin's bow tie. "You were something in your time, old man...." She frowned at him—almost affectionately, Alex thought. "A dapper drake you were."

"And you a dapper dyke," he said with a thin smile. His tiny blue eyes filled with sadness then, and it occurred to Alex that Benjamin wasn't as cheerful about his demise as he had been yesterday, in the meadow. "Well, this is it," he said to Alex. "Mary has agreed to keep Sheeky and...well...the dog will be joining us." He glanced at Boogawoog and Batilda once more. "May our three souls travel together."

"Don't start gettin' sentimental on us," Batilda warned, as Benjamin bid Orielle a farewell. The harpy was fidgeting with the vestigial wings on her back now, noticeably uncomfortable with Benjamin's emotional exchange.

And Alex felt the same way. She didn't like goodbyes...didn't even know how to *say* goodbye, really. "Can we just...*do this*...before I change my mind, please?"

Benjamin held out his arm. "After you," he said. "Twelve steps down, then make a left...you'll see the lighted path. It will take us the rest of the way down...."

Alex patted the bell and the water gun in her vest pockets, then took a deep breath and eased herself into the mouth of the earth.

"Hey, Alex," Batilda called.

Alex stopped on the fourth step and peered up from the darkness. "What?"

Batilda winked at her. "It's been swell," was all she said.

Alex nodded, her throat dry, then continued down.

❧ 26 ❧
Every Dog Has Its Day

The humidity built as they descended into the blue haze, the narrow passageway winding before them like an outstretched serpent. Suddenly, Alex was struck with the disturbing feeling that she wasn't in the subterranean land of New York State anymore, but in the gallery of a European catacomb. She looked up, and passed her flashlight over the enchanting flowstone formations and ancient, water-carved walls. Stalactites, like giant icicles, hung from the vast ceiling, giving the cave a wintry appearance. Beneath her shoes, the floor felt smooth and slick, and somewhere in the distance came the echoing of dripping water.

"What?" Alex asked suddenly, jerking around to face the others.

Orielle looked over at Benjamin and Batilda, then shook her head. "No one said anything, Alex."

"But I heard my name, someone called my..." And then it happened again. A whisper...*Alex...Alex....*

Alex swiveled around, her eyes widening in fear as she searched the shadows behind her. But the whispers, as faint as the sound of the dripping water, seemed to come from everywhere.

"The voice is inside your head," Batilda said.

"It's Lilah violating your thoughts," Benjamin confirmed.

"But—but you hear it, don't you?"

"No," he said, "she cannot invade our minds, Alex...only the mind of the one who keeps her bell." He put a hand on Alex's shoulder and searched her eyes. "Remember this one thing, Alex...evil often hides behind a mask of beauty. If it didn't, it would repel rather than draw us to it." He studied her for a moment. "Don't be seduced by that beauty Alex...it is illusory."

Alex nodded, her lips parting to speak, but then amidst the dripping water and sweet whispers, a rhythmic humming began to sound. Alex looked to Orielle for help.

"That *is* real," Orielle said. "We hear it, too." She took Alex's hand, mentally grounding her. "It is the pulse of the rising energies you hear. The fairies are gathering now...the ring is ready to form."

"Carry on," Benjamin said.

Her heart racing, Alex turned, but Batilda quickly put a gnarled hand on her shoulder. "Wait," she said, "give me the gun."

Alex turned and looked at her. "Why?"

"Because I said so—I've changed my mind."

Alex regarded her with uncertainty, chilled by the rage she saw mounting in those black snake eyes...the eyes of a killer, Alex concluded. "You don't trust me...do you?" she said, as she slowly unzipped a vest pocket and removed the poison gun.

Batilda took it from her. "It's Lilah I don't trust. Besides..." she said, with a rueful smirk, "I've decided the pleasure should be *mine....*"

In single file they pressed on, making steady headway toward the source of blue light. Shadows bounced off the walls, the light shifting, wavering, as if the light were coming from a fire. The trickling and plunking of water grew louder as they crept through the galleries. Then, abruptly, the passageway curved and widened, leaving them standing at the mouth of a spellbinding cavern.

Alex's mind whirled, her senses assaulted by a line of high blue flames which, as if by magic, burned in the center of the cave. And all around the flames were clusters of towering stalagmites, like trees in some primordial forest.

Benjamin held up a finger to his lips, silencing them before anyone could speak, then regarded each one in turn. "Lilah's telepathic powers are focused solely on you, Alex—I don't suspect she is yet aware of the rest of us. And let us pray that she believes Batilda to be dead...a surprise attack may be our only hope. And you, Orielle," he warned, "are not to enter the cavern until I call you in to remove the bell from Alex's pocket. Remember, your powers lie in the ability to heal, not to destroy—you are defenseless here."

Benjamin took a deep breath, slowly exhaling. "You must go in first, Alex. I will sneak in behind you—right behind you, don't you worry. Batilda will find her own way in."

Suddenly Benjamin's words were drowned out by the sweetest, most seductive voice Alex had ever heard: "Where are you, Alex? Come in so I can see you...." The words came in a deep and breathy whisper. And this time they were not inside Alex's head. They were coming from behind the fire.

Hunched behind Alex, Batilda quietly untied Alex's backpack, giving her ready access to her violin and bow. Then the witch gave her rump a push. "Go get her, Kiddo," she whispered. "But don't play until Benjamin cues you. And whatever you do, don't let anyone—or any*thing*—put their hands on that fiddle. Once Lilah knows Benjamin's here, she'll try to destroy anything that makes sound."

Stiff-legged, Alex entered the cavern and Boogawoog followed, growling protectively at her side as they moved several yards into the cavern. Alex paused then, using a hand to shield her eyes from the fire, and watched as Lilah came into focus. Only her face was visible, her body hidden behind the flames.

"Oooh...how very beautiful..." Lilah cooed.

But it was *Lilah* who was beautiful. Even in the blue light her skin was as fair and fine as porcelain, mirrored flames undulating in her eyes and giving them the brilliance of a sapphire-bottomed ocean. Her hair was pulled back, eyebrows naturally arching and accentuating her black widow's peak.

She smiled knowingly, her eyes sparkling with secrets. "How strange..." she commented, "...that you should remind me of someone I used to love...."

Alex heard Batilda spit back in the passageway.

Then, "Come, dear Alex," Lilah's sultry voice beckoned. "Come around the fire and give me what is mine...."

Alex felt a pressure on her eyes; the pressure of Lilah's own eyes holding her stare. She blinked a few times, patted the pocket which contained the bell with its clapper taped, then slowly padded her way around the flames. But the fire wasn't hot; on the contrary, a cool breeze seemed to come from it, as Alex moved around the flames and came into full view of the sorceress.

At the edge of an underground lake Lilah stood tall— barefoot amongst the bizarre cave formations—a shimmering, low-cut gown hugging her body so tightly that one might have mistaken her for a mermaid at first glance. And in her hand was a nearly empty glass of port wine. "What a pleasure it is..."

"The pleasure is mine," Alex heard herself say. She hadn't meant to say it—didn't know why she did.

Lilah smiled seductively, then parted and wet her lips, the tip of her tongue moving from one corner of her mouth clear across to the other. It was a wonderful tongue, really, a wonderful mouth—Lilah was wonderful. More wonderful than...than Orielle...than...any woman she had ever seen.

Alex stopped herself. What was happening to her? What was *wrong*? She was feeling...sort of...*intoxicated*. Not drunk, but strangely relaxed, as though *she* was the one who had just consumed the wine in Lilah's glass. Actually, she could almost taste it.

And Lilah seemed to read her thoughts. She peered into the glass she held and swirled the few remaining drops of wine. "You are tasting my *memory* of the wine...but perhaps you'd like to taste a glass with me...?"

Alex nodded.

Lilah pursed her lips in satisfaction. "How nice," she said, "how nice." And with that, she stepped up onto a low stone platform and moved across to the natural shelves jutting out from the cave walls. Candles burned on one, and on another rested the hundred-year-old bottle of port Batilda had talked about."

"No!" Benjamin called out urgently.

"Let her go," Alex heard Batilda whisper.

"We haven't time," he said, his words hushed but urgent.

"We haven't *time*...!"

"I have all the time in the world," Lilah said, spinning around at the sound of a familiar voice. "Is it you Benjamin, who hides in my gallery like a frightened mouse?"

"FILTHY MOUSE," Boogawoog grunted.

"But then," Lilah said, turning back and chuckling mockingly as she poured the port, "you always *were* more a mouse than a man. Good science, bad sex...and no sense of adventure. How very boring you were," she jeered. "Why, even Batilda was more a man...the man you could never be. Isn't that the truth? Isn't that right, Benjamin? *Isn't it?*"

Despite the swordlike edge to her words, Lilah's taunting tone did not affect the language of her body. Though she spoke harshly, she moved smoothly, sinuously. Lilah was the quintessence of sensuality.

"Lost for words, you impotent fool?" Lilah mocked.

Benjamin didn't say a word, but nearby Alex heard him sniffle. *She's breaking his spirit,* Alex thought.

Alex struggled to say something in his defense, and under normal circumstances would have, but right now she couldn't think of anything to say to this dazzling creature. Couldn't really *think* at all! It was as though her thoughts were...what?...running away with her.

She reached down into her shirt and rubbed the ouanga bag hanging around her neck, the herbal aroma briefly clearing her head like smelling salts. Quickly, she chanced a glance behind her and saw Benjamin crouched behind a stalagmite, its girth, like a tree trunk, concealing him. Only the bent elbow of his sleeve could be seen as he moved about, the antenna of his sound accelerator poking out slightly.

"Where are you, Benjamin?" Lilah playfully called, although his defiance obviously displeased her. "Benjamin...?"

"Leave him alone," Alex finally managed to say.

Lilah stepped down from the stone platform, the full glass of port in her hand, and tilted her head in consideration of Alex's request. "Perhaps *he* should leave *us* alone...to ourselves...." She lifted an exquisite brow seductively. "You *would* like that, Alex, wouldn't you? Tell the truth...."

Alex wasn't sure of the truth anymore. It felt as if there were an octopus on her head, squeezing her skull, its tentacles probing her brain.

"Yes, you sweet young thing, you would," she coaxed, moving closer with the glass, her lithesome form closing in on Alex. "You would like it if I wet your lips with my wine...then wet them with my love..."

Alex's chest heaved, and when the seductress licked her lips again, Alex found herself involuntarily imitating the gesture.

"It is illusory, Alex," came Benjamin's voice. "Her beauty, her love...her promises...they are all illusion."

"Oh, come now, Benjamin..." Lilah said. Then to Alex, "Can't you see he is jealous of me, of my youth...of your youth?" She pushed her lips out in a pouting expression, then gave Alex the once over. "I bet Benjamin—wherever he hides— has told you all sorts of terrible lies about me...hmm? Hasn't he?"

Alex regarded her silently.

"Yes, I see he has," Lilah said, pouting again as she slunk a bit closer. "But surely you understand his motivation for lying...." She reached out, softly tracing a pointy red thumbnail across Alex's strongly defined chin.

Alex winced at the touch of Lilah's razor-sharp nail. There was a burning sensation, like nicking her legs while shaving in the shower. She put a finger to her chin, flinching when she saw the smudge of blood on her fingertip.

Lilah only smiled at the red line across Alex's chin. "You needn't be afraid...it's only blood...the wine...the nectar on which your body feeds. And I, Alex, have the power to keep it clean...and pure...and fresh forever. Give me what I want and you will bathe with me."

"Illusion!" cried Benjamin from the wet and misty shadows. "Her fire burns cold, Alex."

"Show your wretched face, Benjamin—now!" Lilah demanded. "So I can laugh at how time has ravaged your once-young face..."

But it was Batilda who stepped out of the shadows instead, her unblinking eyes deadly in the firelight, her white hair wild like her rage.

The unexpected sight of Batilda instantly disarmed Lilah, and for the moment, Alex felt released from her psychic grip.

"Surprised, eh?" Batilda said, curtly. "Thought I was dead, eh? And I bet you weren't even gonna send a sympathy card." Then she grinned—viciously, Alex thought—and cackled at Lilah's stunned face.

But as soon as she did, Lilah shot her eyes at Alex, and Alex's mind grew fuzzy once more. Immediately, Batilda's resounding cackle began mingling with the rhythmic chanting that sounded somewhere over the water.

Lilah's eyes roved back to Batilda, her supple lips tightening.

But Batilda just shrugged matter-of-factly. "Come now, darlin', don't tell me you actually thought you'd killed me the other night." Batilda smiled menacingly. "You know I was never able to live without you. What makes you think I could ever *die* without you?"

Lilah lifted her lips in a feral grimace. It seemed she would have liked nothing more than to lunge like a wolf and tear Batilda's throat out. But there were rules to be played by here. Lilah knew that. She couldn't *take* the power; it had to be given to her.

Calculatingly, and still holding the glass of wine, Lilah's smile grew confident again. "My old and haggard love," she remarked to Batilda, "what a pity it is to see you in such an advanced stage of decay. To think your rotten face, your putrid mouth, was ever allowed between my legs...."

The words were like a punch in the gut to Batilda, nearly causing her to double over.

Lilah's smile softened, and she gazed at Alex, although it was Batilda she continued to address. "But there was a time, long ago, when your beauty was as grand as your great niece's."

"*SHUT UP!*" Batilda roared.

"Oh, my...have I let out a terrible secret?" Lilah sneered.

"You son-of-a-bitch," Batilda growled.

"B-B-B-B-BITCH!" Boogawoog seconded, challengingly trotting over to assist her mistress.

"Is that horrid little beast still alive?" Lilah asked, as if the dog were so insignificant that she only just now noticed its presence. "Alex *is* part of you, isn't she, Tilly? She is your flesh and blood...I can smell it...I can see you in her."

"Tilly?" Alex asked weakly, confused all over again, and only remotely aware that they were talking about her. "Tilly...?" she hoarsely managed again, a wave of vertigo washing over her. "Not my...my *Aunt* Tilly...."

Batilda fell silent, glaring at Lilah.

"Go on, Tilly...tell little Alex, here, what a terrible aunt you are."

Little Alex...little Alex... Alex began to feel little, as if she were shrinking inside. The pressure started again, a squeezing sensation in her head. "No...*No!*" she moaned, spreading her legs a bit to steady herself as she flashed her eyes at Batilda. "Are you?" Alex shouted. "*ARE YOU?*" she screamed.

"Yeah," Batilda said, her voice dropping in shame, her posture growing worse and worse until it seemed she was caving in on herself. "I am...."

"Alex, dear, you see?" Lilah chortled in triumph, "Batilda has lied to you all along—deserted you all along. She could have rescued you, you realize, raised you in that fabulous house she bought for herself in New Orleans—a big, beautiful house...with a big yard, and a pond, and a treehouse. But the truth is that she didn't want you."

Alex felt as if she were five years old again, and Lilah was shaming her, humiliating her, the way Aunt Sophie always had. She felt her mind, her soul constricting in pain, her head ready to explode.

The harpy narrowed her eyes at Lilah. "Burn in hell, you devil," she sputtered. Then, turning to Alex with tears in her eyes, she said defeatedly, "That's not the way it was. I wanted nothing more than to take you after the accident. I would have loved you, Alex...."

"Aunt Sophie said you *died*," Alex yelled, "that you died in a mental institution."

"A mental instit..." Batilda stopped, a look of surprise on her face. But then her face hardened again and she regarded Lilah. "Somebody *SHOULD* have locked me up to keep my ex-*LOVER* here from driving me mad!"

How could this be, Alex thought...or had she actually said it? She couldn't tell for sure whether she was thinking or speaking.

"Sophie wanted the money, Alex—she would have fought to keep me from taking you," Batilda rambled on. "And the courts never would have found me *fit*—do I look *fit?*"

Alex had to agree. Batilda didn't look at all fit.

"If they'd investigated me, why—why, they'd have linked me to dozens of unsolved poisonings," Batilda pressed on. "Sophie knew that, Alex. She knew something was wrong with me—that I was getting too old to still be alive. She threatened all sorts of things if I didn't stay away from you."

Benjamin began to clap from his hiding place. And he kept clapping. Clapping and clapping, as though he were applauding a play. But the sharp, resounding claps—probably purposeful on his part—served to clap Alex back to sobriety.

"All right then!" he jovially yelled, as though he had just appointed himself master of ceremonies, "Alex, my girl! Let's hear that caprice, shall we?"

Fighting dizziness, Alex nodded, more to herself—to that *part* of herself that still fought to stay in control. She paused, struggling to collect herself. Again, she reached for the ouanga bag and inhaled its fragrance deeply. The haze that surrounded her vanished instantly; the pressure in her brain eased for the moment. Then, in one concentrated effort, Alex reached a hand back over her shoulder and pulled out both her violin and bow. But her hands were shaking; shaking so violently that she couldn't bring it to her chin, and instead lowered her arms at her sides.

Lilah grew suspicious at the sight of the musical instrument, her eyes shifting rapidly between Alex, the direction from which Benjamin's faceless voice came, and Batilda, who now began approaching Lilah slowly.

"Stay back!" Lilah warned menacingly, drawing back her hand as if to pitch a ball. A circular blue light cracked the ground, bursting into another icy flame. For the moment, it held Batilda at bay. And as the flame grew high, Lilah looked up, her expression changing when she caught sight of something amazing.

Way up in the center of the rounded cave ceiling there appeared to be an opening—a natural porthole, no larger than a window—and through it they glimpsed an ethereal red ring shining in the night sky. Only a sliver of the white moon was still visible from where they stood. But as they stared up at it, swishing sounds below drew their attention from the moon. In the cavernous lake, a waterfall was forming, its dark and tumbling surface beginning to pop and fizz with tiny sparks of color. It looked as though myriad fireflies were dancing and lighting themselves over it.

Alex glanced at Lilah, but the sorceress's eyes were already fixed on Alex. "Give—me—what—is—mine! MINE!"

"Yours...?" Alex repeated, her throat so dry she could barely speak.

"Where is my BELL? Where is my SERVANT?" she demanded, staring at Alex's zippered pocket, as if she could actually see the brass object of her desire.

It occurred to Alex that Lilah's eyes weren't so beautiful anymore. They looked like ice crystals now—cold, frozen, devoid of any emotion except anger.

"No..." Alex said, backing away and again raising the violin to her chin.

Lilah dropped the glass in her hand. Crystal shattered against the wet, stone floor, the wine splattering like blood. Lilah was shocked, it seemed—shocked by Alex's refusal, by Benjamin's disobedience, by the threat of Batilda's presence and the potential danger of the violin in Alex's hand.

"Put...that...*DOWN*!" she roared in desperation.

But changes in the atmosphere of the cavern were accelerating now. The water was whirling, the cacophony of humming and chanting presently turning into sweet, female voices, and finally, the colors over the water blending into the ghostly forms of fairies.

Lilah's eyes darted to the water, up to the moon, then back to Alex. She paced herself, her tone deliberately low and breathy. "Give me the bell, Alex...."

"Give me an open G," Benjamin cheerfully called.

"Give me your violin," Lilah urged, "give me my bell...and I will grant you eternal youth." Her smile was dazzling, but her hands were stiff, her long-nailed fingers curling with the tension. It was clear that Lilah had no intention of preserving Alex's youth—she wanted Alex dead, wanted them all dead.

Ignoring her quaking insides, Alex lifted the bow. A knife-like pain stabbed at her temples as she brought it to her strings.

"Put that DOWN!" Lilah commanded again.

Moaning, her teeth clenched, Alex squinted her eyes against the pain and began her caprice.

"That's my girl—bravo!" Benjamin coached her. "Lovely! Magnificent! Stupendous!"

"BEN-JA-MIN!" Lilah screamed, her lips, her hands trembling with a hateful rage which only mounted when she turned back to discover that Batilda had disappeared into the blue flames.

"Whew! Ahhh..." Batilda's voice taunted her. "This fire sure feels good—doesn't burn a bit."

"I'll kill you...!" Lilah swore.

"Oh, I don't think you have that power, darlin'," Batilda shouted over the shaky violin music. "In fact, you know what? Standing here, rubbing the goose bumps on my arms in this doggone HOT fire of yours, it just struck me—a silly revelation—that the only *real* power you ever had was your beauty and psychic charms. And you used them to seduce and slither your way into the minds and hearts of others...all for the sake of making *their* powers your own. So you see, it's me and the birdman who have the *real* powers."

Lilah stood there, silent for a moment. "I will show you *power!*" she cried, throwing back her head and uttering strange words—names—they sounded like to Alex, in a language she didn't understand.

From her hiding place, Batilda feigned a loud yawn. "Don't bother calling your pets...they're busy shittin' themselves in the woods right now."

Lilah looked at Alex, a raw and primitive fear replacing her fury. And again, she flung back her head, wailing the names of her demon-pets once more.

But Batilda, the stealthy opportunist, had already shifted her position. She was hiding somewhere behind Alex now, and as Lilah brought her head forward, emptying the last screams from her lungs, Batilda took aim over Alex's shoulder and shot the poison right into Lilah's open mouth.

Alex saw the stream of poison pass by, the lethal spray of tincture passing straight into Lilah's mouth without so much as touching her O-shaped lips, it seemed. The awesome sight made Alex stop playing for the moment.

"Whoops! I should have made a toast..." Batilda cackled. "Cheers!" she said, triumphantly, "...and here's to your *health.*"

Lilah simply shut her mouth and gulped, barely aware of what had just happened. But as she stood there, glaring at the water gun, a frightful knowledge welled up in her eyes. She staggered back in shocked silence.

There was a loud hiss then, a sudden slapping of wet, rubbery feet against the rock floor.

"Oh, God..." Alex heard Batilda say from behind.

"What?" Alex snapped. "What is it?"

"Don't move, Alex...."

"Why?"

"Looks like one of the imps didn't eat his Wheaties."

"*Shit!*" Alex said, a chill crawling up her spine. She cringed, waiting, just waiting to feel what she could not see—its venomous teeth sinking into the back of her leg. But it didn't. Instead, the slapping feet sounded like they were backing away from her...backing away from Boogawoog, who now padded stealthily toward Alex, ready to spring at the loathsome thing.

Lilah began murmuring to the creature in another language—French, Alex thought—and when Alex glanced up, she saw that the beautiful Lilah was half-naked.

"Don't be afraid, Alex," Lilah cooed sweetly, "It is the little white rat who should fear *you*...."

"White...white rat...?" Alex asked.

"Yesss...." Sinuously, almost woozily, Lilah stepped out of the gown gathered around her ankles, then slowly walked toward the water. As though she were sleepwalking, not fully conscious, she eased herself into a sitting position on the ledge, her legs in the water, her back turned toward Alex. "It's only Fink... your harmless little pet...coming back for a second chance. Don't let the dog kill him, Alex...you already killed him once."

"What...what do you mean?"

Lilah rolled her head on her shoulders, dipping her hands and gently wetting the front of her perfect body. "It's the little rat that Batilda gave you....the rat you killed your parents with...."

"I didn't kill my—that's not true! Not *true!*"

"When all the other children played with puppies and bunnies, you played with a rodent. And you just *had* to insist on taking that filthy thing in the car that day, didn't you?"

"No...no...." That pressure was on her brain again...not too strong now...but it was there, digging into the soil of her unconscious...exhuming the buried memories.

"And do you remember what your daddy was doing when his neck was ripped to shreds by the windshield? Hmmm? He was laughing, wasn't he, Alex? He was looking in the rearview mirror, laughing at his little girl performing a stupid pet trick...." Lilah sighed, her body weaving as though she were drunk. "He never knew what hit him. But your mommy, poor, poor mommy...she saw it coming, didn't she, Alex? She saw her own death...."

"Stop...STOP IT!" Alex screamed, her chest heaving, the curls on the back of her neck drenched in sweat.

"Now look down, Alex," Lilah commanded.

Alex lowered her gaze, and through her tears saw the blurred image of a white rat to the right of her legs. It sat up on its back feet, like a begging squirrel, bubbles of blood about its nostrils. And Boogawoog, still as a statue and ready to strike the moment the rat moved, stood to Alex's left.

"You killed him once...."

"I didn't!" Alex wailed. "Sophie killed him."

"You let her," Lilah said.

"I didn't *LET* her! I couldn't *STOP* her!" The little white rat wiped its whiskers, then peered helplessly up at Alex and coughed.

Eyes locked on her target, Boogawoog lifted a paw to parry the rat's movement, and ever so slowly began advancing. "DIRTY RAT...BOOGIE KILL...."

"No!" Alex shouted at the dog. "Stay!"

"It's not Fink," Batilda shouted. "Fink is in the past...it's all in the past."

But it wasn't, was it? It was here—Fink was here—staring up at her pitifully.

"Don't let the bad dog kill him," Lilah moaned. "It hurt so much to die the first time...the terror, the pain...he choked on his own blood. And to think he trusted you so...to think you betrayed him...just stood there and watched as the blood poured into his little lungs...."

"Let the dog have it," Batilda demanded. "It's not your rat, Alex...it's not real...."

"Pick him up, Alex," Lilah persisted. "Put down your violin and hold him...you can save him this time...if you want to. You have the power this time."

Dizzily, violin in hand, Alex bent halfway down, but hesitated when Benjamin spoke up.

"The water is calm and quiet now, Alex...that is because the fairy ring is moving at the speed of light. We cannot see them...nor hear them now. But they will settle in a few minutes...and when they do, you will see the colors again...hear the music...and the water will be charged. We only have a few *minutes*, Alex. I've taken my measurements...I'm positioned for you...now play for me."

"FILTHY MOUSE!" the Scottie snarled. "BOOGIE KILL FOR ALEC...." Her white canines were exposed now, saliva dripping from her red tongue.

Cautiously, Batilda moved closer. "Don't touch it, Alex...it's not what you think. If you pick it up it will slash your violin strings, then tear the bell from your pocket and your eyes from their sockets...." Batilda spoke softly, evenly, so that it sounded to Alex as though she were listening to some New Age hypnosis tape. "Look into its eyes, Alex...and you will know it isn't Fink."

Alex brought the bow up to her face, wiping away the tears with the back of her hand. And when she looked at the rat again—looked deep into its eyes—something in them smiled devilishly at her.

"All it wants," Batilda persisted, "is what Lilah wants. And Lilah wants Orielle back. You'll lose her, Alex."

Orielle.... Just hearing her name seemed to help.

"I love you, Alex," Orielle called from the darkened passageway. "I am real, Alex...and I am here, waiting for you...."

Alex turned at the sound of the fairy's voice, but the instant she turned her back on the rat, it crouched and leaped.

Boogawoog didn't wait for permission. Perhaps knowing that this time her judgement was superior to Alex's, she sprang, fast as lightning, catching the rat's neck in midair as it sprang up at Alex. Her body almost numb, Alex didn't feel her pant leg tear, nor the creature's hollow, venom-filled teeth lacerate the flesh of her thigh.

Violently, Boogawoog shook her prey and snapped its neck. There was a quick squeal, then the rat fell limp. Boogawoog released it, watching as the animal transfigured into the grotesque creature it was. Its hair was thin and straggled, the open eyes bloodshot, irises as red as the meat hanging from its pointed, bloodstained teeth. And between the amphibious feet and almost human head, there was no substantial body.

"The bag!" Batilda yelled. "Quick! Put the *bag* in your mouth and *suck* it, *chew* on it—NOW!"

"Wha—?" Alex said. She could barely feel the violin and bow in her hands—could hardly feel her hands at all—and her mind, she wondered if it was still her own. A bad time, this was, for an out-of-body experience. But suddenly she felt a gnarled and less-than-gentle finger forcing its way into her mouth.

With her index finger, and cursing all the while, Batilda pulled open Alex's jaw and stuffed the ouanga bag into her mouth. "Wet it," Batilda ordered. "Wet the damned thing and swallow!"

Alex complied, gagging, but forcing herself to swallow the bitter juices mixing with her own saliva.

"That's my girl—swallow!" Batilda pressed.

"Your hands," Benjamin coached. "Move those fingers, Alex. Think of the music and play a song for Orielle."

Defeated, Lilah didn't even bother to turn and look at what was happening. She was lying back against the stone ledge of the lake now, hallucinating, it appeared.

The music of the energies was returning now, sweet voices, like those of children in some celestial playground, sounding over the water.

Lilah was rocking now, a hand held to her heart. It was pounding—Alex could see her chest heaving even from where she stood. And then, suddenly, Alex heard the drumming of that heart. "Alex? This is it!" Benjamin shouted joyfully. "Can I have that caprice, please? From the top?"

With renewed strength, and despite the fact that her hands were still shaking, Alex played loud and hard.

Like colors in a kaleidoscope, bursts of colors began playing like rain on the water. It was as if someone had simply tossed a jar of glitter into the air, then set it all to spinning in fast motion. And as the glittery colors moved round and round, half-formed faces—exquisite, translucent faces—appeared amidst the speeding ring of color.

The violin's music was almost deafening as it reverberated against the walls of the cave. Flailing about in panic, salivating, Lilah struggled to pull herself out of the water. But when she opened her mouth to speak, only the sound of her pounding heart came out of it.

"Stay absolutely still, Alex, don't move from your position," Benjamin instructed. "Orielle is coming up behind you now to take the bell and bring it to me. Just keep playing...."

Alex obeyed. She felt Orielle's arms moving softly around her waist and up to the vest pocket which held the bell.

"Bring it to me," Benjamin instructed the fairy. Then, "Ready? Set...?"

As it had happened in the meadow, the sound issuing from the violin began to climb. Alex heard it off to the left, then off to the right. And just as the ring of color over the water spun itself into a chain of beautiful smiling faces, the sound shot to an inaudible pitch and was gone. Only a ringing sounded over the water now; that and Lilah's heartbeat. It pounded with fear and rage and...and poison.

Writhing with exertion, Lilah had managed to get out of the water. Naked and on her knees now, she stared back at them desperately, her eyes dilated. She tried to crawl toward Alex, her long, red nails curling, reaching for Alex and the bell. She looked at the water, then at Alex, not knowing which would bring her salvation.

But it was too late. She was deafened by the sound of her own exploding heart; horrified as she felt her eyes begin to bulge from their sockets.

Batilda rang the bell, Alex frantically bowed her silent strings and Benjamin pointed his antenna, taking aim at Lilah's body. This was the moment they'd been waiting for.

A look of terror spread across Lilah's face. She tried to scream one last time, but instead, ended up inhaling her own bloodcurdling death cry. Finally, her heart burst wide open.

A flash of red—a ball of blood and fire—shot from her heaving chest. Seconds later, Lilah combusted, her body dissolving as it was pulled into the vortex—the same vortex which had led to Orielle's lifelong prison.

And then there was silence.

We...we did it!" Alex yelled, her own breath coming in short gasps. She didn't know if she was laughing, crying or hyperventilating, but Lilah was gone and Orielle was by her side, her hands moving around Alex's waist.

The water radiated with sparks and flashes of energy, the voices of the chanting fairies echoing softly throughout the cave. But then the voices and the images of a thousand beautiful faces slowly began to fade. Alex stood there gasping, watching in awe, fully aware of her own life energy.

"You have set me free," Orielle whispered. "You have set yourself free."

Alex tried to draw in air so that she might speak, but the air forced itself out instead. Mesmerized, she dropped her violin, then rubbed a trembling palm across her forehead, and felt her waist for Orielle's hand.

"We did it!" Alex yelled again, turning to locate Benjamin and Batilda. But they didn't respond. Excitedly, hardly able to tear her eyes from the water, she glanced around again, her eyes widening in horror as she did.

Both Benjamin and Batilda sat slouched against the wet wall of the cave, their eyes opening and closing as though they'd suddenly gone sleepy.

"Oh, my God," Alex screamed. Then, "Boogawoog... where are you?"

There was a slow dragging and clicking of nails against the stone floor, and then the Scottie emerged from the shadows. She walked stiffly, her beard all white now, as she came up to her friend and nudged Alex's leg with her big nose. "BOOGIE GO WITH MAMA NOW." And then she turned, slowly padding her way to Batilda's side. With a sigh of contentment she settled her aging body at her mistress's feet. Then she looked up at Alex shyly, sweetly, wagging her tail. But even that seemed a strenuous task.

"NO!" Alex heard herself scream. "Don't go...PLEASE!" she begged through quivering lips. "You saved my life."

Alex rushed to them, dragging Orielle along with her. But Benjamin and Batilda's skin was already cool to the touch, and in the blue light of the dying flames their faces already looked dead. They seemed like limp puppets now, as if the uncrossing of the spell had severed their strings. Benjamin managed a thin but peaceful smile, and Batilda, who still had a little strength, attempted to reach out her hand to Alex.

"What?" Alex asked gently.

Benjamin's eyes finally shut, but there was still a spark of life in Batilda—as though she were having a spontaneous idea—and suddenly it seemed to Alex that Batilda was concentrating that one spark of energy on communicating something.

"What?" Alex demanded again, frantically trying to figure out what it was Batilda wanted.

Batilda was too weak to speak, but her eyes kept shifting, as if pointing toward the water.

"What does she want?" Alex yelled to Orielle. "What does she...?" And as Alex followed Batilda's eyes to the water, it finally dawned on her. "The water! Is that what you want?" she asked.

Batilda didn't have the energy to nod, but her eyes seemed to move up and down.

"Quick!" Alex said to Orielle. "Please! Help me get them to the water."

"It's against nature, Alex."

"I don't care! Nature's been against me all my life. Please, Orielle!" she shouted.

They dragged Batilda first, her cowboy hat falling off along the way, and rolled her, with a splash, into the water. Alex crouched alongside, grabbing Batilda's hair the moment she surfaced, and helped her to grasp the stone edge of the lake with her gnarled hands.

"My dog!" Batilda said, spitting water in all directions. "Where's...my...doggone DOG!"

"Coming, she's coming," Alex promised, slipping and sliding on the wet floor, rushing to get Boogawoog to the water, then rushing back.

"Get Benjamin, "she shouted, but Orielle already had the unconscious Birdwhistle by his feet. Alex helped her, grabbing him under the arms.

And when all three were in the water, coming to, as it were, another magical thing happened on this night of celestial magic. Out of the mist, the dancing images of two transparent figures—a man and a woman—took form. The woman looked just like Orielle...and intuitively, Alex knew the young and handsome man could be none other than Orielle's father.

Alex stood up from where she kneeled by the water's edge, her mouth open in wonder, her happy eyes moving back and forth between Orielle and the misty images.

"Mother...Father..." Orielle whispered in wonderment.

The couple smiled and extended their hands, but although they seemed only a few feet away, Orielle could not reach them. They were too far away...a world away.

Orielle smiled joyously, dreamily, as the peaceful images began slowly fading.

"Rutherford? Is that you old chap?" Benjamin hollered, choking and splashing around and trying to compose himself. "You see, old friend, we kept our word."

Orielle took Alex's trembling hand and pulled her close, as if presenting to her parents the special one with whom she had chosen to share her life. And as though wishing them both well, Orielle's parents smiled—smiles too gentle for this world—and bowed their heads in blessing and farewell.

Hand in hand, Alex and Orielle watched in amazement as Steven and his beloved fairy joined hands and began a slow waltz...dancing and spinning, until the energy of their love spun them into a disappearing ring of everlasting light.

Alex and Orielle were still dazedly holding hands when Batilda's gravelly voice jolted them back to the here and now.

"Hey, you two!" the witch yelled. "Come on in—the water's great!"

Alex looked at the water, then at Orielle.

"Come on, now..." Batilda insisted. "Swim tonight...and you'll be kids again tomorrow!"

Alex gazed into Orielle's eyes, brushing the golden-red bangs from her forehead. "I don't want to be a kid again. I don't want to go back." She turned to Batilda, then back to Orielle. "I want to start right here...I'm right where I belong."

❧ EPILOGUE ❧
Enough to Go Around

What sounded like a fog horn roused Alex from a deep sleep. With a start, she sat up in bed, her eyes darting around the room. The sun was just rising; Orielle was beside her. And then the horn sounded again— a car horn, she realized.

"It's your aunt," Orielle murmured.

"My aunt...?" The term still sounded so strange to her. Alex hadn't yet decided if she *liked* calling Batilda *aunt*, let alone *having* her for one.

"Hey, you two! " Batilda yelled from outside the bedroom window. "Wake up and make coffee—we're coming in. We've got donuts and croissants."

Alex dropped back to her pillow again. "Donuts and croissants...*Christ*," she mumbled.

"Alex..." Orielle whispered.

"Just pretend we're not home."

"If you don't go open the door, you know she'll only pick the lock and let herself in."

"We're going to have to move, you realize...and not leave any forwarding address."

"Alex...go on," Orielle said, nudging her.

Alex lay still.

"Alex...?"

"Oh...*shoot* !" Alex grumbled finally, kicking the sheets off herself. "Doesn't that woman have *any* boundaries?"

"Absolutely none," Orielle said softly, sleepily, apparently amused by it all.

But before Alex could tie her robe, Batilda was rapping at the window. "I said, *hey in there!*"

"For heaven's sake..." Alex growled, staggering over to the window, where only the top of Batilda's head could be seen above the windowsill.

But suddenly a powder blue dog appeared, Batilda lifting it above her head and holding it up to Alex's eye level. "Look what I found sleeping in my blueberry patch." Then, "Take her," Batilda said. "Go on now, take her."

Alex opened the screen and took the dog, wondering who had dyed the obviously white dog, whose it was, and why she was being asked to hold it now.

Batilda backed away from the house and grinned up at Alex. It was amazing; she didn't look a day over sixty. Her hair was streaked with black now, and without the weight of the wings on her back—without the weight of the bags beneath her eyes—Batilda's posture was much improved. Only that hideous grin, with each crooked tooth uniquely squared and spaced, gave away her real age.

Batilda winked mischievously. "I didn't *really* find the pup in a patch, ya know. I told you about Mary's sister—remember? The dentist? Well, she volunteers at one of those animal rescue groups...and the dog came from a puppy mill out west."

"So it's Mary's dog...?"

"No, it's your dog—an early birthday present. Just in case we're not back by the third of July." She winked again. "The bird-man and me are takin' the gals to New Orleans for a few days."

"Oh, Alex..." Orielle cooed. "She's darling....Bring her to me."

Alex turned with the dog in her arms, the sight of her waking lover in bed only making her want to shut the window and climb back in bed for a few more days. Instead, she walked over and handed Orielle the dog.

"I guess we have a dog now..." she said, frowning and returning to the window.

"So..." Batilda said, gesturing with her chin toward the car in the driveway, "you wanna meet my new girlfriend, or what?" Alex stuck her head out the window and gave a sidelong glance, utterly amazed by the sight of the two women sitting in Benjamin's Mercedes.

"You've *got* to see this," Alex called to Orielle. Then, "I don't believe it...*twins?*"

"Identical," Batilda said, puffing her chest proudly.

Alex smiled in spite of herself. "Now you and Benjamin don't have to fight over the same woman anymore."

"My thinking exactly. And I know you're gonna like her. She's more worldly than Mary...if you catch my meaning."

Alex shook her head in wonderment. From what she could see, the two sisters *did* look identical—except that Mary's blouse was buttoned to the neck, while Maude's cleavage was showing.

"So snap to it, Kiddo! Let us in," Batilda bossed her. "The sun's just up, and already it's gettin' to me. I'm hot as a pig standin' out here."

"You mean *sweating* like a pig," Alex corrected.

"No...I'm not sweating. Did I say I was sweating? I just said I was *hot*...hot as a pig."

With a roll of her eyes, Alex turned and headed for the door.

"Hey, Alex? One more thing," Batilda called.

Alex returned to the window. "What?"

"Maude's retiring this year, but...well...before she gives up her practice, she says she wants to cap my teeth." Batilda grinned, showing Alex her teeth. "What d'ya think?"

Alex couldn't help but laugh. "I think it's a good idea..." she said, shaking her head and smiling at her crazy aunt, "...a *really* good idea."

She turned away, heading for the kitchen, and stopped to give Orielle a morning kiss.

The End

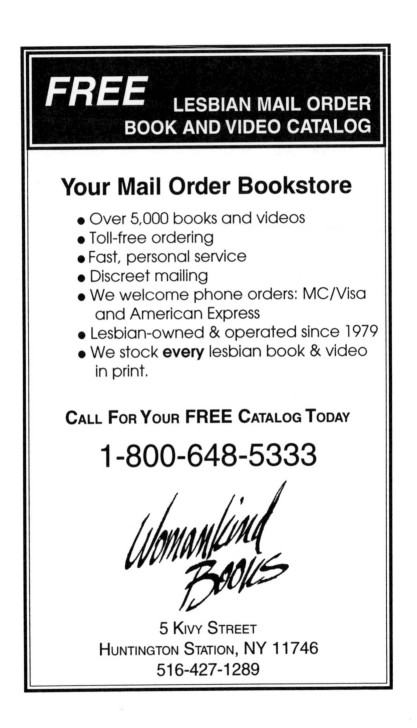

About the Author

Karen Williams spends her leisure time in the mountains of Upstate New York, where she enjoys contemplating life with Stormy, a Scottish terrier who has much to say on the matter...if only she could find the words.

At thirty-five, Williams holds a B.A. and an M.S.W., and in addition to her professional practice, she is the author of two novels. Currently, she is working on a third (the sequel to *Lovespell*) and on—this is a secret—perfecting her recipe for Mumble Munchies. If writing never wins her the Pulitzer, she figures the biscuits will surely make her a contender for the Nobel prize.

In case you're wondering, the hunt for sultry witches continues as usual; however, during her last rendezvous, Ms. Williams stumbled upon a most unusual bell instead....

If You Liked This Book...

Authors seldom get to hear what readers like about their work. If you enjoyed this novel, *Nightshade*, why not let the author know? We are sure she would be delighted to get your feedback. Simply write the author:

Karen Williams
c/o Rising Tide Press
5 Kivy Street
Huntington Station, NY 11746

Our Publishing Philosophy

Rising Tide Press is a lesbian-owned and operated publishing company committed to publishing books by, for, and about lesbians and their lives. We are not only committed to readers, but also to lesbian writers who need nurturing and support, whether or not their manuscripts are accepted for publication. Through quality writing, the press aims to entertain, educate, and empower readers, whether they are women-loving-women or heterosexual. It is our intention to promote lesbian culture, community, and civil rights, nationwide, through the printed word.

In addition, RTP will seek to provide readers with images of lesbians aspiring to be more than their prescribed roles dictate. The novels selected for publication will aim to portray women from all walks of life, (regardless of class, ethnicity, religion or race), women who are strong, not just victims, women who can and do aspire to be more, and not just settle, women who will fight injustice with courage. Hopefully, our novels will provide new ideas for creating change in a heterosexist and homophobic society. Finally, we hope our books will encourage lesbians to respect and love themselves more, and at the same time, convey this love and respect of self to the society at large. It is our belief that this philosophy can best be actualized through fine writing that entertains, as well as educates the reader. Books, even lesbian books, can be fun, as well as liberating.

RETURN TO ISIS
Jean Stewart

It is the year 2093, and Whit, a bold woman warrior from an Amazon nation, rescues Amelia from a dismal world where females are either breeders or drones. During their arduous journey back to the shining all-women's world of Artemis, they are unexpectedly drawn to each other. This engaging first book in the trilogy has it all—romance, mystery, and adventure.
Lambda Literary Award Finalist
ISBN 0-9628938-6-2; 192 Pages; $9.99

ISIS RISING
Jean Stewart

In this stirring romantic fantasy, the familiar cast of lovable characters begin to rebuild the colony of Isis, burned to the ground ten years earlier by the dread Regulators. But evil forces threaten to destroy their dream. A swashbuckling futuristic adventure and an endearing love story all rolled into one.
ISBN 0-9628938-8-9; 192 Pages; $11.99

WARRIORS OF ISIS
Jean Stewart

At last, the third lusty tale of high adventure and passionate romance among the Freeland Warriors. Arinna Sojourner, the evil product of genetic engineering, vows to destroy the fledgling colony of Isis with her incredible psychic powers. Whit, Kali, and other warriors battle to save their world, in this novel bursting with life, love, heroines and villains.
Lambda Literary Award Finalist
ISBN 1-883061-03-2; 256 Pages; $11.99

DEADLY RENDEZVOUS: A Toni Underwood Mystery
Diane Davidson

A string of brutal murders in the middle of the desert plunges Lieutenant Toni Underwood and her lover Megan into a high profile investigation which uncovers a world of drugs, corruption and murder, as well as the dark side of the human mind. An explosive, fast-paced, action-packed whodunit.
ISBN 1-883061-02-4; 224 pages; $9.99

PLAYING FOR KEEPS
Stevie Rios
In this sparkling tale of love and adventure, Lindsay West, an oboist, takes a position with the Filarmonica de Caracas, where she meets three people who change her life forever: Rob Heron a gay man, who becomes her dearest friend; Her lover Mercedes Luego, a lovely cellist, who takes Lindsay on a life-altering adventure down the Amazon; And the mysterious jungle-dwelling woman Arminta, who touches their souls.
ISBN 1-883061-07-5; 256 Pages; $10.99

ROMANCING THE DREAM
Heidi Johanna
A charming, erotic and imaginative love story which is also the tale of how women, together, have the power to make dreams happen. Set in the Pacific Northwest, it follows the lives of a group of visionary women who decide to take over their small town and create a lesbian haven. It will delight you with its gentle humor, beautiful love scenes, and fine writing.
ISBN 0-962838-0-3; 176 Pages; $8.95

DREAMCATCHER
Lori Byrd
This timeless story of love and friendship illuminates a year in the life of Sunny Calhoun, a college student, who falls in love with Eve Phillips, a literary agent. A richly woven narrative which captures the wonder and pain of love between a younger and an older woman—a woman facing AIDS with spirited courage and humor..ISBN 1-883061-06-7; 192 Pages: $9.99

LOVESPELL
Karen Williams
A deliciously erotic and humorous love story in which Kate Gallagher, a shy veterinarian, and Allegra, who has magic at her fingertips, fall in love. A masterful blend of fantasy and reality, this beautifully written story will warm your heart and delight your imagination.
ISBN 0-9628938-2-X; 192 Pages; $9.95

YOU LIGHT THE FIRE
Kristen Garrett
Here's a grown-up Rubyfruit Jungle—sexy, spicy, and sidesplittingly funny. Take a gorgeous, sexy, high school math teacher and put her together with a raunchy, commitment-shy, ex-rock singer, and you've got a hilarious, unforgettable love story. ISBN 0-9628938-5-4; $9.95

NO WITNESSES
Nancy Sanra
This cliff-hanger of a mystery set in San Francisco, introduces Detective Tally McGinnis, the brains and brawn behind the Phoenix Detective Agency. But Tally is no great sleuth at protecting her own heart. And so, when her ex-lover Pamela Tresdale is arrested for the grisly murder of a wealthy Texas heiress, Tally rushes to the rescue. Despite friends' warnings, Tally is drawn once again into Pamela's web of deception and betrayal, as she attempts to clear her and find the real killer. A gripping whodunit.
ISBN 1-883061-05-9; 192 Pages; $9.99

DANGER IN HIGH PLACES:
An Alix Nicholson Mystery
Sharon Gilligan
Set against the backdrop of Washington, D.C., this riveting mystery introduces freelance photographer and amateur sleuth, Alix Nicholson. Alix stumbles on a deadly scheme surrounding AIDS funding, and with the help of a lesbian congressional aide, unravels the mystery.
ISBN 0-9628938-7-0; 176 Pages, $9.95

DANGER! CROSS CURRENTS:
An Alix Nicholson Mystery
Sharon Gilligan
The exciting sequel to *Danger in High Places* brings freelance photographer Alix Nicholson face-to-face with an old love and a murder. When Alix's landlady, a real estate developer, turns up dead, and her much younger lover, Leah Claire, is the prime suspect, Alix launches a frantic campaign to find the real killer. ISBN 1-883061-01-6; 192 Pages; $9.99

HEARTSTONE AND SABER
Jacqui Singleton
You can almost hear the sabers clash in this rousing tale of good and evil, of passionate love, of warrior queens and white witches. Cydell, the imperious queen of Mauldar, and Elayna, the Fair Witch of Avoreed, join forces to combat the evil that menaces the empire, and in the course of doing that, find rapturous love.
ISBN 1-883061-00-8; 224 Pages; $10.99

CORNERS OF THE HEART
Leslie Grey
A captivating novel of love and suspense in which beautiful French-born Chris Benet and English professor Katya Michaels meet and fall in love. But their budding love is shadowed by a vicious killer, whom they must outwit. Your heart will pound as the story races to its heart-stopping conclusion.
ISBN 0-9628938-3-8; 224 pages; $9.95

SHADOWS AFTER DARK
Ouida Crozier
When wings of death spread over Kyril's home world, she is sent to Earth on a mission—find a cure for the deadly disease. Once here she meets and falls in love with Kathryn, who is enthralled yet horrified to learn that her mysterious, darkly exotic lover is a vampire. This tender, beautifully written love story is the ultimate lesbian vampire novel!
ISBN 1-883061-50-4; 224 Pages; $9.95

EDGE OF PASSION
Shelley Smith
This sizzling novel about an all-consuming love affair between a younger and an older woman is set in colorful Provincetown. A gripping love story, which is both fierce and tender, it will keep you breathless until the last page.
ISBN 0-9628938-1-1; 192 Pages; $8.95

EMERALD CITY BLUES
JEAN STEWART
When the comfortable, yuppy world of Chris Olson and Jennifer Hart collides with the desperate lives of Reb and Flynn, two lesbian runaways struggling to survive on the streets of Seattle, the result is unexpected and wonderful. As their very different worlds become intertwined, the college professor, the renovator of Victorian homes, and the two young runaways discover they have much in common.

A warmhearted, gritty, enormously readable novel of contemporary lesbigay life, which raises real questions about the meaning of family and community, and about the walls we construct. A celebration of the healing power of love.
ISBN 0-8836061-09-1; $11.99Avail. 2/96

How To Order

TITLE	AUTHOR	PRICE

- ❑ **Corners of the Heart**-Leslie Grey 9.95
- ❑ **Danger! Cross Currents**-Sharon Gilligan 9.99
- ❑ **Danger in High Places**-Sharon Gilligan 9.95
- ❑ **Deadly Rendezvous**-Diane Davidson 9.99
- ❑ **Dreamcatcher**-Lori Byrd 9.99
- ❑ **Edge of Passion**-Shelley Smith 9.95
- ❑ **Emerald City Blues**-Jean Stewart 11.99
- ❑ **Heartstone and Saber**-Jacqui Singleton 10.99
- ❑ **Isis Rising**-Jean Stewart-11.99
- ❑ **Love Spell**-Karen Williams 9.95
- ❑ **Nightshade**-Karen Williams 11.99
- ❑ **No Witnesses**-Nancy Sanra 9.99
- ❑ **Playing for Keeps**-Stevie Rios 10.99
- ❑ **Return to Isis**-Jean Stewart 9.99
- ❑ **Romancing the Dream**-Heidi Johanna 8.95
- ❑ **Shadows After Dark**-Ouida Crozier 9.95
- ❑ **Warriors of Isis**-Jean Stewart 11.99
- ❑ **You Light the Fire**-Kristen Garrett 9.95

Please send me the books I have checked. I enclose a check or money order (not cash), plus $3 for the first book and $1 for each additional book to cover shipping and handling. Or bill my ❑Visa ❑Mastercard ❑Amer. Express.

Or call our Toll Free Number 1-800-648-5333 if using a credit card.

CARD # _____ EXP.DATE_____

SIGNATURE_____

NAME (PLEASE PRINT) _____

ADDRESS _____

CITY_____ STATE_____ZIP_____
- ❑ New York State residents add 8.5% tax to total.

RISING TIDE PRESS

5 KIVY ST., HUNTINGTON STATION, NY 11746